the LEAGUE of PICKY EATERS

the LEAGUE of PICKY EATERS

STEPHANIE V.W. LUCIANOVIC

CLARION BOOKS
An Imprint of HarperCollins*Publishers*
BOSTON NEW YORK

Clarion Books is an imprint of HarperCollins Publishers.

The League of Picky Eaters

clarionbooks.com

Library of Congress Cataloging-in-Publication Data is available.
ISBN: 978-0-358-37986-7

The text was set in Carre Noir Std.
Cover design by Kaitlin Yang
Interior design by Kaitlin Yang

Manufactured in the United States of America
1 2021
4500833823

First Edition

For my 2017–18 Bookopolis Bookclub and picky eaters everywhere

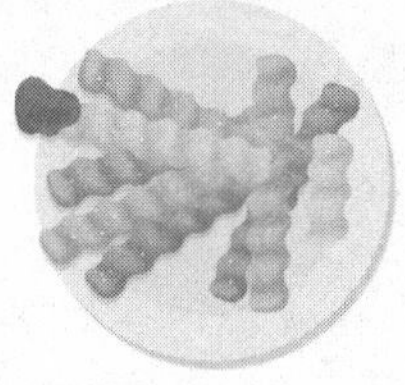

The proper development of one's tongue is the education that will speak highly of them for the rest of their lives.

— Muffuletta Town Motto

Welcome to St. Julia Child Elementary and Middle School!

Ever since our beloved town of Muffuletta was founded decades ago by chefs, food writers, gastronomes, and gourmands, St. Julia Child has been proud to serve up an innovative food-infused curriculum unparalleled by any other in the world. While we do provide an education that teaches to all subjects, we believe that exceptional instruction in the subject of Eating is one of the most important things we can provide to our children. And, as I am so fond of saying to all our parents, the children of today are the adults of tomorrow, so they better eat like it!

Parents, rest assured that when your children leave our school, they will be able to eat just as well as they can read or do math, if not better!

This year, we at St. Julia Child are setting our sights to win the Silver Tongue, which is awarded to the school with the highest taste test scores in Muffuletta. If we win it, we will have the privilege of displaying the trophy in our courtyard for everyone to admire—and to try to guess the number of taste buds!

Hungrily yours,

Sharon Butcher

Sharon Butcher, Principal
St. Julia Child Elementary and Middle School

CHAPTER 1

Standing outside of St. Julia Child Elementary and Middle School, I choked on the stink. Raw eggs covered practically every inch of the pavement in front of me. And some had started to rot.

It was absolutely sweltering, and sunscreen was sliding off my pale and easily burned skin. A heat wave had been roasting the entire town of Muffuletta for over a week now, so of course the Camp Egghead summer campers would try to fry eggs on the sidewalks in the courtyard. Normally, I wouldn't go anywhere near the school during the annual Eggsperiment, because the sight and smell is beyond shuddersome. Unfortunately, that was also the day of my sixth-grade Eating placement test.

Back when my parents went to St. Julia Child, which was so long ago they didn't even have microwaves in the classrooms, Eating placement tests were taken right before high school. But a few years ago a bunch of parents complained that their kids' mouths weren't being challenged, so the Muffuletta School Board decided to start dividing sixth-graders based on their Eating skill. Excuse me, please, but taking a test is not the nicest way to end summer vacation.

The placement test determines whether we get into the Gifted and Gourmet class, the Becoming a Real Foodie class, or the Remedial Eating to Change Habits class. (Pretty much all the students at St. Julia Child call these classes GAG, BARF, and RETCH, but only when the teachers or Principal Butcher aren't around.) RETCH is what you get put into if you fail the placement test, and if you don't pass out of RETCH by the end of the year, you have to go to summer school. That's exactly the kind of embarrassment that would actually kill you very dead, no matter how much my parents try to convince me otherwise.

I shaded my eyes to see how far the Eggsperiment extended. Going around it would take too long, and I was already worried about being late. I was going to have to walk right through the oozing yellow minefield.

I slapped a hand over my nose and mouth, took a deep breath, and started leaping from one patch of clean pavement to the next. Maybe if I concentrated really hard on total egg avoidance, I could forget how nervous I was.

If it had been a test for any other subject, my stomach wouldn't feel like it was being put through a meat grinder. I get Satisfactorys in almost everything except Math and Science (where I get Exceptionals) and Eating. Here and there,

I might get a Needs Improvements, but if I'm unlucky, which seems to happen a lot, I get Pickys—the worst Eating grade. Even though teachers at St. Julia Child try to infuse all the subjects with food-related curriculums or examples—like, for Reading, making recipe collections of all the food that's mentioned in a book, or in Math, learning fractions by cutting up a pie—Eating is the only subject at school that requires a placement test. An *oral* placement test.

I don't try to get Pickys in Eating, but I'm just not as good at it as other kids. It's boring and gross and hard.

There was this day in kindergarten when I didn't want to make meatballs for a Touch! Make! Taste! lesson. I told Mrs. Courgette that the raw ground meat squishing and squelching between my fingers felt like the time I picked up a slug from the garden and accidentally squeezed it too hard.

The next day, Mrs. Courgette called my parents in for a chat.

"So," Mrs. Courgette said to my parents, "Minerva is struggling in Eating. She doesn't want to try new things, she disrupts the class with awful faces and gagging noises, and her food group sorting, well, just see for yourself."

My parents looked over at the big display of paper plates on the class bulletin board. Using pictures from food magazines, we were supposed to fill the smallest section of the paper plate with things like chips and cookies, to show that they were less nutritious. And then we were supposed to fill the other, larger sections of the plate with the basic food groups—fruits, vegetables, grains, meat, and dairy products—according to how much we were supposed to eat of them per day. But in the small section I had glued magazine cutouts of all the foods I hated and labeled it "Iky Fud."

The rest of my plate was filled with pictures of food I liked: macaroni and cheese, mashed potatoes and baked potatoes (both with lots of butter), french fries, grilled cheese, pasta, cheese pizza, roast chicken, cheese, ice cream, cookies, pickles, and ketchup. I had drawn lots of arrows pointing to those foods and written "YUM!" I didn't even bother to sort them into the proper groups.

My parents exchanged worried glances.

"It is very important that you work on Eating with Minerva at home as much as possible so she can catch up with the rest of the students," Mrs. Courgette went on, picking up a neatly piled sheaf of flavored nori and holding it out. "I have some worksheets you can have her eat at home."

My parents would have the same conversation every year with all my other teachers. And it always ended with more seaweed worksheets. Teachers think that sending worksheets home is the answer to everything. I think the only thing they answer is: What would it taste like to lick the wall of a moldy old dungeon? The worksheets come in flavors like onion, barbecue, and even bacon, which is supposed to help "expand your palate." But I still taste dank dungeon walls.

I hopped over another dark yellow egg slick. Getting across the Eggsperiment wasn't as hard as I thought it would be. In a few more seconds, I'd be home free.

I just needed to take one last leap.

Too late and in midair, I realized my leap wasn't going to be long enough.

I landed hard. The heel of my flip-flop slashed right through the middle of an egg yolk and sent me skidding through several others.

"MOTHER EARRRRTH!" I hollered.

I windmilled my arms as hard as I could to stay upright, but I slipped and slid across the courtyard sidewalk before I finally *splurched* to a stop on egg-free pavement.

I leaned over my knees to catch some of my breath. That was the closest I had ever come to getting a concussion.

Last week my parents and I watched an interesting but also sort of scary television program all about the science of concussions. I had been reading a lot of books and articles about concussions ever since. I did the same thing after we watched a special on shark attacks. My parents don't like it when I do this. They think it makes me even more anxious, but if you ask me, it's good to be as informed as possible about the scarier things in life. That way it's easier to avoid them. In my concussion research I learned that pretty much ANYTHING could give you a concussion: driving in a car, taking a shower, stuff falling from the sky when you happen to be outside without a hardhat—even walking around in the middle of the night in your own house. You just never know when concussions might strike.

Still panting, I scraped egg off my flip-flops on the pavement and flapped my shirt.

Just for a second I thought about Sons of Seitan, Muffuletta's vegan K-8 school. They had air conditioning, which really helped with how hot classroom ovens made everything. But honestly, if I ever had to give up real cheese for nut cheese, I would most certainly die a horrible death.

The door on the testing classroom had a big sign taped to it in the shape of a poufy chef's hat: SIXTH-GRADE PLACEMENT TEST. (We made those hats out of coffee filters in first grade, and they're really called toques, but I like calling them poufy chef hats.)

Before I grabbed the door handle, I closed my eyes and reminded my stomach to think positive. If I took calming breaths, drank water, and didn't concentrate too hard about what was in my mouth, there was no reason why I couldn't do well enough to get into BARF.

The lights were off and the windows were open, but the room still stunk a bit from last year's classes—old potatoes, hot fish, and the fartiness of raw broccoli. Some students were twisting around in their seats, looking at everyone else.

Others sat with their hands folded and their napkins already in their laps. Akshay Bhargava, a boy I knew slightly from having the same teacher in second grade, tried to inch up the lid of the covered plate in front of him, until Mr. Kreplach stomped over and smacked it back down again. "Ashkay, you will lose points if you try that again!" Mr. Kreplach snapped, his perpetually pink face turning even more so than usual.

"Akshay, not Ashkay," Akshay said in an undertone. Like he was hoping no one else would hear him. But also hoping they would.

"What?" Mr. Kreplach said, turning back around.

"Nothing," Akshay said, flushing under his deep brown cheeks.

Teachers were always getting Akshay's name wrong. When he played on the boys' basketball team last year, they misspelled his name on his jersey. And when his team won the championship, the school newsletter spelled his first *and* last name wrong. I didn't understand it. They were always bugging students about knowing how to spell everything correctly, why didn't they do the same for kids' names?

I looked around until I spotted my best friends, Patricia Jenson and Cindy Kobayashi, sitting next to each other. Cindy had pink ribbons patterned with tiny yellow butterflies threaded through her long, shiny black braid. Cindy's grandmother in Japan was always sending her the cutest hair accessories. Then I noticed that Patricia's copper-colored curls were pulled in a high ponytail and tied with the same pink and yellow ribbon. Huh.

I ran my hand through my own sweat-damp brown hair in a basically pointless attempt to neaten it up a bit, and tried to get Patricia's and Cindy's attention. But they were too busy whispering with each other to see me standing there—or, I noticed with a frown, even to save a seat for me. On the other side of the room there was an empty desk with a covered plate. I sank down in the seat, gave a loud sigh, then quickly looked over at my friends. They finally looked up and waved, smiling. I gave an unsmiling wave back.

Neither Patricia nor Cindy looked even a smidgeon as nervous as my stomach felt. Of course, I reminded myself, neither one of them has ever gotten a Picky in Eating, either, so there was really no need for them to be nervous at all. Cindy's dad works at the business school at Stanfork University in Muffuletta, where my dad is a math professor, and whenever they run into each other on campus, Mr. Kobayashi tells him how great Cindy is doing in Eating. "Don't worry," my dad always says to me, "I never forget to tell him how great you're doing in Math." And Patricia . . . well, even the kindergartners knew how amazing Patricia was in Eating—Principal Butcher made sure of that.

"Not everyone is going to be naturally good in Eating," my dad told me over and over. "That's why you're going to school: to learn."

"But we do need you to try your best," my mom always chimed in.

That was easy for them to say—both of them had been good at Eating all their lives, and their love of all food seemed to have skipped me and gone right to my brother. Hugo ate everything I didn't and more. And by the way, I *did* try, but eating food after food after food that you don't like is so hard.

I jiggled my leg under the desk and forced myself to take a breath. The test changes every year, so it was very possible it would be something I could handle. Last year, the test included grilled octopus, so at least I didn't have to worry about dealing with that today. I crossed my fingers and jammed them under my thighs. Then I counted off my luck on my crossed fingers: I made it through the Eggsperiment without gagging or getting a concussion, the classroom oven was off, and I was wearing my favorite flip-flops.

I was still trying to think of one more piece of luck when Mr. Kreplach left the room. Inch by inch, I leaned forward as far as I could without my face actually touching the silver lid on the plate.

"No sniffing!" someone hissed behind me.

I flinched away from the lid and was about to hiss back "No snitching!" when Mr. Kreplach came back with our knives and forks, and all at once I found the ceiling incredibly fascinating.

"Mr. Kreplach?" Patricia called out, waving her hand in

the air. "There won't be any clams, will there? Because I'm allergic."

"Yes, Patricia, we do know you're allergic. There won't be any clams on the test, and no student at St. Julia Child would ever be given a food that is listed on their medical or religious 'do not eat' form," Mr. Kreplach said. Then he turned to me. "Proper testing conditions at St. Julia Child require sitting up straight, elbows off the desk, and napkin in lap."

I snatched my elbows back and picked up my napkin from the floor. Then I crossed my arms really hard across my chest so my hands wouldn't try to peek under the cover.

Mr. Kreplach walked to the front of the class and waited for the high school students, who were acting as teacher's aides for the test, to finish setting glasses of water on every desk. When they were finished, Mr. Kreplach clapped his hands to get our attention.

"Now, class," he said calmly, "as soon as the lids are removed, you may begin. Remember to keep your mouths on your own work and chew with your mouths closed. The cleaner your plate, the better your grade. If you meet standards on today's test, you will return for a more advanced test tomorrow to determine your final sixth-grade Eating placement."

I raised my hand, "And if we don't meet standards today?"

Mr. Kreplach raised his eyebrows. "That will also determine your sixth-grade Eating placement."

He lifted a finger. "And begin!"

With a metallic zing, the aides whipped the lids off everyone's plates. I thought it was pretty amazing the way they did it all at the same time, and I was about to ask them how long they had practiced and how many lids they dropped or how many kids they had clonged in the face and given concussions. I thought it was a very good thing to learn about before I took this test. Maybe we'd even have to have a long, interesting discussion about it and would run out of time for the test. But when I opened my mouth, Mr. Kreplach narrowed his eyes and glared pointedly at my plate.

I looked down, and when I saw what was there, I glared, too.

CHAPTER 2

Meatloaf.

But the problem was, it wasn't like my mom's meatloaf, which I love and ask her to make at least once a week. My mom's meatloaf is plain ground beef and pork patted into a loaf pan. That's the way meatloaf is supposed to be. The meatloaf in front of me had *stuff* in it.

I saw shiny bits of onions (which I'm fine with, actually), orange cubes of cooked carrot (which I am *not* fine with), celery (which I don't even understand), and green pepper (which is the worst possible thing you could ever think to stick in a food).

Cooked green pepper isn't even really green anymore. It's a gross sort of grayish brownish green that the crayon makers call khaki. No food should ever be khaki.

I looked around the room, hoping to catch sight of what the vegetarians had on their test. Mostly, the vegan families in town went to Sons of Seitan, but St. Julia Child Elementary and Middle School did have a bunch of vegetarians. In fact, Akshay might have been one. I knew his family didn't eat beef. But that might have been the only meat he didn't eat. I squinted over at his plate. He had a slice of something that looked sort of like meatloaf but paler. A few other kids had loaf slices that looked like Akshay's. The slices were probably mashed-up mushrooms and lentils or tempeh instead of meat. My stomach shuddered.

The next problem on the test was a neatly stacked pile of green beans. Of course they were probably cooked perfectly, which, we had been taught, meant they were still crisp and not mushy. But "cooked perfectly" or not, I still hated green beans. They tasted so bland and green and just *beany*. They were also sitting in a puddle of greasy liquid. It wasn't exactly water, but wasn't exactly butter, either. It was . . . bean juice.

As soon as the words *bean juice* flashed through my brain, my entire body gave such a hard shudder I almost fell right smack out of my chair. Trying not to think about all the concussions people probably get all the time from falling out of chairs, I forced myself to do more of my calm breathing.

Calm breathing is the best way to stop myself from gagging super loud. It settles me down. I do it at home a lot because when my gags get out of my mouth, my parents have to give me the lecture about how vomiting noises don't belong at the dinner table.

I heard a muffled *"Hoarf!"* several rows behind me. I felt sorry for whoever that was, but it also made me feel a tiny bit better that I wasn't the only one having a hard time with the test.

Once I felt I could handle it, I took another look at the test plate and almost fell out of my chair again. This time in relief. I had been so distracted by the meatloaf and the green beans, I hadn't even noticed that there was a dollop of mashed potatoes on the test. Mashed potatoes are one of my favorite foods in the world—this part was going to be a cinch!

I piled my fork high with a huge bite and opened wide. And then my mouth went haywire with confusion. Because whatever was in my mouth was the wrong texture for mashed potatoes. It was too slippery. Slick. And it was also completely the wrong flavor. It sort of had that from-the-ground dirt taste (people call it earthy because it's nicer to say that instead of dirty), but it was also sweet. And mashed potatoes are definitely not sweet.

What was this? I flicked the pile with my fork tips and took another taste. Parsnips. These weren't mashed potatoes, they were puréed parsnips. I sighed. It was a trick question.

Honestly, I don't mind parsnips all that much; it's more that I really, really, REALLY love mashed potatoes. And it seems to me that since everyone knows that meatloaf and mashed potatoes are perfect together, putting pureed parsnips in their place is a dirty (not earthy) trick.

Moving on to the meatloaf, I was about to stand up to get the ketchup. But then I saw that the classroom condiment shelf was empty. As in nothing was on it: not the usual six kinds of mustards nor the array of hot sauces, and definitely not a single bottle of ketchup. Did they really expect us to eat meatloaf . . . bare? How does that even make sense?

I took a quick look around, totally expecting to see that everyone else was just as confused as I was. But they all had their heads bent over their plates and were concentrating on the test. Patricia had even finished the string bean section. I shook my head in admiration.

As long as we'd been friends, Patricia Jenson had never met a food she didn't love. In kindergarten she once brought a plastic container of haggis in for Show and Taste. Haggis, Patricia explained, was a traditional Scottish dish that a famous Scottish poet loved so much he wrote a poem about it. I was fine with that part. I could definitely write huge books of poems about grilled cheese sandwiches. But then Patricia went on to say that haggis was made up of sheep heart, sheep liver, and sheep lungs, all ground up with onions and oatmeal and stuffed in a sheep's stomach. And then she actually ate it right there in front of us.

I had to do some serious calm breathing while I watched her chew and swallow every bite, but Patricia didn't gag once. She even said it was delicious! That's how good she is at eating—she can eat an entire sheep's insides like it was chocolate pudding with whipped cream and rainbow sprinkles.

That night, Principal Butcher called Mr. and Mrs. Jenson and told them that Patricia was the most promising student eater she had come across in all her years at St. Julia Child. Patricia's mom loves to tell that story to almost everyone she meets. Whenever I hear it, it makes me feel all puffed up and warm, like I'm full of popcorn. I'm not as good in Eating as Patricia is, but she's still best friends with me.

We have been in the same class since kindergarten, which is kind of rare, since St. Julia Child has enough students to mix about five classes per grade level. For a while I thought it was just luck that Patricia and I always got to be together. But then she told me that we got to be together because she told her mom she wanted us to be.

"And Principal Butcher always listens to my mom," Patricia told me. "Because of her volunteering and all the money she raises." Mrs. Jenson raised enough money for the school to put brand-new blenders in every classroom as well as get the most up-to-date refrigerators and food processors. From what I can tell, she does it by throwing huge parties that snooty rich people call galas and then charging people money to come to them. Seems kind of weird, but it works.

Mr. Kreplach clinked a fork against a glass to get our attention. "You have ten minutes left."

Ten minutes! I looked around. Half the class had left already. My stomach sank, but I shoved the feeling aside and plowed through pureed parsnips as best I could, although some of them ended up on the floor, which I mostly didn't mean to happen.

Then I turned to the meatloaf problem. It was going to be the toughest. First I used my fork to gouge out every bit of carrot, celery, and green pepper, leaving them in a tidy little pile on the plate. When I was pretty certain that the meatloaf was totally cleared out, I took a deep breath and a bite.

Maybe this time it would work.

I eased the fork into my mouth and closed my lips. The instant that celery, carrot, and green pepper–free piece of meatloaf hit my tongue, I knew.

Bleeeeeeeeecch!

All my poking and prodding had saved me from feeling the bits of carrot and celery mushing around in my mouth, but no amount of meatloaf dissection could stop the green pepper chunks from leaving behind flavor fingerprints everywhere. Like a smudgy bathroom mirror. And my tongue tasted every single one.

You know how everybody has something weird about them that they can't exactly explain? Like how Cindy can curl her tongue or my little brother can pick up crayons with his toes and write with them? Well, my tongue is really, really good at tasting things. It can even taste things that aren't there anymore.

If you remove something I hate (green pepper) from something I like (meatloaf), my tongue still knows it was there, which makes it impossible for me to eat it. My tongue is a lie detector test for food. But instead of finding lies, it finds grossness. It might sound like a cool talent, but it's actually pretty awful, and it makes it so hard for me to get good grades in Eating.

"Five minutes," Mr. Kreplach warned. Now there were only two of us left in the classroom.

I pinched my nose and shoved the green beans into my mouth. Then I took a big gulp of water, chewed furiously, and swallowed it all. If you can stop your brain from thinking about what you're eating and swallow vegetables like you're taking medicine, they slip right down your throat without a lot of chewing and tasting.

But there was no way I could do that with the meatloaf, and I was out of time. As soon as Mr. Kreplach turned away to examine the other student's plate, I scraped the rest of the meatloaf onto my lap and scrunched the napkin around it. Then I raised my hand to show I was done.

Mr. Kreplach checked over my plate. He looked down at the floor around my feet and frowned. "You could have done better on your parsnips, but . . ." He pursed his lips and narrowed his eyes at me.

I held my breath.

"You may be excused," he finally said.

"HOORAY!" I yelled, tossing my napkin over my head to celebrate. Too late, I realized what I had done.

The meatloaf soared free from the napkin and smacked Mr. Kreplach right in the face before landing on the floor with a damp *splatch.* "Oh, mother earth," I whispered.

Mr. Kreplach put a hand to his face and looked at it in wonder before staring down at the floor. When he finally found his voice again, he only had one word: "OUT."

CHAPTER 3

Two weeks later, I was driving back to school with my family. It was a Wednesday, the day before school started. It was also the day everyone checked the posted lists to find out what class they were in. I bounced so hard in my seat that my dad told me to calm my body because I was shaking the entire car.

I tried clutching my legs with both hands, but there was no way I could sit still. The heat wave had finally broken, and the air was crisp and fresh and ready for a new school year. Everything around me had the kind of energizing fall feeling that prickled my insides and made me want to jump, scream, dance, and run as hard and fast as my legs would let me.

The school parking lots were long past full, so my mom poked around for open spaces in the residential streets surrounding the campus.

"Hurry, hurry!" I whispered as she inched around a particularly wide trunk of a tree that had been allowed to grow tall and thick with age right in middle of the street.

The residents of this neighborhood prized their trees greatly and resisted any effort to cut them down. Even the ones that could scrape off a side mirror or slow cars. *Especially* the ones that could slow cars. If anything, the trees acted like vertical speed bumps, slowing down any passing driver. The city had even been so accommodating as to stripe the trunks with wide bands of white, tree-safe paint so drivers could see them in the dark.

As my mom made another pass through the neighborhood, hoping a spot had opened up, I saw Mr. Kreplach carrying bags of groceries to the school. I scrunched down out in my seat. Staying out of sight. Two weeks was a long time to stay mad at a little meatloaf in the face, but I wasn't taking any chances.

When the school didn't call me in to take a more advanced test, I knew that meant I hadn't come close to making it into Gifted and Gourmet. Which, as I told my parents a few nights earlier in my most believable voice, was quite fine with me because Becoming a Real Foodie was probably going to be more than enough work for me.

One tiny, dark, pitted area of my stomach worried itself into knots every time I pictured the meatloaf flying out of my napkin. But I kept telling my stomach the same thing my mom tells me — how if you blow things out of proportion, you'll make a mountain out of a molehill, and that's where trouble looks for you instead of you looking for it around every corner of your eye. Or something like that.

After all, I reasoned with myself, I got the green beans down and I did okay with the parsnips, so as long as Mr. Kreplach was willing to overlook the whole meatloaf-in-the-face thing, I should easily get into BARF. Ease.I.Ly.

And it's not like I threw all my meatloaf at him. I had eaten some of it.

Plus, I reminded my stomach, everyone knows that your memory can play tricks on you and make you remember things being much worse than they actually were. Of course I wouldn't be in RETCH.

Finally, my mom maneuvered our car into a space. I whipped off my seat belt the moment the car was in park. "Hurry up, you guys!"

As I flung open the door and scrambled out, I saw a dog staring at me from a front yard. It looked hungry. It also looked like the dog that followed me home from school last year. That was the day I hadn't finished my beef stroganoff in class, so my teacher assigned it as homework.

"Why don't you go on ahead, honey," my dad said. "We'll catch up with you later. Go find Patricia."

"And Cindy," I reminded him.

It had always been me and Patricia at first, but in the fourth grade, Cindy had started playing with us at recess.

Sometimes I thought she tried a little too hard to make Patricia like her. She was always complimenting Patricia's hair or clothes or table manners. And I worried whether Patricia liked her more than she liked me. But I tried to push those thoughts from my mind.

"And Cindy," my dad repeated. "You don't need to wait for us."

"Okay," I said. I flipped open my purple notebook and glared at the dog. "Just a sec."

On my desk at home I have stacks of purple notebooks. They are filled with things like haiku, stories about cats that come from outer space to save humans on Earth, drawings of trees, lists of words I've invented, and a bunch of potential names in case my parents let us get another cat someday. But this particular purple notebook is more important than any of the others, and I don't go anywhere without it. This notebook contains everything I plan to do as president of the sixth grade.

I haven't exactly been elected yet, because class elections don't happen until later in the school year, but I had already written "President Minerva's Ideas for the Improvement of the Students at St. Julia Child Elementary and Middle School" on the cover. I even used my neatest block lettering to make it extra true.

I found a clean page and wrote, "do not assign homework that might attract a slothering pack of dogs." My dad says *slothering* isn't a word, but it actually is because it's one of my invented words. I mashed together slobbering and blathering, since *blathering* means talking nonsense, and I've noticed that's what all dogs do when they're hungry and telling you about it.

It wasn't a whole pack of dogs that followed me home that day. It was just the one. But I am convinced it told all its friends about me.

And it was definitely slothering that day.

My purple presidential notebook already has a lot of other great ideas in it, like how we should have more dance parties during vocabulary time because it probably helps learning, and that cats should be allowed to be classroom pets. But my most important idea is that the school should add grilled cheese, macaroni and cheese, and french fries to the hot lunch menu. I plan to talk to Principal Butcher about it just as soon as I win the election.

I took off for the school, skipping by houses that were either old and stately, with fancy white trim and iron balconies at every window, or huge steel boxes with entire walls made out of glass windows. This tree-thick neighborhood also had knobbly roots that bubbled through the bricked sidewalk, which can trip up the unaware. But Patricia lives here, and I come over a lot, so my skipping feet knew what they were doing.

I passed one enormous green lawn after another. We

had just been through a heatwave with no rain and yet, even with city water restrictions because of the drought, these lawns never seemed to get brown and crispy like the ones in my neighborhood did. I paused to glance up at one of the houses. It was boxy and looked as though it were made entirely of glass and steel.

"Clean lines," my dad always said about these types of houses. "Modern."

"Museums," my mom always responded. "Cold. Exposed."

I agreed with my mom. I didn't understand why anyone would want to live in a house that looked more like an office building than a home and had so many windows that anyone walking down the street could see your entire life—like you picking your nose or your brother having a tantrum—going on inside it.

I liked the iron-balconied houses better. Somehow they seemed cozier than the museum ones, even though they were just as huge, and *cozy* is really a word people use for the smallest kinds of houses. Our house, which is in a very different neighborhood, with not as many trees and hardly any lawn, is so "cozy," I share a room with my brother.

There was already a huge crowd of parents and kids outside the school office. I wedged my way through a group of shrieking third-graders and ducked under arms of parents who had their phones out, snapping shots of the lists to send to families who didn't come in person. I liked that my family always came in person because at some point it had become a back-to-school tradition to eat out at Amy's Delish Diner after checking the lists.

Some people might think it's boring to eat at the same place every year, but the thing about traditions is that they are comfortable. They make you feel safe. With traditions, nothing unexpected happens and there are no bad surprises, like the kind of bad surprise you get when you bite into a cookie thinking it's oatmeal chocolate chip but discover it's actually an oatmeal raisin cookie and everything in your mouth is ruined.

I wriggled my way over to the postings for the upper grades. I bypassed the GAG lists and went straight to the BARF classes. But I didn't see myself. I checked again, going down the list even more slowly and mouthing every name listed to make sure it wasn't my own. Then my eye caught my name on a totally different classroom list.

With Mr. Kreplach as my new teacher.

It was the worst kind of raisin surprise ever.

I couldn't believe I was really in . . . "RETCH?!"

I slapped my hand over my mouth. Too late. The shrieking third-graders overheard and started making retching noises at me. My cheeks prickled with heat. I tried to give them my best "I am a sixth-grader now" look, but I was too upset to make it properly withering.

I quickly looked for Patricia's and Cindy's names. And

my shoulders, which my anxiety had hitched up to my ears without my realizing it, slumped. They were both in GAG. Patricia was in Mr. Cornichon's class, and Cindy was in Mr. Pomelo's.

I stumbled my way back out of the crowd, not paying attention to where I was going, just needing to get out of there.

I trudged past the giant fork flagpole, where the school emblem—two baguettes crossed over a wedge of blue cheese—ruffled in the evening breeze. That tiny area of worried knots in my stomach, which I'd been doing such a great job ignoring the past few weeks, suddenly got much bigger.

"At least they aren't together without me. At least they aren't together without me," I kept repeating in my head. That was something to feel slightly better about. It would be way worse if they were in the same GAG class and I was stuck in RETCH alone. At least we'd all be alone together.

I was so dumb to think we'd all be in BARF together. Dumb, dumb, dumb. RETCH dumb, in fact. And Patricia and Cindy weren't RETCH dumb. They had always done better than I did in Eating. Even when we worked on the exact same projects together, they still got better grades.

Take last year, for example, when we did the Fruit in Fables unit in History. At first I didn't even want the Trojan War apples to be our topic, but after Patricia talked me into it, I worked really hard on it.

"We can dress up like the goddesses who fought over the golden apple and started the war," Patricia said. "I'll be Hera. Minerva, you can be Athena, and Cindy, you're Aphrodite."

"Ooh, can I make the goddess costumes?" Cindy asked. "I can use my mom's sheets!"

"Or you guys could dress up like Hades and Persephone, and I'll be the pomegranate Persephone eats after she's kidnapped," I said. "Like in the Greek myth about the seasons."

Patricia wrinkled her nose, "I don't want to be Hades."

"Me either," Cindy said.

"Okay, then I'll be Hades," I said.

"But my mom already bought me a ton of edible gold leaf just so I could make the golden apple," Patricia said. "I told her we had already agreed to do the Trojan War apples."

"A real golden apple? That will be soooo amazing!" Cindy said, clasping her hands together. "I have gold ribbon from my grandma that I could use in our goddess hair!"

"Min, all you have to do is write a short oral report about the apple. Maybe we'll do Persephone and pomegranates next year," Patricia said.

"Totally," Cindy said.

They both looked at me.

I didn't want to argue anymore. Also, I had no idea how to even start making a pomegranate costume, so I nodded.

The golden apple did sound pretty cool, and it had given me an idea of what I could write for the oral report.

Mrs. Mulligatawny went crazy over Cindy's costumes, and she couldn't stop admiring Patricia's apple in the sunlight coming through the classroom windows. But she was less happy with my oral report.

"In conclusion," I read, standing in front of the class, "when you think about Adam and Eve being thrown out of the Garden of Eden and also about Snow White being put to sleep, and now the Trojan War with that huge body count, people should stop eating apples because they cause too much trouble."

"People should stop eating apples because of the Trojan War?" Mrs. Mulligatawny repeated. "Minerva, the point of your report isn't about blaming apples."

"Well, I don't exactly blame all apples. I guess some are okay," I said. "But not the ones that call themselves Red Delicious when they're the exact opposite!"

"They are red," Mrs. Mulligatawny pointed out.

"But they aren't *delicious,*" I said.

Mrs. Mulligatawny opened and closed her mouth a few times. Finally she put out her hand for my report. When I got it back, there was a big red P for Picky on the top. Cindy and Patricia both got Exceptionals.

Afterward, Cindy and Patricia had tried to make me feel better, saying we'd definitely do Persephone and pomegranates next year. But now it was "next year," and we weren't going to be in the same class, and all at once everything was starting to feel really messed up and wrong. It wasn't losing out on doing Persephone and pomegranates that was so awful, it was losing out on doing *everything* with them.

And by now I was so used to having my best friend in my class, I never even thought about what it would be like without her. Or Cindy, either. Cindy and I hadn't been friends as long as me and Patricia, but she was still my next best friend. Being in the same class with them was as much a tradition as going to Amy's on the last day of summer vacation.

But we couldn't be in the same class if I was in RETCH, no matter how many ovens or pressure cookers Patricia's mom got for the school.

"Okay," I told myself in firm tones as I paused in front of the giant teakettle in the courtyard. "But it's not like we're going to stop being friends or anything. We're still going to eat together at lunch and play with each other at recess."

The courtyard teakettle was made out of bronze that had dulled and darkened over time. But there was one area that had stayed bright and shiny from kids rubbing it for luck over the years. For some reason, that spot bothered Principal Butcher, and she occasionally grumbled about having the whole kettle polished to make the entire surface bright and shiny again. But that was expensive, and St. Julia Child alumni were too attached to their own kettle-rubbing memories to want to raise the money.

I took a deep breath and put my hand on the bulbous belly of the kettle. It felt warm from the sun and reassuring under my palm. I told myself that as a sixth-grader, I was getting too old to really believe in luck.

"Yeah, but," the arguing side of me said, "does that stop you from blowing on every dandelion you find or searching for four leaves in a clover patch?"

"And what about birthday candles," it argued on. "Are you going to stop wishing on those now, too?"

"Okay, okay!" I said. "Point taken."

A seventh-grader carrying an armload of used cookbooks from one of the classrooms looked at me out of the corner of her eye and quickened her pace.

I bit my lip and gave the kettle a quick swipe. Then I walked away before anyone else saw me arguing with myself.

I mean, when you really thought about it, it one hundred percent wasn't going to matter at all that we were in different classes. Especially since Patricia had double-pinkie-thumbed-nose promised me this summer that she and Cindy would both help me become sixth-grade president. We'd be together all the time just like usual, because that's the way friendship works.

"That's just the way friendship works," I repeated to my brain as relief spread over me.

I passed the enclosed kindergarten yard and saw my parents talking to Hugo's new kindergarten teacher. I thought about reminding them that Hugo had tried to sneak off with the raw lamb chops before dinner last night and how Mr. Collard would need to keep any and all classroom foods out of his reach.

But I knew Patricia and Cindy would be on the playground waiting for me, just like every other year, and I really wanted to find them as soon as possible. After all, my parents had reassured me that the kindergarten teacher already knew that Hugo was a "precocious" eater who was still learning what was socially and culinarily appropriate and what wasn't, so maybe I didn't have to worry about it. As I continued over to the big kids' playground, I thought about how we could start making presidential plans immediately. That would prove that nothing had changed. So what if I was in RETCH —my friends weren't going anywhere.

"Whoa!"

My feet stuttered to a stop right before I collided with someone coming from the opposite direction.

"Oof!" was all I said as an arm shot out to steady me.

The arm belonged to Alice Who Only Eats White Food. She was in RETCH now, too. I saw her name on the list along with Akshay's. The three of us hadn't been in the same class since second grade.

Alice had on a purple polka-dotted gaiter pulled up over

half her face and completely covering her nose. All I could see were her curious blue eyes staring out at me and her pale, slightly sweaty forehead. Alice wearing a gaiter in late August without a ski slope or even a cool breeze in sight is exactly the kind of thing she does all the time. It's *so* weird. It also makes the teachers really mad. Which kind of doesn't make much sense because the gaiter isn't breaking any school rules that I know of, but that didn't stop the teachers from telling her off about it.

Alice Who Only Eats White Food actually has a real last name, but kids don't bother with last names unless you have two kids with the same first name in the same class. And even then they just become Henry L and Henry X or something.

But even without last names, everyone knows Alice Who Only Eats White Food, just like everyone knows Alejandro Who Sneezed Blood Boogers in the Water Fountain That One Time. They are the kind of kids who don't have to be in your classroom for you to hear about them. Because of her name, the entire school knew that Alice was bad at Eating. And now we were in the same Eating class, so everyone would know I was just as bad.

"Sorry," I muttered.

Alice dropped her arm. She didn't say anything.

"Aren't you hot?" I finally asked, flicking my hand at the gaiter. Even though it felt more like fall every day, it's not like it was close to being cold enough for something you'd wear if you were on a sled getting pulled by a pack of howling (and probably slothering) dogs. It never even snowed in Muffuletta.

"It's cozy," Alice said. "And it's a good sunblock. I burn really easily," she added, staring at me from above the purple polka dots. The way she was looking at me made me feel like I had something stuck in my teeth or, even worse, something hanging out of my nose.

I hadn't eaten anything green that wasn't candy in a long time, so I pinch-swiped at my nose just to make sure I was in the clear there, too.

"I heard about the meatloaf and Mr. Kreplach's face," Alice said, still staring. "He's our teacher now."

I gave my nose another pinch-swipe.

". . . Okay?" I said, getting annoyed. I was pretty sure that by now the entire school had heard about how I had meatloafed Mr. Kreplach's face, so I didn't know why she was bringing it up.

"Okay."

I decided it was a good time to be done with this non-conversation, so I stepped around Alice Who Only Eats White Food and started scanning the playground beyond her for Cindy and Patricia.

"Your *friends* are on the turkey baster," Alice said.

There was something about the way she said *friends,*

almost as if it had a very different meaning to her, that made me turn back.

"Where are *your* friends?" I asked. I was almost annoyed enough to add, "Do you even have any?" But I didn't.

Back in second grade, when Alice and her older brother, Ty, first started going to St. Julia Child, Ty was instantly popular. He was tops in every subject, including Eating, and he was good at every sport he tried out for. Everybody liked him. But unlike her brother, Alice wasn't instantly popular. Or any kind of popular, really. In fact, Alice used to go to the potato-shaped Spuddy Bench at recess. That's where you're supposed to go when you need a friend or when you want to signal to everyone that you're available to be a friend to anyone who needs one that day.

The Spuddy Bench makes teachers and parents feel better about any lonely kids who might be having a hard time at school. They think it solves everything without getting them involved. But all kids everywhere know the truth, which is that sitting on the Spuddy Bench basically hollers to all of mother earth that you have no friends. And no kid wants to do that. Except Alice.

Mostly, when kids sit on the Spuddy Bench, they hunch up into themselves and stare down at the ground so they can't see all the kids who *aren't* coming over. Alice didn't sit like that.

One time she stood on the bench, walking up and down

and yodeling. Yodeling sounds like what a flamingo would sound like if you tried to turn it into an accordion. I had only heard people doing it in movies or on TV. I definitely had never met anyone who could do it in real life.

Another time, Alice was lying down flat on the Spuddy Bench, her arms crossed over her chest like a mummy. She lay there so still, I almost went over to see if she was actually asleep, but Patricia pulled at my arm, hissing, "Where are you going? Everyone will think you're a weirdo freak just like her." Myself, I never considered sitting on the Spuddy Bench. I had Patricia and Cindy.

At some point, Alice stopped sitting there. I wondered if she had been sitting there because she needed a friend or because she wanted everyone to know she could be their friend if they wanted one. Before I could untangle my brain to figure out if those two things were the same, Alice answered me.

"They're around," she said.

"Around?" I repeated.

"My friends. Keep an eye out for them, okay?" she said. And then she walked past me, off the playground, and into the tall shadows of the late afternoon.

There was no mother earthly way to respond to that. Now I really had to find Patricia and Cindy so I could tell them everything Alice Who Only Eats White Food said.

CHAPTER 4

The turkey baster is the tallest play structure on the playground. It has THYME'S A-BASTING painted in big green letters down one side of it. I used to wonder why it was called a turkey baster, since Mr. Haricot explained to us in second grade that basters are used to squeeze juices over *any* meat or roast to keep it from drying out. But then I ate turkey and realized that when you're the driest meat of all, you get to have your name on the thing that tries to make you better.

On school days, the turkey baster swarms with kids trying to race one another to the top at recess. But a lot of kids had already headed home with their families for dinner. Cindy and Patricia were the only ones peering down from the top.

"We saw you're in RETCH—did you see what class we're in?" Patricia called as soon as she saw me.

"We're in Mr. Cornichon's Gifted and Gourmet class!" Cindy yelled before I had a chance to answer.

I froze in place on the blacktop. Everything that Alice Who Only Eats White Food said to me was knocked right out of my head. "Wait, I thought Cindy was in Mr. Pomelo's GAG class."

"She was, but I told my mom to talk to Principal Butcher. So they're going to put her in with me," Patricia said.

"You're both in the same GAG class together," I said, trying to make my brain stop freaking out.

Even from way down on the ground I could see Patricia scrunch her nose at me. "Don't call it that."

"GAG? Why not? We've always called it that. Besides, you say RETCH."

"Well, we're not supposed to do it. Besides everyone knows that RETCH is so very RETCH, and Gifted and Gourmet is so the exact opposite of GAG," Patricia said.

I didn't see what the difference was, but instead of arguing, I climbed very slowly and very carefully up to meet them. I was kind of regretting having watched that TV show about concussions. Knowing all that I knew definitely felt more scary now than interesting.

"Well," I said when I reached the top, "at least we can still sit together at lunch and go to recess together."

"Yeah, sure," Patricia said, examining her nails, which were painted a shimmering pearl-white today. Cindy's were painted the exact same, and the color glimmered against her tawny skin. I looked at my own nails. All the chewing I had done to them had mostly destroyed the purple polish, which now looked ugly and pointless.

"Great!" I said, trying to sound more excited than I was truly feeling. "So we can do all my election planning at lunch and during recess. And also after school. And on weekends."

Then there was the longest silence that has ever happened in the entire world.

"Actually . . ." Patricia said, shaking her mass of bright red curls off her pink, freckled face and smoothing down a pair of new gold and green shorts. I noticed that Cindy was wearing the exact same pair. Had they gone out and bought them together? Was it the same time they painted their nails or was that another time they were together without me? My mind flashed back to the ribbons they both had in their hair at the placement test. But the unhappy thought that they were possibly doing a lot more things without me was knocked from my head when Patricia said, "I'm going to run for president of the sixth grade."

"What?" I sputtered. "But *I'm* running for president! And excuse me, please, you know I've been talking about it all summer!"

"Ugh—it's not like you *invented* the idea of running for president, Minerva," Patricia said. "I mean, did you even ask *me* if *I* wanted to be president?"

"Well, no, but . . ." I had no end to that sentence. I was

supposed to be president this year; it was all arranged except for the getting elected part. This was something we all had been planning! Patricia had never shown even the tiniest interest in being president.

"Oh, come *on,* Min," Patricia said. She stood up and looked down at me. "I have a ton of amazing ideas."

"She does, Min, she really does," Cindy said.

"But—" I started to say.

Patricia went right on just as if I hadn't said anything at all. "Like how we should build a bread maze for the Culinary Arts Show. That's something I was actually going to put you in charge of because you like bread so much, but if you're going to be like this . . ."

"A bread maze?" I hadn't thought up anything like that. The Culinary Arts Show was a time when our art teacher, Ms. Naan, pushed us to get creative with food and ourselves. It's a really cool event, but I hadn't thought up any plans for it yet. Patricia was right—I really do love bread. And I didn't want to get into a fight with her. That always made things weird with us. Last year, when we got into little fights or had misunderstandings, we were almost always able to fix things before the school day ended. Or it would all be forgotten when we saw each other in class the next day. But that would be harder to do now that we were separated.

"You could totally help with the bread maze!" Cindy said, nodding so hard her black braid bounced against her back.

"Yeah. Maybe," I said, dragging myself to my feet.

We stood there for a little bit longer, not saying anything or even looking at each other, until Patricia glanced over my shoulder and said, "Oh, Min, I think your mom and dad are leaving."

I turned around. Mom and Dad were waving me over. Hugo had my mom's shirt in both fists and was trying to backwards-drag her toward the car. A clear sign that he was very hungry.

"Going to Amy's again?" Patricia asked.

I didn't trust myself to open my mouth and not have all my crazy stew of so many different emotions come spilling out, so I just nodded as I started down the ladder.

"So you gonna order a cheeseburger with avocado and mushrooms and tomatoes and gobs and gobs of mayonnaise, right?" Cindy said.

"Now, why would she do that, Cindy? You know Min eats only grilled cheese at Amy's!" Patricia said, shaking a finger at Cindy.

"Ohhhhh, riiiiight." Cindy giggled. "I forgot."

"So what? I like grilled cheese," I muttered. I was in no mood to joke with them.

"Oh my gosh, don't be so sensitive! You know we're just teasing!" Cindy said.

"Yeah, but honestly, Min, you might want to think about

trying something else. I mean, we're sixth-graders now. Not kindergartners," Patricia said.

Because of her deadly, dangerous allergy, clams are the only thing Patricia doesn't eat, and if you ever get her started on the subject, she will go on and on about how much she *wishes* she could eat clams because she knows she would just *love* them.

I don't get how you could love something that wants to murder you. Patricia says that's exactly why I don't understand food. But her pushing at me to try new foods kinda shows that she doesn't understand me in a way. And like she doesn't listen to me.

"I don't know if I would like something new, and if I tried it and didn't like it, I'd be stuck with a whole plate of it," I said, as if I hadn't said the same thing to them a million times before.

I usually shrug off their teasing me about what I like to eat—or at least I try to—but what really bothers me is that what I eat is none of their business. It's my mouth the food goes into, not theirs. Do I go on and on about Patricia not liking math? Nope. Did anyone ever make a whole big thing about how books about mermaids in outer space were the only books Cindy would read? Never.

Why does everyone have to fixate on the things I'm bad at instead of the things I'm good at? Like, I'm one of the top math students in my grade, and I'm also awesome in science (mainly because it's full of mysteries I want to solve). But noooooo, people have to bring up Eating. All. The. Time. I wasn't in the mood to hear it, especially not that day.

I had almost reached the bottom of the turkey baster when Cindy called, "Hey, were you talking to Alice Who Only Eats White Food?"

"Yeah. I guess we're in the same class now," I said.

"Why is she wearing that neck warmer again?"

I shrugged. "She says it's cozy."

"She's *so* weird," Cindy said.

"So weird," Patricia agreed. "No wonder she doesn't have any friends."

"Yeah," I said, thinking about what Alice said about keeping an eye out for her friends. Why had she said that? What did it even mean? It *was* kind of weird. Like everything about her.

At the bottom of the turkey baster, I paused. Then I tipped my head back to call up. "Hey, Patricia, I—" I swallowed down all the stinging feelings that wanted to surge out of my throat. "It will be fun to help you with the bread maze."

"Of course it will," Patricia said. "It will be the most fun thing we do all year!"

"Yeah, maybe," I said. "So I guess I'll see you guys at lunch tomorrow?"

"Look for us," Patricia called back.

On the edge of the playground, I passed a clump of parents. As I got closer, I caught snatches of them complaining about which teachers let students watch too many online videos.

"I mean, if they were watching shows that actually taught them something, like better table manners or the difference between a yam and a sweet potato—" one said.

"Oh, I agree—it's the competitive reality shows, like *Bagel Battles* and that chewing one with all the yelling, that are a complete waste of valuable learning time," said the other.

"It's certainly not going to help get them onto the Gourmet track. That kind of screen time should just be for the Remedial Eaters."

This was going to be a very long year.

CHAPTER 5

On the car ride to Amy's Delish Diner, Hugo launched into a long, complicated explanation about the colored squares on his new kindergarten classroom's carpet. He listed all the colors in rainbow order and explained which square he'd choose to sit on for each day of the week.

He stopped to take a breath.

"So, Minerva—" my mom began, making the mistake of thinking he was done when he clearly wasn't even close.

"Hey—you're *erupting* me!" Hugo protested, aggrieved, and then proceeded to go through the entire explanation all over again. From the beginning.

Normally, it bugs me when my little brother takes over all conversation, but the longer I could put off talking to my parents about RETCH, the better. I hadn't been exactly honest with them about the placement test. For weeks I had been telling them that I'd done so well on the test, I was sure I got into BARF. And now they were going to ask why I didn't, and I'd have to tell them that, once again, I'm a big disappointment to them on the Eating front.

Plus, there was that whole meatloaf-in-the-teacher's-face thing I was going to have to own up to.

By the time we parked, Hugo had changed his mind and come up with an entirely new plan for the colored squares in kindergarten, which involved instructing all the other kids about where they should sit on what day. His teacher was gonna be thrilled.

While my parents went to place our order, Hugo ran along the rows of shiny red vinyl booths lining the walls. He dove into the one with the best view of the freight train tracks and started yanking wads of napkins out of the dispenser for each member of the family.

"Move over," I told Hugo, nudging him with my knee.

"DON'T TOUCH ME, I'M DELICATE!" Hugo bellowed.

I snorted. Excuse me, please, but there is nothing delicate about my little brother.

I looked around Amy's, my favorite of all the restaurants in town. It wasn't fancy, you didn't have to put on uncomfortable, dry-clean-only clothes just to get in the door, and your plates never had strange foams or gel-like smears on them. And Amy never made things that looked like one thing and tasted like something else entirely. You always knew exactly what you were getting, and it was always delicious. There were a ton of restaurants in town that made confusing and serious-looking food—the kinds of places that so many people in Muffuletta flocked to and then talked about loudly. This seemed to be most important when a new restaurant opened in town. Everyone wanted to be the first to go, and then they wanted everyone to know that they had eaten there before anyone else. But even those kinds of people—people like Patricia's mother—loved Amy's because the diner had dishes that would satisfy even the most "advanced" eaters.

"Well-made," is what my parents said about the food at Amy's. All the meat and produce came from the local farms that clustered around Muffuletta, the seafood came from the coast, which was about forty miles away, and everything was always cooked exactly the way it should be to bring out the best flavors. If you wanted to order a side of seasonal vegetables (which I never did unless it was corn on the cob), you could be sure they wouldn't come out mushy and overcooked, like the ones my dad sometimes served when he got to daydreaming about math when he should have been paying attention to the stove. Dad never *means* them to come out that way, but when they do, my parents and Hugo just shrug and eat them anyway. I can't do that. At all. So I always try to find ways to make the grody vegetables disappear in places that aren't my stomach.

What I like most about Amy's is that it's the only restaurant in town that lists "easier" foods, like plain, uncomplicated grilled cheese sandwiches, right there among the artisanal pulled pork sandwiches and the locally caught Dungeness crab roll slathered with house-made lemon aioli. Unlike at other restaurants in town, where I have a hard time ordering anything off the menu and an even harder time finishing what I get, I never feel like an underachieving eater when I go to Amy's. I just feel normal.

My dad slid a red plastic basket in front of me. Tucked in next to a heap of hot fries still glistening with fat from the fryer was the best grilled cheese sandwich ever made. I took a deep breath and inhaled the delicious, toasty, comforting fragrance.

"Ketchup? Pickles?" my dad confirmed with me and Hugo before going to the fixings bar to load up.

I unwrapped my sandwich and smoothed the wax paper out on the table. Another thing to love about Amy's is that they cut the grilled cheese sandwiches into two triangles, not two rectangles. They know as well as I do that the best part of a sandwich is the middle. A sandwich cut into two triangles gives you a larger non-crust-to-crust ratio, so you get less of the dried-out, hard-to-swallow crust in each bite. Triangles also give you much better corners for dipping into small paper cups of ketchup.

My dad explained that I'd have an even larger ratio of non-crust to crust if the sandwich was cut in an *X*, giving me four little triangles instead of two. But that's how little kids eat their sandwiches, so I'd feel kind of babyish asking Amy's to do that for me.

My mom waited until I had crunched into the first bite of my sandwich before she asked, "So, Min—excited about sixth grade?"

I was not at all fooled by the ho-hum-everything-is-okay voice she was using. Like somehow acting casual was going to trick me into talking about RETCH. "I guess."

My dad sat down, handing out paper trays of thick-sliced tomatoes, raw onions, and crispy stacks of lettuce to my mom and Hugo. He pushed over two small paper cups of ketchup and smiled at me. Along with the best grilled cheese sandwiches, Amy's also has the best ketchup of any restaurant in town. And unlike the other places, which are always trying to come up with new flavors, she never changes her recipe, so I always know I'm safe to dip right in.

"So," my dad said. "Not BARF this year, but RETCH?"

My mom rolled her eyes at my dad for his complete lack of casualness.

"You're not supposed to call them that," I muttered.

"Honey—" my mom began.

"Do we really have to talk about this?" I asked. "Hugo, tell us again what square you're going to sit on."

My mom put her hand up to stop Hugo. “Eat your cheeseburger, Hugo. Minerva, I think you should tell us about the test. You walked away from it thinking you did okay, so what happened?”

The expression on Mr. Kreplach’s face when the meatloaf hit him flashed before my eyes. I squirmed in the booth.

“Minerva?” my dad said.

“The test had green beans and pureed parsnips, and the meatloaf part had green peppers in it.” I carefully dipped a corner of my grilled cheese into the ketchup.

“Hmm,” my dad said, taking a huge bite of his turkey-avocado burger.

“And I suppose you couldn’t just . . . pick the green peppers out?” my mom asked.

Of course I couldn’t. Didn’t she know me and my lie detector tongue at all?

“I did pick them out. But it didn’t work. I still tasted the—”

“Flavor fingerprint,” my parents said at the same time. My mom heaved a sigh. I hate it when she sighs in that tone of voice.

“You guys just don’t understand how it feels to have a stupid tongue that tastes everything,” I muttered.

“My tongue tastes everything, too!” Hugo said loudly.

“It’s not the same thing, Hugo. I can taste stuff that’s not there anymore.”

Hugo lowered his brow over his brown eyes as he thought about this. "But *how* do you taste it if it's not there?" he asked.

"I don't know. I can't explain it. I just do."

"That's weird." Hugo leaned into me. "You're WEIRD."

"Okay, okay—enough, Hugo. Minerva is not weird." My mom reached across the table to push him away from my face.

But the thing is, he's right. I am weird. I don't know anyone else who tastes things the way I do. Certainly no one in my family. They're all really good at eating. In fact, Hugo's probably going to do so well at St. Julia Child, I bet he never gets a single P in Eating.

"Soooo, where did Cindy and Patricia end up?" my dad asked.

I snapped my head up to look at him. Now *he* was using the ho-hum-everything-is-okay voice, and I knew exactly why. My parents were always nice to Patricia and Cindy, but my mom has hinted so many times how great it would be if I made other friends. Like she didn't understand that they were my best friends. Why would I need other friends when I had them?

"They both got into Gifted and Gourmet, okay? Are you happy now that I have no friends in my class at all and I'm going to be lonely for the entire year?" I dropped my sandwich back into the basket. It tasted like sand now.

"Okay, well, who *is* in your class?" my mom asked.

"I don't know. They're all kids I don't really know. I mean,

I know who they *are,* but I'm not *friends* with them," I said. "Oh, and Alice Who Only Eats White Food—she's in there, too. I'm a weirdo just like her, and now everybody knows it."

"WHERE ARE MY PICKLES?!" Hugo demanded suddenly.

"Hang on—Hugo, don't interrupt your sister. Your pickles are right there next to your milk—Alice . . . who?" Mom asked.

"Alice Who Only Eats White Food," I repeated. I peeled a strip of melted cheese off the wax paper.

"Do you mean Alice Pepin?" my mom asked. "The Alice from your second-grade class?"

I nodded.

"But WHY does she eat white food?" Hugo asked, his voice thick with pickle slices.

I shrugged. "Because that's what she likes, I guess."

Hugo was silent for a second. "Milk is a white food, and I like it!" he finally said, grabbing his carton and chugging it. Tiny streams of milk ran down his chin.

I scowled at my now-cold fries. "Everything is awful."

"Everything is not awful, Minerva," my mom said. "You have to look on the bright side—"

I interrupted her. "The only people who tell people to look on the bright side are the ones who don't understand how it feels to be in sixth grade with no friends because they're both in another class together. And I'll probably never be able to find them at lunch or recess and I'll just spend the whole time looking for them while they plan Patricia's presidential campaign without me. And on top of that, I'll probably fail RETCH and have to go to summer school!"

I ran out of air. It was hard to breathe, listing all the ways my life was ending.

Hugo launched himself at me, locking his chubby arms around my neck and pressing his soft, chunky cheek against mine.

"I will play recess with you, 'Nerva," Hugo promised solemnly, squeezing me so hard his five-year-old body quivered with the effort. Even Hugo's hugs can give you bruises.

"Thanks, Hugo," I said.

I decided not to tell him that kindergartners aren't allowed to leave their own yard. Hugo, being, well, *Hugo,* will most likely see the fenced-in playground as an interesting obstacle to overcome by the end of the first day of school. Better not give him extra time to prepare for it.

He broke his painful hug by pushing my face away with pickle-stinky hands, and he reached for his milk again. "I'm very drink," he explained between gulps, which is Hugo-language for thirsty. He started saying it that way in preschool, and we all loved it so much we have never corrected him.

"I thought *you* were going to be the sixth-grade president," my dad said, and then gave my mom a look. She gave him the exact same look back. I hate it when they do that. It's like they think I don't know what they're thinking when I know exactly what they're thinking. And they're thinking that Patricia pushes me around, but they just don't understand how things are. It's fine that she does that. I mean, sure, it bothers me *sometimes,* like today when I was in a bad mood, but we're still friends. And that's the most important part.

I shrugged, to show how much I didn't care about being president anymore. And then I yawned for good measure. Nothing like a yawn to show how very unconcerned you are about whatever is being talked about.

"What about your purple notebook and all the presidential plans you had cooking over summer vacation?" my mom asked.

"I don't know. Maybe we can use them to help Patricia," I said.

"But they're *your* plans," my dad said.

"Yeah, and they're *my* friends!"

The table was quiet, except for Hugo's loud chewing and slurping. He enjoys his food with such energy, my mom always has to pick up the stuff that has fallen under the table. She feels bad leaving behind a Hugo-size mess for someone else to clean up.

"You know what I think?" my mom said, choosing her words in a way that made me tense up. I knew exactly what was coming.

"I think that being in a different class with all new kids might actually be a good thing. Maybe you'll—"

"I threw meatloaf at Mr. Kreplach's face!" I blurted out.

My dad nearly choked on a bite of his turkey burger.

I hadn't meant to tell them that, but I could not bear to listen to my mom telling me again how I should make new friends. I *had* friends. *Best* friends.

While my dad was busy coughing and wiping his eyes, my mom said, "You did what?"

"I, um, threw meatloaf at Mr. Kreplach's face," I said, then added quickly, "but I didn't mean to. It was an accident!"

"Minerva Van Zoren, how do you *accidentally* throw meatloaf at your teacher's face?" Mom demanded.

"It was in my napkin, and I got so excited when Mr. Kreplach excused me that I sort of . . ." I couldn't go on. I'd rather they just read my brain instead of having to say all of it out loud. Saying it made it so much worse.

"You 'sort of' what?" Dad asked, taking a sip of his drink, his eyes watering.

"I flung the napkin in the air, and the meatloaf flew out of it," I whispered.

My mom reached for an onion ring. "What was the meatloaf doing in your napkin in the first place? No—wait." My mom held up a hand. "I don't want to know. I can guess."

"Oh, Minerva," my dad said, shaking his head. "We just—"

“I know, I know,” I said quickly. “You need me to try. I will. I promise I will not throw meatloaf at another teacher’s face. Ever.”

“TRAIN! TRAIN!” Hugo shouted, jumping up on the seat and smearing his face against the window so he could watch the long, slow-moving freight train.

I picked up my grilled cheese sandwich, relieved that the discussion seemed to be over. I had no problem promising my parents that I would try. I knew it was a promise I could keep. Well, at least I was pretty sure it was one I could keep. I just didn’t want them to make me promise to make new friends this year. I didn’t need new friends—I needed to make sure I kept the ones I had.

CHAPTER 6

Before I walked out the door on the first day of school, my mom pulled me aside. She had the same worried pinch between her eyes that showed up every time my report card came home.

"Min, you'll really try your best today, right?" she said. "You'll listen to the teacher and pay attention and just . . . try?"

I busied myself readjusting the straps on my backpack to avoid looking her in the eye when I answered, "I always try."

"You didn't get enough sleep last night, did you?" she asked.

I shook my head. Mom gave me a hug and a gentle push out the door. "I'll see you this afternoon."

I was always too excited to sleep very well on the night before the first day of school, but the night before my first day of sixth grade was different. Instead of being excited for the morning, I was super dreading it. And even when I did sleep, I had the worst nightmares.

I dreamed that my mom decided to make her own cheese in an oozing bag hanging over the sink, like so many other Muffuletta parents do, instead of buying it in blocks at the grocery store. I woke up sick to my stomach and shaking. At breakfast, I checked the sink: no oozing bag of cheese. But just to be safe, I wrote "cheese" three times on a shopping list and taped it to the fridge.

There might have been a lot of changes happening in sixth grade—new teacher, way harder lessons, much, much smaller class (there were only five of us!)—but there was one thing staying very much the same: Eating lessons were still scheduled to come immediately after PE. Ugh.

The school had this idea that putting Eating after PE, instead of after Social Studies or Writing or something else, was best: after all that running around and throwing things at each other, we'd supposedly be good and hungry. I thought the exact opposite. Sometimes just looking at a food I hate is enough to make me lose my appetite. It was real unlikely that getting sweaty in a smelly gym was ever going to change anything.

At the start of our first Remedial Eating lesson of the year, Mr. Kreplach bent over his desk and shuffled through a stack of manila folders. When I was in kindergarten, I thought Mrs. Courgette called them vanilla folders. I was really disappointed when I sneaked a lick of one and discovered that it tasted nothing like my favorite flavor of ice cream. I have this whole theory that the best way to judge an ice-cream brand or shop is to taste their vanilla. If they can get that right—an even balance of rich vanilla bean flavor without being too sickly sweet—then you can usually trust them to get the rest of the flavors right, too. (Except rum raisin because there's no way anyone can make that flavor good.)

I explained my ice-cream theory to my mom once, and she said, "For such a picky eater, you really think a lot about food."

But the thing is, when I love a food, I really *LOVE* it, and I think very hard about what it is that makes it so great. Unfortunately, I do the same thing with the foods I hate. I kind of can't control it.

"Now, before we begin today," Mr. Kreplach said, holding up the stack of folders for us to see, "these are your Eating records. They list all the foods you are struggling with. For some of you, it's a handful of things, but for others"—he squinted watery blue eyes down at me—"it's quite a bit more."

My cheeks burned. I fixed my eyes on my desk. I was finding it difficult to look at Mr. Kreplach without seeing a piece of meatloaf flying into his face. I had to dig my fingernails into my leg skin as a wild giggle threatened to surge out of my throat. Mr. Kreplach dropped the folders back on his desk with a bang.

"That all changes now," he said. "There might be only

five of you in RETCH this year, but it's still five too many for this school. You're all going to learn how to be better eaters.

"Okay," he said, grabbing an oven mitt and pulling a pot off the classroom stove. "Since it's the first day, we're going to start with something easy."

He set the pot on a side table and removed the lid. Steam billowed out.

"Oatmeal."

All of us let out groans, except the girl with warm brown skin and long black braids who was sitting next to the window. That was Willa Lewis. Willa's parents were both veterinarians at the clinic where my mom took our cats. She was one of those super quiet kids. I didn't know if she was shy, but I was pretty sure I had never heard her say more than three words when we ran into her at the clinic a few times. Even now, instead of groaning, Willa just stared out the window and whispered, "'Double, double toil and trouble. Fire burn and cauldron bubble.'"

Mr. Kreplach pulled a stack of brightly colored plastic bowls from the classroom supply cupboard and started ladling out lumpy portions of beige oatmeal. I clutched my stomach and thought about the worried pinch between my mom's eyes. Then I took calming breaths. "Just try, just try," I whispered between breaths, looking around at the other RETCH kids.

Surprised, I saw that none of them seemed as disgusted

as me. Although it had *sounded* like everyone was grossed out by the mention of oatmeal, nobody actually looked all that bothered. Even more puzzling, some of them were even smiling. I slumped in my seat. If they were all happy about oatmeal, I was going to be the worst student in Remedial Eating, and I was going to fail and have to go to summer school, and my life would end forever.

I snuck a look at Alice, who sat behind me. She had on a different gaiter from the one she wore the awful day of the class lists. The day when she said weird things about looking out for her friends. This gaiter was rainbow striped and looked hand-knit, but just like all the others she wore, it was pulled up and over her nose. There wasn't enough of her face left for me to figure out how she in particular was feeling about the oatmeal. Feeling me looking at her, she looked up from her desk and stared right back at me over the fuzzy wool. Then, before I could look away quick enough, she winked.

I absolutely did not know what to do with that, so I just turned around again and waited to start my dreaded assignment.

"Alice, please take that thing off during Eating," Mr. Kreplach said when he got to her desk. "Clearly, you can't do your assignment with your mouth covered up."

We all shifted to see what Alice would do. Everyone loved to talk about the elaborate excuses Alice had for why she had to keep her gaiter on. Once, she said it was her security blanket. Another time, she claimed to have an infectious rash that would spread to everyone in the school if she took it off. That was the day she spent hours in the office being examined head to toe by the school nurse.

I wondered what she would say this time, but without a word, Alice pulled the gaiter off over her head and ran a hand through her staticky blond hair. Then, seemingly unaware, or uncaring of everyone staring at her, Alice neatly folded the gaiter up, gave the rainbow stripes a tender pat, and tucked it away in her desk.

I don't know exactly what I expected to happen, but I couldn't help but feel a little let down by the lack of spectacle.

"This is not oatmeal," Akshay said from the other side of the room, without raising his hand.

"Of course it is, Ashkay," Mr. Kreplach said, placing a mustard yellow bowl in front of me.

Akshay opened his mouth to correct Mr. Kreplach's mispronunciation of his name, then closed it with a frown and a shake of his head.

I looked down at my bowl. Akshay was right. It was not oatmeal.

"But there's *stuff* in it!" Alice argued back.

Mr. Kreplach corrected her. "It's not 'stuff,' it's savory oatmeal with Spanish goat cheese, pickled shrimp tails, sautéed kale, and sieved eggs."

"'Eye of newt and toe of frog,'" murmured Willa. She spoke so much to her lap, I wasn't even sure I heard her correctly.

"What kind of eggs? Sifted?" Akshay asked. "Like flour?"

"No, *sieved*—it means to push something through a fine mesh screen," Mr. Kreplach said.

"Like a window screen?" Willa asked so quietly that Mr. Kreplach asked her to repeat herself. Willa had a huge book open in front of her. There were a lot more words on the broad pages than I had ever seen in a book. I squinted—the words were really tiny, too.

Willa blushed and raised her voice slightly. "You mean like a window screen?"

"Exactly," Mr. Kreplach responded, motioning at her to move her huge book to make room for the bowl of oatmeal. "Please put the Bard away during Eating."

The what? The bar? Did she have a granola bar? I didn't think we were allowed to have any outside food at St. Julia Child. I looked over at Willa in time to see her put *The Complete Works of William Shakespeare* into her desk. Wow, was she reading Shakespeare for fun? I was impressed. My mom took me to a Shakespeare play once, and I didn't really understand anything. Like, I understood the words, but not what they were *saying.*

"Well, that doesn't seem very sanitary," Willa went on.

"Have you ever *seen* a window screen close up? They're covered in dirt and bugs and fur and cat vomit."

"Cat vomit?" Mr. Kreplach boggled at her.

"Hunca Munca, my cat, sits next to the kitchen window to keep an eye on the birds. Sometimes he throws up on it," Willa said. "He gets hairballs." Then she closed her mouth abruptly and fixed her eyes on her desktop, as if she suddenly realized how much she was talking.

Mr. Kreplach looked like he had a lot of questions for her, but didn't know how to ask a single one of them.

"I have two cats!" I exclaimed without thinking. "They are Needles and Bean. Bean's got black fur, and she gets tons of hairballs, and when she throws them up, they look like long black sausages."

"Gross," Willa said, ducking her head and giving me a slight smile.

"So gross," I agreed, and smiled back. Talking about vomit and hairballs made me feel better than I had all day. All week, even. And yeah, I knew that was a super weird realization.

"Mr. Kreplach," Alice called, "if we have hair, but cats have fur, why do people call them hairballs when they throw them up?"

"I—uh . . ." Mr. Kreplach struggled to respond. He ran a hand through his yellow hair, making it stand up on end.

"Do you think we could study it in science?" Alice persisted. "Maybe Willa and Minerva could bring a few in for us to look at."

"We could dissect them!" I said. I loved dissection. Cutting things open to see what was inside was like cutting open a puzzle. Not that there would be anything too puzzling to find inside what Bean hoarked up, since it was probably just more fur, but I really liked the way Alice thought.

Mr. Kreplach's face went slightly green.

"HOARFF!" a white, freckled boy named Ralph Leebens announced.

"Excuse me?" Mr. Kreplach said, whipping around to him. "Did you say something?"

"I'm done!"

"Me too!"

Willa and Akshay waved their hands in the air. Wait, they were done already?

Mr. Kreplach started to walk over to them.

"HOARRRRFFFF!" Ralph said again. Louder. More insistent. His pale cheeks turned bright pink with the effort.

Mr. Kreplach turned back to Ralph, who had his hand over his mouth.

"Mr. Kreplach, should we wash our bowls for you?" Akshay called.

"Fine, fine," Mr. Kreplach said, still eyeing Ralph. "Take them to the sink."

As they slipped behind Mr. Kreplach's back, I got a closer look at the bowls. My eyes widened: the bowls were not empty! Not even close. But Mr. Kreplach was distracted by Ralph and didn't see what I saw.

"Ralph—" he started to say.

"Mr. Kreplach," interrupted Akshay, running the water, "I think Minerva is done, too. Should we just—"

"*Yes yes yes*—just collect all empty bowls, please and thank you," Mr. Kreplach said, rubbing his eyes.

Willa reached for my bowl. "Oh, but—" I started to say, then stopped as Willa gave a tiny, urgent shake of her head. I snapped my mouth shut and stared at her. What was going on?

Mr. Kreplach stared down at Ralph. "Do you actually have anything to say?" He crossed his arms to show just how much he would not put up with today.

"I'm not saying anything," Ralph explained. "It's just the sound I make before I think I'm going to throw up."

"You're going to throw up," Mr. Kreplach stated.

"Not necessarily. Maybe. It could happen," Ralph said, then clapped his hand over his mouth.

Mr. Kreplach glared. "I'm not going to fall for that." But he stepped back quickly and banged right into Alice's desk.

It didn't seem as though he banged *that* hard into Alice's desk, yet her desk sort of jumped up and teetered in reaction, sending her bowl of oatmeal skittering across it. Alice's arms were stuck way under her desk, and she didn't even try to grab for her bowl. Without thinking, I reached out to catch the bowl as it tipped off the edge. But Alice bugged out her eyes at me. Shocked, I snatched my hands back and let the bowl clatter to the ground, splattering oatmeal, shrimp tails, and sieved egg everywhere.

"Darn," Alice said, grinning. "You almost had it."

As Mr. Kreplach stared at the mess on the floor, Ralph jumped up and scurried his bowl over to Akshay, who quickly rinsed everything in it down the drain.

Mr. Kreplach sighed, looking very, very tired. "Alice, please get a damp cloth to clean this up. There's a stack of clean ones behind Morty, the weeping fig tree in the corner. And please be more careful. I'll have to give you an Incomplete for today."

At that moment the announcement system squealed to life, making everyone jump.

"Forgive the interruption, teachers. Please send Minerva Van Zoren to the office. Minerva Van Zoren to the office, please."

The entire class *oooooooohed*, the way entire classes always do when anyone is called to the office. They think it means someone is in big trouble, but I am going to tell you something right here and right now: it doesn't actually mean that. It usually means that their parents brought in homework they left at home or they have a dental appointment or something totally boring like that.

That's what I tried to tell myself as I walked to the office. I couldn't think of anything I had done since the meatloaf incident, and school had only just started. But I've also learned that it can be pretty difficult to predict when you're going to get into trouble. And that always worried me. It worried me that it was possible to have done something that got you into trouble without your knowing it.

In the school office, Ms. Morel was busy on the phone, so when I walked in, she pointed at some chairs. I sat down on the edge of one and waited. Ms. Morel sits at the front desk, makes the schoolwide announcements, knows every child by name, comforts crying kindergartners who want to go home on the first, second, or eighteenth day of school, and basically knows everything about everything at St. Julia Child.

"No, Mrs. Landingham," she was now saying into the phone. "The school simply doesn't have the resources right now to make its own salt. Yes. I— Yes, everyone at St. Julia Child agrees that it's important to eat local, Mrs. Landingham, but maybe the PTO president can help you with this? You could fundraise or something?"

Ms. Morel sighed and then tried to say a few more things, but I could tell it wasn't working by the way she couldn't get a full sentence out. Finally she motioned me to her desk.

Covering the receiver with one hand, she whispered, "Just go into Principal Butcher's office. They're waiting for you."

I opened my mouth to repeat "They?" but Ms. Morel was now talking to her caller about growing peppercorn plants in the school gardens.

Principal Butcher's door was slightly open. I knocked anyway. Even though I'm a girl, that's called being mannerly.

"Yes?" Principal Butcher called out.

I poked my head around the door. Hugo was sitting on a chair by the principal's desk, swinging his legs. He had both hands wrapped around a half-eaten ear of corn. I groaned inside of myself.

"Ah, Minerva," Principal Butcher said. "Thank you for coming. I'm sorry I had to interrupt Mr. Kreplach's very important lesson, but we have a situation with your brother and have been unable to reach your parents. We thought you could help."

A few corn kernels dropped off Hugo's chin. "I'll clean it up," he said, sliding off the chair and rubbing the kernels deeper into the thick carpet with his foot.

Principal Butcher's eyes went all boggly and round. But she dragged her eyes away from Hugo and spoke in a voice that sounded like it was being forced through a meat grinder. "Hugo took every ear of corn from Mr. Collard's snack trays, and he won't tell anyone what he did with them. We were hoping he might tell you."

"All of them?" I repeated.

"Yes. Twenty-three ears."

"Was it . . . cooked?"

"Not yet."

"You're eating that raw? And no butter, salt, or anything?" I asked my little brother, already knowing what the answer would be, Hugo being Hugo. As far as any of us in my family could tell, Hugo hadn't yet met a food he didn't like, and everything seemed to taste good to him. Or, at least, it didn't taste awful, the way many foods did to me. He was an eating machine.

"I'm jus' taking a bite," Hugo said, finishing off the ear.

"Did you eat all the other corns?" I asked, kneeling next to him.

Hugo leaned forward and put his mouth right on my ear. "Nope. It's treasure," he whispered loudly. "I've never seen so much corn at once! I don't like sharing." He frowned. "Just sharing with you."

I groaned.

"He likes to hide things in our yard," I explained to Principal Butcher. "He digs holes, buries his favorite things, and then 'finds' them later. He's done it with buttons, broken pieces of chalk, pill bugs—anything he's decided is treasure."

Principal Butcher stared at me. "So the corn is in . . ."

"Maybe check the sand area in the kindergarten yard," I said.

Principal Butcher sat back in her chair, her eyes closed, and groaned softly.

"That's Ecstatic Palate Farm corn. Their fish oil–infused soil is imported all the way from up north. The farmers perform midnight madrigals in the summer months to help the crop grow to its fullest. It costs eight dollars an ear."

I raced through the math in my head. "One hundred ninety-two dollars?" I was so fast with the calculation, I wish my dad was there with a stopwatch. At home sometimes, we made a game of him timing my mental math calculations.

Principal Butcher nodded wearily.

Look.

I don't know what a school is doing giving $8.00-an-ear corn to a bunch of kindergartners when—oh, my mother earth—$192.00 could buy so much other stuff. Like, *SO* many purple sparkly notebooks! I might be only a sixth-grader, but at least I know that grownups have no reason to get upset if they let five-year-olds get that close to something so expensive. Especially if the five-year-old is my brother.

"You can take Hugo back to his classroom," Principal Butcher said, reaching for the phone. "I'll let Mr. Collard know where he can find . . . it all."

I had an idea. Since I'd be helping Patricia become president and wouldn't be having all the meetings with the principal that I had planned, I decided to seize my moment.

"Wait . . . can I ask you something first, Principal Butcher?"

"I'm very busy, Minerva. You and your brother's antics have taken up a lot of my time already."

I really wanted to tell her that "antics" are exactly what they'd probably find all over the corn, but decided I better not. I don't think Principal Butcher enjoys laughing.

"I'll be fast," I said, taking a deep breath. "I was wondering if we could put macaroni and cheese, grilled cheese, or french fries on the school lunch menu."

Principal Butcher raised an eyebrow at me. "We have all those things on the menu already, Minerva."

"Not exactly. Because we have lobster macaroni and cheese with unagi breadcrumbs. And we have truffled sweet potato fries with seaweed flakes and smoked paprika, and our grilled cheese has string beans and creepy corn stuff in it."

"It's not 'creepy corn stuff,' Minerva, it's corn *smut,* which is more properly known as huitlacoche—the fungus that grows between corn kernels. It's a delicacy, and our school is the first in town to put it on a hot lunch menu."

"Sometimes I have fungus that grows between my toes, but it doesn't taste good," Hugo announced. I shushed him.

"Couldn't we just have *plain* macaroni and cheese or fries or grilled cheese without any fungus anywhere at all?"

Principal Butcher looked at me as if I had just suggested

that everyone should wear their underwear on their head and sing the school song while banging on a pasta pot.

I tried to explain. "You know, so kids who don't like all that extra smut will have something to eat? Like those of us who are in RETCH?"

"First of all, Minerva, you know better than to use that *odious* acronym. The proper name of the class is Remedial Eating to Change Habits, and second of all—"

Principal Butcher stood up and planted both hands flat on her desk so she could look me right in both of my two eyes.

"Second of all," she repeated, "before we are through with them, every student who attends this school will leave this school with elevated, elegant, *exceptional* palates. Muffuletta is known all over for producing the best chefs, food writers, and restaurant critics in the world. We don't do *plain* at St. Julia Child."

"But," I said, "since I was helping out with the corn, I just thought you might at least consider adding them."

Principal Butcher pressed her mouth in a line. "How about I thank you for your help and 'consider' forgetting that you made such a ridiculous request, which goes against everything this school and the town of Muffuletta stands for?"

I decided it was best to talk to her about this another time. I also decided not to point out that she didn't actually thank me.

CHAPTER 7

"Come *on,* Hugo—you're going to make me late for lunch!" I dragged my little brother back to the kindergarten yard, where Mr. Collard and a few other kindergarten teachers were already going at the sand area with shovels.

"I need to find Patricia and Cindy to tell them—" I stopped myself. I actually didn't want to tell them about Principal Butcher's reaction to my hot lunch idea. Patricia would probably be a know-it-all about how right she was, and Cindy would agree with her. But the entire school heard me being called to the office, so if they asked, I'd just tell them about Hugo and the corn and leave out the hot lunch part.

Hugo banged through the kindergarten gate and ran straight to the sand area. As I walked away, I could hear him yell encouraging things at the teachers, like "You're getting warmer!" and "Nope, you'll never find it. It's very, very deeper!"

The giant copper teakettle whistled for lunch, sending kids streaming out of classrooms into the courtyard. Heading to the lunch lines, I raced past the kosher and halal windows and jumped into the third line before it got too long. The only thing on the hot lunch menu that I could comfortably stick in my mouth was the plain cheese pizza with a really good crust. And there have been horrible, dark days when Chef Rocco has run out of it.

The description on the hot lunch menu fancies the pizza up by calling it "Pizza with sauce pomodoro, sprigs of fresh basil, and aged mozzarella." But it's red sauce and it's cheese and it's all smacked on a nice, chewy crust. It's cheese pizza.

A small part of me always wants to ask how old the mozzarella really is. And are mozzarella years like dog years, where you have to multiply them by seven? But Chef Rocco doesn't give me time to ask a single question. Not anymore. Not since I asked him if he thought the cold tongue sandwiches could taste us when we ate them. Or why he serves bratwurst when it tells you right in its name that it's the worst kind of brat.

Once I had my little pizza box warm in my hands, I looked around for Cindy and Patricia. I found them sitting at a table and laughing with their GAG classmates. They hadn't saved me a seat.

"Hey," I said, tapping Patricia on the shoulder. She turned around.

"Oh. Hi, Minerva," she said.

"Hey." Cindy waved a forkful of veal stew at me. "Osso buco today!"

I lifted my pizza box. "Pizza."

They nodded but didn't say anything else.

"So, um, how's your first day going?" I asked.

"It's so great," Patricia said, scooping up a spoonful of mealy yellow polenta and mushy lumps of carrots. "Gifted and Gourmet is amazing and so much fun, and Mr. Cornichon is the nicest teacher ever."

"So great," Cindy repeated.

"We had oatmeal in RETCH," I blurted out. "It was really disgusting."

The rest of the kids at the table stopped their conversations and stared at me.

"Oatmeal?" Patricia said, astonished. "Oh my gosh, that's sooooo easy."

"It was savory. It was disgusting," I repeated. Hadn't she heard me the first time?

A girl at the table snorted, then plastered a napkin over her mouth. She wore a yellow St. Julia Child hoodie with blue splotches all over it. It was supposed to look like the cheese on our school flag, but mostly it looked like the fabric was rotting through a bad case of mildew.

I shifted my weight from one foot to the other. I couldn't bring myself to tell them about Hugo and the corn with the entire GAG table listening, and it felt really awkward to keep standing there while saying nothing. Plus, my pizza was getting cold.

"Okay, well, I guess I'll find you at recess?" I said.

"Okay," Cindy said.

I waited for Patricia to say something else, but she had already turned back to her lunch.

"Okay," I said again. "See you later."

Cindy nodded, and then she turned around, too.

Before I walked away, I thought I saw Patricia nudge Cindy with her elbow. But really, it's actually pretty hard to eat lunch at those tables without constantly bumping into people next to you. I'm sure it was nothing.

I carried my pizza box to an empty table and flipped it open.

And then I am pretty sure I died.

And if I didn't die, I must have fallen off my seat and gotten a concussion *AND* brain damage because there was no other explanation for my pizza looking the way it did.

Was that an . . . egg?

Not scrambled. Not hard-boiled. Not omeletted.

But sunny-side up! And staring at me with a filmy yellow eye, like a quivery white cyclops.

I grabbed my box and went straight to the front of the hot lunch line, explaining to all "No cutting!" protestors, "This is an emergency!" I stuck my head under the service window and called into the kitchen, "Chef Rocco—an egg got on my pizza by mistake!"

Chef Rocco slid a bowl of osso buco around me to the next student in line and jerked his flour-covered thumb in the direction of the wall outside the kitchen. "New pizza this year."

With rising panic, I walked over to the school lunch menu. Every day a new one is posted, but since cheese pizza had been on there forever, I hadn't actually looked at the menu in years. Sure enough, there was "Pizza alla Romana" instead of "Pizza Margherita" written out in Chef Rocco's curliest handwriting. Things were getting worse and worse. And the day was only half over.

Back at the table, I stared at the egg. It stared right back at me.

Cooked egg white is not a problem for me. It doesn't leave a flavor fingerprint behind. I could lift it right off and still eat the pizza, no problem. The actual problem was, if the yolk broke, it would send a river of yellow ooze streaming over everything. That would make the entire pizza—cheese, sauce, amazing crust, everything—taste the way a wet dog smells.

I shuddered convulsively, shaking the table slightly. The egg responded in kind, and there was a clear threat of yolk breakage in every wobble. I had to think fast. There was a chance that if I moved more slowly and more carefully than

I've ever moved in my life, I could separate a few slices from the whole pizza without breaking the yolk open.

I was working on my first slice when my RETCH class, Alice, Akshay, Willa, and Ralph, walked up to my table.

"WHAT THE?" Akshay yelled, looking at my pizza. None of them had opened their boxes yet.

"Sidewalk egg pizza," Alice groaned, and flopped down on the bench next to me.

"Don't. Bounce. The. Table," I said, not taking my eyes off my pizza. My jaw ached from clenching it.

One false tug, one overly impatient *yoink,* and the yolk dam would burst.

For the next ten minutes the lunch table was silent as everyone copied my careful egg movements.

"Gotcha!" I breathed at last, sliding one piece free. I gobbled it down faster than anything I had ever eaten and went to work on another piece.

Just as I slid my second piece to egg-free safety, Ralph wailed, "NOOOOOOOO!"

Bright yellow yolk surged over his whole pizza, leaving no slice un-egged.

Everyone gasped. Ralph burst into tears.

Alice, who I just noticed was wearing swimmer's nose clips, examined the damage and tried to console Ralph.

I looked down at my hard-won piece of pizza. One piece

of a personal-size pizza didn't come close to filling my gaping, growling stomach, but one piece was still better than the nothing that Ralph now had.

I handed my second piece over to Ralph. "Here."

Scrubbing tears off his face, Ralph picked up the slice.

"Thanks," he whispered between shaky bites.

The teakettle blew the whistle for recess. I gently nudged my box at them.

"You guys can have the rest of my pizza if you want to keep working on it," I said. There wasn't any time left for me to try for more slices. Patricia and Cindy's table was empty, and they hadn't come to get me, so now I needed to go to look for them.

I was about to walk away when I decided that I just absolutely had to ask Alice about the nose clips.

"What's that for?" I said, pointing at her nose.

Alice grinned. "I have allergies."

"You have allergies," I repeated.

She nodded. "The pollen count is reaaaaally high today."

I was about to ask how a nose clip helped with allergies when I realized something.

"Hey, you ate pizza!" I blurted out.

Alice gave me a strange look. "So did you."

"But I thought . . ."

Then I stopped my mouth from saying something rude.

"You thought I only ate white food?" Alice said.

"Kind of?" Saying it like I wasn't sure if I ever really believed it in the first place seemed less rude.

Alice twitched up one side of her mouth in a half smile, "You can't believe everything you hear from Patricia Jenson."

"Oh, I didn't hear it from—"

I stopped. Of course I had heard it from Patricia. She was always talking about how weird Alice was. And I was always listening.

"In second grade, before the school made that rule that everyone should eat from the hot lunch menu as part of the Eating curriculum, I only ever brought plain pasta with cheese and sometimes a cream cheese sandwich. Patricia started telling everyone that I would eat only white food," Alice said.

I fingered the hem of my shirt, looking for a loose string that wasn't there. "Are you sure it was Patricia who started it? Not someone else?"

But even as I asked, I knew the answer. Patricia's favorite subject was making fun of other people. Especially about how they ate. It all seemed funny at the time, and because Alice was so weird in so many other ways, with the gaiters and the Spuddy Bench yodeling, it also seemed believable. I frowned. I never thought about how Alice might have felt. On the other hand, Alice didn't seem to care what people thought about her.

Alice asked, "Do you remember your *Titanic* report back in second grade?"

In second grade I was totally obsessed with the *Titanic.* I spent all my sharing time telling the class *Titanic* facts. Mr. Haricot told me I could get extra credit in Eating if I did a report on the food the rich passengers ate for their last meal.

"Yeah, that was actually really fun," I said. "But the food I had to report on was so gross—remember all the fish stuff? The salmon mayonnaise and the potted shrimp and the—"

"Soused herrings!" we both said at the same time.

Alice smiled at me. After a moment, I smiled back.

"My mom told me 'soused' meant drunk, which I don't even understand. How do you get a dead fish drunk?" Alice wondered.

I couldn't remember exactly. "It was something about it being cooked in beer or cider or something."

"Oh, and what was the name of that soup? The one that made Akshay laugh so hard Mr. Haricot told him to go sniff lavender in the herb garden until he calmed down?"

"Cock-a-leekie," I said.

It was kind of funny how you could be in a class with kids you thought you didn't know at all just because they weren't your best friends. But then you remembered things about them years later that you had always known. Like how people were always mispronouncing Akshay's name or that his family didn't eat beef. Or how Willa was quiet. And how

Alice yodeled, wore things on her face, and didn't care what people thought of her.

"Oh, right." Alice snorted.

"Wait," I said, pulling myself back to the conversation. "What does my *Titanic* project have to do with you eating . . . or um, you know, *not* eating only white food?" I asked.

"Remember that blancmange iceberg Patricia brought in the next day and sort of upstaged you?"

"She didn't 'upstage' me," I said, getting irritated. "She just—I don't know—she really got into *Titanic* stuff after my report. That's how we are as friends. We inspire each other."

Alice was silent as she chewed on her lip.

"I inspired her to make the blancmange iceberg," I insisted.

I didn't want to admit it to Alice, but at the time, I was, like, maybe the tiniest bit annoyed that Patricia made the iceberg. I actually needed the extra credit in Eating, and she didn't, and it did seem that as soon as she saw how much attention I got for my report, she wanted to grab some of it for herself. But I never said anything to her about it because it would have started a whole argument, and I would end up apologizing later. And it's gotten worse since Cindy became friends with us. If we have a disagreement now, Patricia goes off with Cindy, and it's awful and uncomfortable and lonely.

"Do you remember when Mr. Haricot explained what 'blancmange' was?" Alice asked.

"Yes," I said. I never could forget that. "It's a completely disgusting dessert that you make with milk and gelatin and vanilla and sugar. And you can pour it into molds, and after it sets, it jiggles horribly."

"What about the name?" Alice said.

I struggled to remember what Mr. Haricot told us that day while Patricia cut sections of her perfect iceberg and handed it out for people to eat. I remember *not* eating it.

"It's French?" I said. "And it literally translates to . . . white eat?" I stared at Alice with sudden realization. "She made it to make fun of you?"

Alice shrugged. "She handed me a bowl of it and said, 'Even you can eat this, right, Alice Who Only Eats White Food?'" She looked down and dropped her voice a bit. "And then everyone started calling me that, even if it's not totally true. But it stuck anyway. It was my first year here, and my older brother got lots of friends and good grades, but what I got was a nasty, not-true nickname."

"I'm so sorry," I whispered. I didn't know what I was apologizing for, exactly. But it still came out.

"Minerva," Alice said, looking up and waving my apology away with a slight shake of her head, "it's not your fault that Patricia is the way she is."

I wanted to argue with Alice and tell her that Patricia wasn't like that. I wanted Alice to understand that Patricia was one of those people who could occasionally be mean

—even super mean—and everyone would still want to be her friend. It was like you could burn your tongue on a mug of hot chocolate, but it never stopped you from drinking it. Because the pain doesn't last that long. And by the next time you want a hot chocolate, you have pretty much forgotten that underneath the sweet pillow of marshmallows is something that could hurt you. But only if you aren't careful.

I wanted to explain to Alice how special and proud it made you feel to be one of Patricia's best friends. And that even though she teased me for always ordering grilled cheese, she did it the way friends tease.

I wanted to say it wasn't mean teasing when you were teasing your best friend. Not really.

But all I said was, "I have to go."

As I wandered around the playground searching for Patricia and Cindy and dodging the runaway four-square balls that were painted to look like watermelons, I tried to shake off my conversation with Alice, but something about it wouldn't leave me alone. It wasn't so much that I couldn't possibly explain to Alice what it meant to be friends with Patricia because, when I thought hard about it, I really didn't owe her an explanation about anything. What was getting to me was that Alice said it wasn't my fault that Patricia made fun of her.

"It's not my fault," I repeated to myself. And it wasn't. It was Patricia's fault. She's the one who acted mean like that. Or maybe it was even Alice's fault for being so weird. Why did she have to be that way if she didn't want people to make fun of her?

"She doesn't have to be so weird," I said to myself. "She could choose not to be weird, and then people wouldn't make fun of her."

The teakettle whistled, ending my argument with myself. Recess was over, and I still hadn't found my friends. Frustrated, I flapped my arms against my sides and trudged off the blacktop. It would have been nice if Patricia and Cindy had tried looking for me even half as hard as I had looked for them.

As I walked back toward my classroom, I gave myself a pep talk. Patricia's sleepover birthday party was this weekend, and sleepovers with Patricia and Cindy were always something to look forward to. There'd be popcorn, movies, and just hanging out and laughing. One missed recess wasn't going to change that. I exhaled. Things were going to be okay.

I peered over the kindergartner yard and saw that the facilities crew had mobbed the sand area. They were now using a mini bulldozer to scoop up all the sand, and Principal Butcher herself was directing them on where to dig next. "We can't risk another ant infestation in this school!" she hollered on her megaphone.

How deep had Hugo buried that corn?

Entranced kindergarten faces were pressed up against classroom windows watching the digging. I picked out Hugo, still gnawing on the same ear of corn. He seemed determined to suck every last bit of flavor from the cob. He waved his cob at me, and I waved back and turned away. Passing the teakettle, I gave the lucky spot a good, hard glare.

Nothing about today had made me feel as if any measure of supposed teakettle luck was working for me: horrible oatmeal, the principal rejecting my menu ideas, *egg* on my pizza, feeling sort of ditched at recess, and—and it wasn't my fault that Patricia used a wobbly iceberg dessert to make fun of Alice in second grade. It wasn't! Alice herself even said so, with words and an entire sentence and everything. She's the one who would know.

But I also didn't ever try to be friends with Alice, and—at the coat hooks, I froze, my arm halfway down the depths of my backpack—it wasn't what Alice said. It was what she *didn't* say.

I never tried to stop Patricia from making fun of Alice. Not once. Maybe I was too wrapped up in what Patricia was doing to me with the blancmange iceberg to know what she was also doing to Alice, but there were so many other times I could have stood up to Patricia. Told her she was mean. Told her to stop. I yanked my math notebook out of my backpack.

By my calculations, saying nothing made me just as mean as Patricia. My stomach curdled.

CHAPTER 8

It was Saturday, and Patricia's birthday party was not off to a great start. The day before, I had spent another recess looking for Patricia and Cindy without ever finding them. As soon as I got Patricia alone at her party, I asked what happened and she told me, without even saying sorry, that she and Cindy had decided, without even telling me, to go to the library and read cookbooks.

And then it turned out that I was the only one at the party who wasn't in Gifted and Gourmet.

I wouldn't have thought much of it until Patricia retold a story about something Mr. Cornichon did while preparing a cheese-tasting lesson for Eating.

"And then he said, 'I feel Gouda!'" Patricia said.

All the other girls went off into gales of laughter. And I joined in until one of the girls, Janelle, looked at me and said, "You're not in Mr. Cornichon's class, are you?"

"No," I admitted. "But it's pretty funny. 'I feel Gouda!'" I tried to copy how Patricia said it, but no one laughed.

"Gouda, I get it—like good, but Gouda!" I explained.

"You have to understand how Mr. Cornichon *talks* for it to be funny," Cindy explained.

"Oh. Okay." I felt stupid and lame and totally pointless.

And that's how the rest of the afternoon went. There was a lot of "You had to be there" or "It's a Gifted and Gourmet thing." Finally I stopped trying to join in and just sat on the edges of the party while everyone else nudged and laughed and talked about stuff I didn't know anything about. It was awful.

I tried to get Patricia alone a couple of times, but she was always surrounded by the gaggle of GAGs. And it didn't seem like she wanted to talk to me anyway.

"Haaaaaappy biiiiirthdaaaay, to yooooou."

Mrs. Jenson pushed through the swinging door from the kitchen carrying Patricia's birthday cake to the dining room table. We followed in the glowing wake of the lighted candles and finished the song the way we learned it at school.

". . . happy birthday, to you! Cha-cha-cha! A-ha! Chocolate Chunks! Mama Mia! Pizzeria! EAT! MORE! CHOCOLATE!"

Patricia leaned over the glossy mahogany table and blew out the candles on—well, actually, on closer inspection, what was sitting on the table wasn't something that anyone would ever call a cake. It was pale yellow and jiggly. A slimy, brownish, liquidy top oozed down the sides. And raisins bulged out of its yellow skin like fat black flies drowned in honey.

In the past, Mrs. Jenson had for-real cakes or pastries for Patricia's birthday. They were all completely fancy and filled with stuff like jam and buttercream or wrapped in chocolate and papery pieces of crumpled edible gold. But they were *delicious* fancy. But what was now sitting in front of us, swollen with raisins and doing a shimmy every time anyone slightly bumped against the table, did not look delicious at all. I pressed the heel of my hand against my mouth to hold back a gag.

"Crème caramel, Minerva," Mrs. Jenson said, placing a shivering slice in front of me.

"Ph-phlegm caramel?" I asked. That couldn't really be the name. (On the other hand, my parents once tried to get me to eat a bowl of organs and intestines. They told me it was called offal, and that's exactly what it was.)

"Crrrème car-a-mel," Mrs. Jenson repeated, drawing out each syllable and rolling the *r* in a way my tongue refused to copy.

"This one in particular happens to be a recipe from Florence Fabrilous, the famous food writer," Patricia's mom said, narrowing her eyes at me.

"Oh," I said, shrinking. "Thank you."

Patricia's mom is kind of prickly. I don't think I've ever seen her smile in way that made you believe she meant it. She also has a lot of rules, which makes me feel like I've broken every single one of them before I even step foot in their house. Whenever I go there, she's always watching or hovering or checking on what we're doing. Patricia's house is not a comfortable house.

I waited until Mrs. Jenson was safely back in the kitchen getting the rest of the food before I pushed my dessert plate away. Dessert is always served first at Patricia's birthday parties. That tradition started when we were in kindergarten.

Patricia's mom loves themed birthday parties, and the year Patricia turned six, the theme was an English garden tea party. There was a lace tablecloth spread out on the lawn for us to sit on and china plates and teacups to eat and drink from. There were also baskets of sugar-covered roses for party favors. That's when I found out that sugared roses look much prettier than they taste.

Stationed at the edge of the lace tablecloth were wooden trays and plates of super small sandwiches that Patricia's mom called finger sandwiches. I avoided them until I found out that they were filled with cream cheese and sliced cucumbers, not actual fingers. But when Mrs. Jenson brought out a silver tray of stuffed eggs, Patricia hurled it away and screeched, "WHERE'S MY CAKE?! I WANT MY CAKE!"

Patricia's mom immediately tried to hush her and explain

that the cake came later, but Patricia wasn't having it. She threw herself onto the lace tablecloth, kicked over a few teacups, and screamed until her face was red and shiny with furious sweat. Finally Mrs. Jenson dragged her inside. But her screams could be heard even after the heavy front door slammed shut behind them. All the kids scrambled to the big picture window to watch whatever was going on inside. Birthday party tantrums are fascinating when you aren't the one having them.

While everyone was distracted, I took the opportunity to squeeze the red-speckled yellow insides of my deviled eggs into the bushes and pop the whites into my mouth. They are the only part worth eating when it comes to hard-boiled eggs.

"MINERVA WANTS CAKE NOW, TOO!" Patricia bawled, pointing at me looking through the window. "AND THAT'S BECAUSE SHE'S ALWAYS MY BEST FRIEND IN THE WHOLE WORLD!"

Patricia's mom looked up and saw everyone staring through the window. Her eyes locked with mine. I grinned through my egg whites. That was the very first time Patricia ever said I was her best friend. For days, I had been hoping and hoping we were, but now I knew for sure. I never had a best friend before, and I didn't know that being declared someone's best friend could feel so wonderful. So safe. Like nothing could hurt you.

I gave Patricia and her mom an enthusiastic thumbs-up. Patricia was my best friend, and I definitely wanted cake right then, too. She gave me a watery smile, and Mrs. Jenson's face went redder than Patricia's. I think that's when she decided not to like me.

Now Patricia insists on dessert first every year. I don't know if Mrs. Jenson approves of this way of doing things, but it seems like she doesn't want to risk another public tantrum. Getting to have dessert first is always the best (duh, of course), but for me especially it's even better because it means I can fill myself up with cake or pastries or chocolate mousse or whatever and not worry about starving to death if I don't like the rest of the food. But that all changed at this year's Gifted and Gourmet–themed birthday party; I couldn't bear to eat a single bite of that raisiny phlegm caramel. And as I clenched my napkin in my lap, I wondered what else was in store for me.

"Ta-*da!*" Mrs. Jenson emerged from the kitchen carrying a steaming platter. She set it down on the table, and everyone crowded around to get a look at it.

"Oooh," Patricia breathed, admiring the platter.

I nudged my way through and stared at a sparkling mountain range of salt crust covering a long object. Using two large silver serving spoons, Mrs. Jenson cracked the crust open to reveal an enormous cooked fish. Ugh, fish? At a birthday party?! But then it got so much worse. As Mrs. Jenson cleared away more salt, a tiny moan escaped my lips. The fish still had its head, its eyes, and every last inch of its skin.

Patricia and all her friends squealed with delight. I had to grab my arms around myself to stop myself from doing something really awful, like flipping the dining room table over and running away, screaming my lungs off. Anything to get far away from that staring fish. I closed my eyes instead and took a few deep breaths.

To my huge relief, Mrs. Jenson disappeared into the kitchen again and returned with a pan of macaroni and cheese. "Straight from the oven," she said. "So be careful, girls."

Everyone started serving themselves portions of fish. I shuddered and dug into the macaroni and cheese. By then I was so hungry, I didn't even care how hot it was. I blew quickly on an enormous bite and shoveled it into my mouth. After a few seconds I stopped chewing, but not because it was too hot. Because of something horribly, disastrously, disgustingly else. I gulped down my water before I struggled any words out.

"Is there squash in this? Acorn squash?" I gasped.

Patricia barely flicked her eyes in my direction. "My mom purées it and adds it to the sauce. It's the best."

Squash is truly one of my worst food enemies—it's all the way up there with green peppers, raisins, bananas, and milky casseroles with suspicious things swimming in them.

"Mmmm, soooo gooood," Cindy said, closing her eyes as she took a bite of the mac and cheese.

"Yummy," said Janelle.

I put my fork down.

"What's the matter?" Janelle asked.

"She doesn't like food," Patricia explained, serving herself more fish and some squashed mac and cheese.

"No, that's not true," I said with a stab of hurt plunging into my stomach. "I do like food. Just not all food. And definitely not squash."

"I don't understand how you can not like all food," said Britta, another GAG girl.

"Because I just don't. I can't help it," I said.

"But, like, what's the big deal?" Britta said. "Why can't you just eat it anyway?"

"Because . . . I don't know," I said, feeling trapped. "I just can't. I hate it too much."

They all looked at each other.

"I mean," I went on, desperate to make them, anyone, finally understand at last, "can you choose what music or books you like? No. You like some things, but not others. That's how it is with food and me."

"Yeah, but really, Minerva, there is so much food you

won't eat. It's not normal," Patricia said. "The only thing *I* won't eat is clams, because of my allergy. But I wish I could eat them. I'm sure they're delicious." Her voice took on a mournful tone, and all the girls made sympathetic noises and shook their heads.

"So if you don't like squash, why did you bother to eat the macaroni and cheese at all?" Janelle asked me.

"I didn't know it had squash in it until after I took a bite," I said to my plate.

"That's another weird thing about Minerva," Cindy said, rolling her eyes. "She says she can taste everything even if she doesn't know it's there."

"I can!" I insisted. "Well, not everything. Just the things I don't like."

"And Minerva really only likes grilled cheese—which reminds me—" Patricia jumped up and ran through the swinging door to the kitchen.

Janelle laughed. "*Only* grilled cheese? Are you three or something?"

"Oh, wait, you're not even in Becoming a Real Foodie, are you? You're in RETCH, right?" Britta asked. "You guys are weird—Eating is so easy."

"Excuse me, please, but I don't like only grilled cheese," I mumbled. Heat pricked behind my eyes, and I clenched my napkin even tighter.

The other girls whispered to each other until Patricia

came back with a plate stacked with grilled cheese sandwiches, all a perfect shade of toasted brown.

"Here, made especially for you!" Patricia said with a wide smile.

Speechless, I looked from the grilled cheese to Patricia. She was looking out for me. She was still my best friend. I scolded myself for letting my feelings get hurt over the squashed macaroni and cheese. After all, if that's the way Patricia liked macaroni and cheese, it's the way she should have it at her birthday party. It was so nice of her to make grilled cheese for me.

"Thank you, Patricia!" I smiled in relief as I bit into a toasty warm sandwich. Then my mouth froze. I peered down at the sandwich. All I saw was bread and lovely, oozy cheese, and yet . . .

"Green pepper?" I said, squinting.

Patricia giggled.

I took another bite. Green pepper. My lie detector tongue wasn't lying to me. Green pepper flavor was in there. My tongue knew it was in there.

Then I bit into another sandwich.

Green pepper.

I pulled both sandwiches apart.

There was nothing even resembling the smallest speck of green pepper inside.

Patricia burst out laughing. "You're not going to find

anything, because I took all the green peppers out before bringing the sandwiches to you! Isn't that a great trick?"

"Ohmigosh, you did that just to see if she really could taste it, didn't you?" Cindy asked.

Patricia nodded, still laughing as if it were the greatest joke in the world.

"But why?" I asked, irritated that I could feel tears pin-prick my eyes again. "I've told you for years about my tongue. Didn't you believe me?"

Patricia shrugged. "I thought it would be an interesting experiment. Maybe you were telling the truth, maybe you weren't."

"Wait—you can taste things even if they're not there anymore?" Janelle asked. "That's really weird."

If I didn't leave right then, I was going to start crying in front of everyone, and that would make everything so much worse. I shoved my chair back and ran out of the dining room.

"Come on, Minerva, you're not going to make a big deal about this, are you? It was just a joke," Patricia called after me.

The times I've caught my parents crying—over a book or a memory or an athletic shoe commercial—it's a quiet kind of crying. I guess at some point in your growing up, you somehow learn how to make your sadness less noisy and obvious to others. But I wasn't there yet.

In the hall bathroom, I twisted the faucets on and sat on the edge of the toilet. Not until I had the faucets blasting as full and loud as possible did I let go and cry. It felt like I was wringing days of hurt, anger, and disappointment out of every last corner of me. I had stuck all my hopes on this total disaster of a birthday party as proof that Patricia was still my best friend. Even if everything else was changing around me, that was something I was supposed to be able to rely on. But the only proof of anything I got was that my stupid lie detector tongue was in great working order.

I didn't realize how long I had been in the bathroom until I blotted at my face with one last fistful of soggy tissues and crept back out into the hallway. There was silence in the dining room, which meant that everyone was already done eating and was down in the basement watching movies. Patricia hadn't even come to check on me. Nobody had.

While I was trying to figure out how to make myself go down to the basement and face them all with my swollen eyes and blotchy face, Mrs. Jenson came around a corner carrying a huge bowl of fragrant popcorn. Her hair was, as usual, pulled into such a tight blond bun that it seemed to pull her sallow cheeks back into sharp edges.

"Oh, Minerva. I was wondering who was in there all this time. Was it really necessary to use quite so much water?"

I didn't think I could open my mouth without starting to cry all over again, so I nodded without saying a word. Even Mrs. Jenson didn't notice that I'd been missing from the dining room. Or she didn't care.

"You know, Minerva, I've actually been meaning to speak with you," Mrs. Jenson said. "Patricia really wants to be Muffuletta's Princess Head Cheese one day." She paused. "I don't imagine that is something you're even interested in, am I right?"

I shook my head.

Every year, the best high school Eaters in Muffuletta compete to be crowned Muffuletta's Prince and Princess Head Cheese. The ones who win get to ride on a sandwich float in the Founders' Day parade and wear crowns made of salami sticks. Because I love cheese so much, I actually dreamed of becoming Princess Head Cheese when I was little. I made a crown out of string cheese and wore it all around the house until the cats got at it. There wasn't much left to wear after that.

But a few years later I found out that head cheese isn't cheese at all. It's actually meat taken from the head and face (and sometimes lips) of a pig or cow that gets chopped up and made into a chunky spread. People spread the head cheese on bread. And *eat it.* After learning that, I decided nothing in the world could make me go for the salami-stick crown.

While Mrs. Jenson was talking on and on about all the requirements and responsibilities that come with being Princess Head Cheese, I couldn't help giving a sideways glance into the living room. Showcased on the mantel in refrigerated glass display cases sat four salami crowns on velvet cushions.

They were from Mrs. Jenson's high school years. She had been Princess Head Cheese four times.

"Patricia has so many Eating aspirations, you know? She will most likely be the next great chef or food writer to come out of Muffuletta. And I am just so, so, so glad you girls all agreed that she was the best choice for sixth-grade president. After all," Patricia's mom singsonged, "better eaters make better leaders."

I started to say we never "agreed" any such thing, but then I realized that's exactly what I had done. After all the tears I squeezed out of myself in the bathroom, I didn't think it was possible to feel any more shrunken down than I already did. This one time, my dad had accidentally put my favorite green wool sweater in the dryer, and it came out too small for anyone but a doll to wear. I rubber-banded its sleeves to two of my bedposts and tried to stretch it out, but after a week, nothing changed, and I knew I could never wear it again. That's how my entire self felt.

I pressed my trembling lips together, and Mrs. Jenson went right on, not even noticing that I hadn't said a word.

"The rest of the girls are in the basement, watching the first movie. Be a dear and bring them the popcorn, will you? It's Vermont maple syrup and rosemary flavored." Mrs. Jenson held out the bowl to me and added, "Then you can come back up and finish your dinner in the dining room. You girls are old enough to understand that polite guests clean their plates. Even at birthday parties."

I didn't take the bowl. Instead, I whispered, mostly to the shiny wood floor, "I think I need to go home. I don't feel very well."

Mrs. Jenson pulled back the bowl, giving me a long look and a tiny nod that said she had finally checked off a box about me in her head. "It's really too bad you don't try harder to get over your eating habits, Minerva. Patricia was so looking forward to you celebrating her day." She paused. "I did tell her that not inviting you at all might actually be a kindness, since you might feel . . . a bit out of place now."

I could have told her that it seemed like the only reason Patricia invited me was to tease me in front of other people. I could have told her that I didn't understand how Patricia could be so horrible to someone who had been her best friend since kindergarten. But you're not supposed to talk back to adults. Anyway, I was pretty sure that Mrs. Jenson did not care at all how I felt.

When I didn't say anything, she sucked in her cheeks and said, "I'll go call your mother. You can wait by the door until she gets here. No need for you to interrupt the movie."

My sleeping bag and pillow were still in the living room pile with everyone else's. As soon as I was alone again, I reached into my pillowcase for Patricia's presents.

That morning, I had dragged my mom to five different stores to find wrapping paper in Patricia's favorite shade of lemony yellow.

There was this day in Art when Ms. Naan showed us the color wheel and talked to us about complementary colors. I thought it was cool that my favorite color, purple, and Patricia's favorite color, yellow, were complementary. This meant that when they were next to each other, one made the other shine more brightly. They were supposed to bring out the best in each other.

Along with some pretty, sparkly pens that smelled like lemons and a tiny yellow coin purse shaped like a lemon, I had decided to give Patricia my purple ideas notebook as a birthday present. I wanted to show her that I really was one hundred percent supportive of her running for class president. I even made a new cover by taping construction paper over my name. Now it said "President Patricia's Ideas for the Improvement of the Students at St. Julia Child Elementary and Middle School" in shimmering gold glitter glue. Patricia could use my ideas if she wanted, but there were still tons of blank pages to add her own ideas or include the ones we would come up with together.

If I had been standing next to the giant teakettle in the school courtyard, I would've put my hand on the lucky spot and made a wish that when Patricia opened her present, she'd remember how important our friendship was to her.

She would feel sad that I went home without saying goodbye, and she would bike over to my house right away to tell me she missed me, and then everything would be back to normal by Monday. I closed my eyes and hugged the wrapped notebook until the paper crinkled against my chest.

Then I set my present on the stack with the others and ran out the door.

CHAPTER 9

Kids were out in the streets and yards playing night games on bikes and scooters. The low, mellow light of early evening dappled down from the canopy of trees above and made it feel like it was still summer. I wished it was still summer. I wished I could go back to when the placement test hadn't happened and Patricia's birthday party hadn't happened and Principal Butcher saying no to all my menu ideas hadn't happened. Sixth grade had barely started, and it was already a colossal mess. I rested my head against the car window.

In the front seat, my mom cleared her throat—the grownup's way of warning you that they are about to say something you might not like, so you better get ready.

"Patricia's mom said that maybe you weren't feeling well because you didn't eat a single thing at the party. She kind of made a point of saying 'anything.' "

Of course Patricia's mom would make a point of saying "anything."

"Min?"

My mom was looking at me in the rearview mirror, but I kept my eyes on the kids beyond my window.

"Honey, is there anything else? Any other reason why you wanted to leave?"

I was absolutely in no way going to tell her what happened at the party. Instead of just listening, my mom would bring up all the other times Patricia had been mean to me. And I didn't want to be reminded of those times. Especially not when I was in the middle of this one. One of the worst feelings in the world is talking about how awful you're feeling at the moment you're feeling awful. It just makes the awful so much louder and bigger inside you.

To remind myself of why we were friends, I combed through my brain, trying to remember the last time she had actually been nice to me. Over the summer, things had been fine. Hadn't they? There had been times when it occurred to me that I was the one doing all the calling and asking to hang out. It seemed like she barely called me. And when we did hang out, she didn't act all that interested in anything I told her about becoming president or my trip to the ocean or anything. I didn't want to notice it at the time, so I tried hard to avoid thinking about it. It's not that any of it was really and truly mean. But it didn't feel exactly nice, either. Somehow, being nice had to be much more than just not being mean.

I couldn't tell my mom any of this. Hearing myself say it

out loud would make it too real. As long as I kept it inside of me, I could keep it quiet until I could fix it. Then there would never be a need to talk about it.

My mom sighed as she parked our car. I stared out the window. Our house is pretty small. It's got only three bedrooms—one for my parents, one for me and Hugo, and one that is filled with stacks of boxes and papers and a lot of junk my dad promised my mom he'd throw out but just hasn't gotten around to yet. Dad calls that room his study because sometimes he crams himself into the corner and works on the scratched-up old desk in there.

Patricia's house is huge. Humongous. She's an only child, so she has her own room and doesn't have to share anything. Her house also has an enormous basement filled with toys and a big TV and an indoor trampoline. It was perfect for sleepovers. The basement even has a bathroom, so if you needed to pee in the middle of the night, you didn't have to go looking around in the dark upstairs. Right now, everyone would be down there, laying out their sleeping bags and inflating the air mattresses. Then they'd whisper late into the night. I had an uneasy feeling that I knew what they'd be talking about.

I tromped inside. My dad was standing in the kitchen. "Well, hey there, Pumpkin—would you like me to make you a grilled cheese?" Dad was using his ho-hum-everything-is-okay voice again, though there's no way he didn't know what happened at the party.

I scowled at him.

"Not hungry," I said, and headed down the hall, lugging all my sleeping-over stuff with me. I hate when my parents act like everything is okay when it's obviously totally awful. I didn't want them to *talk* about how awful it was. And I didn't want them to make me talk about it either. I just wanted them to do or say something that would make everything okay again. I had no idea what that something was, but I wasn't a parent. Parents were *supposed* to know how you felt and how to fix it.

In our room, Hugo's rainbow-striped pajama legs were sticking out from under his bed. I threw my sleeping bag in the corner and sank down on my comforter.

There was a warning meow that I knew came from Bean. Her voice is not like any other cat I've heard in my life. She doesn't so much as meow as she bleats like a baby goat. "Hugo, what are you doing?" I asked, hugging my pillow against me.

Hugo's reply was muffled. "I'm loving Needles and Bean."

"You know Mom said that when the cats go that far under the bed, it means they're done with your loving."

Inch by inch, Hugo squiggled himself back out. He was

covered in dust bunnies and clutching a battered copy of his favorite book.

Seizing their chance, both cats streaked out from under the bed and out the door.

"I'm very read," Hugo explained as he dropped the book in my lap and crawled up next to me. That was Hugo-talk for wanting to be read to. "Why are you sad?" he asked.

I took a deep breath and then let it go as a shudder.

"I have mean friends who think it's funny to embarrass me." It was often easier to tell Hugo things. He didn't ask me questions I didn't want to answer.

Hugo placed a small, sticky hand on my cheek and laid his head against my chest. Then he gave me one of his bruising hugs and pulled at my face so I was eye to eye with his solemn little face.

"You smell like hair," he told me.

"Thanks, Hugo." I opened the book.

Hugo fell asleep against me before I got to his favorite poems about Paul the sausage-shaped dachshund and the furious strawberries. I eased myself out from under the curl of his body and tucked one of my blankets around his small shoulders. He turned toward the wall and resettled, his thumb in his mouth.

I stepped into the hallway outside our room and stopped. I could hear hissing coming from the kitchen. My parents were whispering. And whispering meant they were either talking about Christmas presents or they were talking about me.

Avoiding all the creaky parts of the floor, I crept down the hallway until I got close enough to hear what they were saying.

"—her pickiness. It's become so difficult."

That was my mom.

"Look, I know, but remember what Dr. Claussen said at her last checkup? She said she's not worried about her growth or development or anything. She'll be fine."

That was my dad.

Then there was a bunch of clangs, clinks, and slams as one of them loaded up the dishwasher.

"—something happened tonight, but she won't talk about it. All I know is that Patricia's mom said Minerva didn't eat anything." My mom again.

"We just have to be patient. The Eating curriculum is much more challenging now than when we were in school. All we really had to know is how to eat all the vegetables they threw at us. But now everyone seems to expect kids to be able to eat grilled squid and pâté as soon as they can walk!"

"I know. I just wish—"

The dishwasher shooshed to life, drowning out most of what my mom said.

"—it would be so much easier!"

The dishwasher was making it impossible to hear

anything else, which was good because I had definitely heard enough. I crept back to my room and climbed onto my bed, where Hugo was still sleeping.

Of course it would be "so much easier" if I liked more foods or didn't have such a freaky tongue. Then my parents could cook whatever they wanted and I'd eat all of it. Actually, they already cook whatever they want, and if I don't like it, they just make me take three bites and leave the rest. Unlike Patricia's mom, who makes everyone clean their plates.

There was only one time my parents tried that on me. When I was three, they said they wouldn't let me get down from the table until I cleaned my whole plate. I stayed at the table until I fell asleep smack-dab in the middle of my unfinished pot roast. They never made me do that again.

Excuse me, please, but I wasn't *trying* to make life difficult for my parents—or anyone else for that matter! Why doesn't anyone get that? Don't they understand how perfectly wretched it is to hate so many foods? Going out to dinner, or even just over to a friend's house, is beyond scary when you have no idea what you're getting yourself into. There are so many potential dangers lurking in other people's kitchens, like gross and mushy vegetables, or stinky fish that watches you while you eat it, or green-pepper-covered anything. And that's just the beginning.

Stupid tongue! I punched my pillow. Hugo rolled over against me.

“Can I tell you something that’s a secret, ’Nerva?” Hugo murmured, half awake.

“What?”

Hugo put his mouth right against my ear.

“We have raccoons at school now!”

“Raccoons?”

Hugo nodded around his thumb.

“How on mother earth do you have raccoons at school?”

Hugo took his thumb out of his mouth.

“We’re watching them before they are butterflies,” he explained.

“Those aren’t—actually, never mind. Raccoons are very cool to watch.” I was quiet for a minute, then asked, “Hugo, how can you like everything you eat?”

“Because I do. It’s just how I be me. *You* know that, ’Nerva,” he said.

Yeah, I knew.

I went out of my way to avoid my parents for the rest of the weekend. They seemed to know what I was doing and gave me lots of space to do it. It made me grateful and angry at the same time, which mixed me up inside even more.

When Monday morning rolled around, I had a really hard time getting out of bed. I had waited and waited all Sunday, but Patricia never called to apologize or thank me for the birthday present or anything. I wished I could stay home instead of facing a whole day of school feeling like this, but my mom would ask too many questions. So I hauled myself to the bathroom to wash up and get dressed. I couldn't even bring myself to care what I looked like. I just wanted to fade into the background forever. After pulling on whatever clothes I grabbed first, I dragged myself into the kitchen with a giant stone in my stomach.

Breakfast tends to be one of the easier meals. It's usually just cereal, milk optional, or a breakfast bar. On the weekends when they have more time, my parents will try to push scrambled eggs or bacon on me. I love the bacon, but I know how to avoid the egg part using a secret trick.

I divide the eggs into smaller pieces and then spread them out around the plate with my fork. All that empty space between the egg bits makes it looks like I eat way more than I do. One morning, though, my dad figured out what I was doing.

"Min, what you're doing right now is basically known as the Banach-Tarski theorem," he said.

"What is?" I pretended not to know what he was talking about.

"The way you're moving your eggs around your plate to make it look like you ate them when you actually didn't."

I put a confused look on my face, which made me look very innocent.

Dad went on. "The Banach-Tarski theorem says that it's possible to cut something up into a certain number of pieces and then rearrange it and have it end up being half the size it was to begin with."

"Really?" Now I was interested. Math is one of those crazy, beautiful subjects where it feels like anything can happen. It's not just about right and wrong answers, it's about future possibilities.

He nodded. "No one's actually physically done it, but the math has proven that it can be done."

At Stanfork University, my dad spends most of his time writing exams, getting his students to work on the Ham Sandwich Theorem, and talking to Professor Concord about the unsolved Pieman Hypothesis. At home he likes to tell me and my brother about other cool math things he knows. I like it, even if he did catch me out on my egg trick. Now I just use ketchup to get my three bites down. Cereal's still easier.

But before I could pour cereal into my bowl that morning when I was dreading everything, my mom set a plate in front of me.

I frowned at the green-smeared triangles of toast. "What is that?"

"Avocado on toast with a bit of sea salt, some capers, and feta cheese." My mom returned to the kitchen without allowing me time to react.

"Where's the ketchup?" I asked.

"No ketchup today." And there was a decided briskness

in my mom's voice that told me she wasn't going to give in on this.

"But I like toast as just toast. With butter. Not with all that other stuff." I pushed the plate away and stood up. I wasn't going to eat avocado toast for anything. Not even three bites. Not today.

"I thought you might want to try something new this morning."

"Why would you think I'd *want* to try something new? Do I ever want to try something new?"

I didn't realize I was raising my voice until Hugo clapped his hands over his ears and yelled, "TOO LOUD!"

But I kept going, and I kept getting louder. "Do you even care how I feel, or do you just want a perfect child—like Hugo, who's *easier?*" I didn't wait for an answer. I yanked my backpack off the back of the chair and slammed out the front door. My mom didn't try to stop me. She probably thought it was *easier* not to.

I trudged to school, eating the crackers and orange segments I keep hidden in my backpack for emergencies, and thought about just how much I hated being a picky eater.

CHAPTER 10

The next few days were awful. Worse than awful, they were *horrendful.* I didn't say a word to a single human being, and I got so good at not looking anyone in the eye that all I saw for days was pavement, pavement, cracked pavement, yellowy egg-stained pavement, pavement. I also got a slight crick in my neck, but I'd rather deal with that kind of pain than the kind that can't get rubbed away.

I almost saw Patricia and Cindy a few times. Except I didn't so much see them as be aware of exactly where they were. Of their voices coming closer. Of a flash of a favorite shirt or a familiar flip of the hair that I caught out the corner of my eye. And then, before I could fully focus on it, before I could let my brain tell me, "Hey, that's Patricia coming through the door," I turned and ran in the opposite direction. Almost as if, by not looking directly at them, I was somehow safe. Or at least not seen by them. Which amounted to the same thing.

Even in RETCH, I shrank away as much as possible from

any class participation. At the edges of my brain I was aware of how busy the other four were, sneaking their Remedial Eating lessons away down the drain or even deep into the soil of the plant named Morty. But when Alice or Ralph paused at my desk like an unasked question, I answered them by staring at my desk and holding tight to my lesson bowl. When I turned assignments in untasted, I shrugged at Mr. Kreplach's frustrated face. I knew I was racking up rows of glaring red Incompletes in his grade book, but I couldn't bring any part of myself to care. When lunchtime came, I leaned against the wall in the cold tiled bathroom and waited for the teakettle to whistle. No one could make me eat with everyone else if I didn't want to.

I hated everything about school and myself.

But everything changed one evening. I was trying hard to distract myself in the minutes before my parents told me for the fifth and final time that I had to get to bed. Night and dark and the quiet under my covers with my wide-open brain was always the time when all my worries couldn't be packed away any longer.

On that particular night I was cleaning out my backpack, sorting through binders, textbooks, uncapped pens, and broken erasers. Stuffed all the way down at the bottom of the backpack among the pencil shavings, a sticky plastic baggie, and a random rock I collected because of how strange and potentially dinosaur eggy it looked was a bunch of papers I was supposed to give to my parents but had totally forgotten about. There were at least six screaming salmon-pink flyers advertising an eighth-grade bake sale that was raising money for new classroom stand mixers and another few about the Food Science Fair. As I was taking fistfuls of these papers to the recycling bin, a folded white square flipped to the ground.

Before I could hold it back, my heart leaped all the way from my rib cage and stuck itself in my throat, beating hard. A note! From Patricia! I dumped the other papers, grabbed the square, and opened it—my shaking fingers nearly ripping it in half. Would it be nasty? An apology? A plea to be best friends again?

As I ran my eyes over the unfamiliar handwriting, my heart sank back to the soles of my feet. It wasn't from Patricia. And I didn't even know who wrote it, because it wasn't signed. The only thing it said was, "Wear lots of pockets to school." At the very bottom was a drawing—some sort of symbol.

When I was finally in bed and waiting to fall asleep, with Hugo snoring gently across the room, I was still puzzling things over. Who was the note from? How long had it been in my backpack? What did it mean? "Wear lots of pockets"? *POCKETS?* Why on mother earth?

The next morning, my brain felt as if I had spent the entire night with question after question trollomping all over it. All thoughts of Patricia and Cindy, the birthday party, and the past few days were stamped down under the discovery of the note and the question of how I would "wear lots of pockets to school" that day.

After brushing my teeth superfast, I looked at the clothes strewn all over my room. I had clothes with some pockets, but lots? What did that even mean? How do you wear lots of pockets? And how big should the pockets be? Where should they be? Why did I even need pockets? And who on *MOTHER EARTH* gave me that note?

"Pockets!" I ordered myself, yanking open my dresser drawers. I dug out every piece of clothing I could find that had pockets. None of my favorite skirts or dresses had them, which was kind of annoying. Where else were you supposed to put everything you wanted to carry?

Finally I pulled on a pair of basketball shorts that had a hip pocket on either side. Would that be good enough? Just to be on the safe side, which is always the best side to be on in most matters, I slipped my arms into my purple aloha shirt. It had one pocket over my heart.

I studied myself in the mirror, frowning as I tried to finger-comb the snarls out of my brown hair. I really hoped three pockets would be enough for whatever this day was going to be about, because I looked downright goofy. And everyone at school was probably going to laugh at me. Patricia would laugh at me, I thought with an abrupt twist in my stomach.

Maybe I should just dress more regular.

Maybe I should put on things that wouldn't call any attention at all.

Maybe I should forget about the whole pockets thing and pretend I never even saw the note. It was probably some sort of trick anyway. One of the GAG girls or something.

I started to crumple up the note, but the drawing at the bottom caught my eye again. It kind of looked like a shield or a coat of arms, and there was something weirdly familiar about it. I had the feeling that I had seen it somewhere before. But I couldn't think where. And there were letters inside the symbol! I had missed that detail the night before. The letters were written in a curly kind of cursive—the kind of writing you see on menus when the restaurant is trying to hide the fact that their dishes have brains and intestines in them. I squinted.

LOPE

LOPE? What did that mean? Was it a secret code? Ooh, maybe there was invisible writing somewhere on the note! At last year's Food Science Fair, a fifth-grader demonstrated how to write secret messages using lemon juice.

I switched on my desk lamp and held the note close to the light bulb. If there was a secret message, the fifth-grader had explained, the bulb's heat was supposed make it show up. But there was nothing there.

Could *lope* be an actual word itself? I grabbed my dictionary. I hardly ever use it, because it's easier to keep asking my mom what a word means until she finally gives in. But I didn't want to do that today.

I thumbed through the pages until I finally found it between *loot* and *lopsided*. *Lope* meant "an effortless way of moving with long, smooth steps." I flipped the unhelpful dictionary closed and went to breakfast.

"Why are you walking weird?" Hugo, well into his bowl of cereal, asked me.

"It's not weird, it's loping," I told him, and went to grab a bowl.

I loped all the way to school and across campus. I didn't even care who gave me strange looks. And I got a lot of them. When I loped up to my classroom door, I paused. It suddenly struck me that there was something about being in RETCH that felt . . . so totally okay to be weird. Not even just okay, but also a relief. I lifted my chin, pulled open the door, and loped in.

Alice looked up from her seat as I reached my seat. She smiled. "Hey."

"Hey," I said, and sat down. And that was the first word I had said to anyone at school since forever. Could Alice be the one who put the note in my backpack? Just as I opened my mouth to ask, Mr. Kreplach walked into the room and announced, "Class, I'm very excited to tell you that today we are beginning our very first Remedial Eating to Change Habits immersion lesson!"

Everyone looked around, uneasiness pricked out on all of our faces. Immersion lesson?

"Mr. Kreplach, um, I've already been baptized, so can I skip the lesson?" Ralph asked.

"No, no, Ralph—it's not that kind of immersion. Although, by the time we are done with all the lessons, you might feel as though you've had a religious experience." Mr. Kreplach giggled at his own joke. (No one else laughed.)

Clearing his throat, he continued. "Yes, well, ahem—here at St. Julia Child, we are piloting a new and innovative curriculum for Remedial Eating, where you will be fully immersed in foods—"

"Like stomping grapes to make wine?" Ralph spoke again without raising his hand.

"No, Ralph, not like that. At least"—Mr. Kreplach

frowned and flipped through a binder on his desk—"I don't think so.

"Well, not today anyway," he concluded, still frowning at the binder. "Instead, we're going out to the garden to 'Be One with the Brussels Sprouts.'"

"Be one of what?" That was Ralph again.

But this time Mr. Kreplach pretended not to hear him. He opened the side door that led out to the school gardens. "Follow me!"

We filed outside and were met at the vegetable beds by a very tall lady wearing a fluttery pale green dress draped over dark green yoga pants. Wrapped around her neck was a spangled scarf embroidered with radishes, carrots, and deep red beets. She flapped the ends of it at us in greeting.

"Class, this is Madame Bouche," Mr. Kreplach said. "She is a specialist in food immersion therapy, and her techniques are truly groundbreaking. Starting today, you and Madame Bouche will have a weekly session where she will help you experience foods in a whole new way. After she is done with you, you'll come back inside and have your Eating lesson with me." He nodded at Madame Bouche and went back to the classroom.

"Hellooooo, my picky little eaters! I am so glad to meet you! As your wonderful teacher said, I am Madame Bouche, and I am here to help de-pickify every last one of you!"

"Is that like delousing?" Ralph wanted to know. "Because

my dog really didn't like it when we did that to him. He howled until my mom closed all the windows, and then he anger-peed in my sister's closet."

I could have sworn I saw a flicker of irritation break through Madame Bouche's intensely tranquil expression. But as soon as I thought it was there, it was gone.

"Oooh, you're a cute one. I could just eat you up, yes I could!" Madame Bouche cooed.

"HOARFF!" Ralph responded.

Everyone took a step back from Ralph.

But Madame Bouche simply smiled very hard at Ralph. "What a creative noise that was, my dear. But actually the noise we're going to make is slightly different. It's a noise that will get us in what I call the mood for food."

Next to me, Alice groaned.

"Yes, very good dear, that was quite close! Now, everyone sit on the ground—yes, yes, right *in* it. Crisscross tartar sauce."

Reluctantly, all five of us sat down in the dirt and crossed our legs.

"Now," Madame Bouche said, beaming at the group, "take a deep breath in, and when you let it out, say 'Nummy.' Okay? I'll show you, like this." Madame Bouche closed her eyes and exhaled. "Nuuuummmmmmyyyyy."

"Seriously?" Alice muttered, echoing my exact thoughts.

Madame Bouche clapped loudly. "Ready? Okay!"

We all took a deep breath in and nummied it out again. It wasn't that different from the calm breathing I did to stop gagging, but saying *nummy* as a class sort of made me want to crawl away in embarrassment.

"Wonderful! Wonderful! Do it again, and keep going."

The garden hummed with our nummies for many excruciatingly long minutes until . . .

"NUUUUMMMOOOOOOWCH! OWCH!" Akshay screamed, clutching his bottom. *"A bug crawled up my shorts and bit me!"*

We all scrambled to our feet and hurriedly brushed our backsides to make sure we didn't get bitten as well.

"Well, that was simply spectacular!" Madame Bouche squealed. She clapped her hands at Akshay. "Come! Come!" Akshay, holding half his bottom, limped up to her. "Now, while—tell me your name, dear?"

"Akshay," Akshay said.

"Ak-shay—oh, I'll never get that right. Can I call you Shea?" Madame Bouche asked, and then, without giving Akshay a chance to respond, she said, "While Shea goes to the nurse to have his, ahem, *posterior* attended to, the rest of us can move right along to the Food Is Love portion of our immersion lesson." Madame Bouche made a shooing motion at Akshay, who limped out of the garden.

I heard Willa whisper in a warning tone, "'Weeds are shallow-rooted. Suffer them now, and they'll o'ergrow the garden.'" Her dark amber eyes flashed a glare at Madame Bouche.

"What?" I hissed back, unable to help myself.

"It's Shakespeare," Ralph explained. "She did drama camp one summer, and she really got into it. Every so often she says stuff like that. We're used to it."

"According to your files," Madam Bouche said, "Brussels sprouts are something you all need to work on. So please go find your special Brussels sprouts plant and stand next to it."

Along with the rest of the class, I walked over to the Brussels sprouts bed and stood uncertainly at the edge of it. Brussels sprouts are truly the weirdest-looking vegetable ever. They're like alien palm trees from outer space, with the Brussels sprouts growing from their trunks like enormous green warts. No one wants to eat enormous green alien warts from outer space.

"Good! Good! Now, what I want you to do is reach out and caress the Brussels sprouts. Give them a gentle squeeze or a pinch. Get to know how they feel while they are growing," Madame Bouche instructed.

I had no idea how this was going to change my mind about eating enormous green alien warts from outer space, but I tentatively squeezed a few of them anyway.

"Next, I want you to kiss the Brussels sprouts. Tell them how much you *love* them and that you can't *wait* to share your stomach with them."

Someone snorted, but Madame Bouche ignored it.

"Go ahead, *kiss them!*" Madame Bouche encouraged.

Alice raised her hand. "You're not supposed to kiss anyone without permission. It's called consent." Her voice sounded stuffed up—like she had a cold. I looked over at her and saw that she had put on her nose clips.

Drawing her mouth and lips into a very shiny, bright pink pouch, Madame Bouche frowned pointedly at the nose clips.

"They're to stop my nose from growing too fast," Alice explained. "I have a prescription from my doctor."

"Of course, you are absolutely right that you must get consent before kissing anyone, my dear," Madame Bouche said, refusing to allow her class to be derailed.

"Oh, Brussels sprouts," Madame Bouche called out. "May we kiss you?"

She cupped her hand over her ear and grinned wide. She had a smear of bright pink lipstick on her upper teeth.

The entire class waited while Madame Bouche made a series of faces and then nodded, as if she could hear what the Brussels sprouts were saying. Maybe she could.

"Thank you, sweet and wonderful and *delicious* Brussels sprouts!" she finally trilled, and then she curtseyed. "You may all kiss the Brussels sprouts!"

No one wanted to be the first to kiss a plant.

"Kiss them!" Madame Bouche urged. *"Kiss them!"*

"Oh, fine!" Alice finally grumbled. "Let's just get this over with." She shoved her face into a stalk, lips first, and made a loud smacking noise.

I exchanged shrugs with Willa, and we both leaned into our stalks. It was definitely the dumbest thing I had ever done at school.

When the smacking noises around the garden subsided, Madame Bouche walked us back to the classroom door. She put her hands over her heart and looked at all of us, saying, "Until we eat again." And then she left. Probably to go cuddle a cauliflower or something.

"Now that you have immersed yourself in the Brussels sprouts, you will surely enjoy *eating* the Brussels sprouts!" Mr. Kreplach announced, motioning us to sit down as we reentered the classroom. He started dishing spoonfuls of steamed Brussels sprouts into bowls.

Have you ever smelled a steamed Brussels sprout? It's really foul. Like rotting garbage smeared on fried-egg pavement on the hottest day of the year.

Everyone looked up when the classroom door swung open and Akshay limped in with a very bunchy butt cheek. A bit of cotton gauze trailed from the bottom of his shorts. He handed Mr. Kreplach a note and sat down gingerly, tipping a little to one side.

"Are you okay?" Alice whispered to him.

"I think a fire ant got me," Akshay said. "This is my worst bug bite reaction ever. Huge swollen welt down there now."

Mr. Kreplach read the note, and his eyes widened. "Madame Bouche left the school premises without filing an incident report on Ashkay!" He dashed out of the room, muttering, "Oh my goodness. We could end up like Sacred Artichoke Heart Academy. Disaster!"

Some years ago, a fourth-grader at Sacred Artichoke Heart on the other side of town burned his tongue on some hot Bolognese. He couldn't taste food for a few days and had to get physical therapy for his taste buds. His parents were so upset about how far behind he fell in Eating that they sued the school for serving food at an "inappropriate temperature." The Sacred Artichoke Heart administration tried to argue that if the fourth-grader had just waited until the sauce cooled off, he would have been fine, but then the parents gave an interview to *The Muffuletta Gobbler* and all the local food blogs picked up the story, and it turned into a whole big thing. Now, when anyone gets even slightly hurt during Eating, every school in the district has to fill out piles of paperwork.

As soon as the door closed behind Mr. Kreplach, Alice hissed, "Okay, we probably don't have much time. Akshay, go watch the door!"

Akshay struggled back out of his seat and over to the door. He waved an arm up and down, saying, "Go! Go! Go!"

Willa, Ralph, and Alice started stuffing their pockets with Brussels sprouts. My eyes widened. They were all wearing cargo pants or cargo shorts. With "lots of pockets"!

"If you run out of room, you can probably fit some in Morty's soil. Just push it as far down as you can," Willa whispered.

"And maybe leave a few leaves on your plate. It will look less suspicious," Alice added.

"Oh, that's good thinking," Ralph said, nodding.

I was listening to these exchanges with my mouth hanging open. Pockets! The note!

Just as I was about to ask a whole bunch of questions, Akshay shout-whispered, "Shoot—he's coming back already!" and started limping as fast as he could back to his desk, where he still had a full bowl of Brussels sprouts.

"I'm not going to make it," Akshay whimpered. "And Brussels sprouts are the only vegetable I just can't stand!"

I leaped over to his desk, grabbed the Brussels sprouts, and stuffed the entire mass into my pockets. Then I did the same with mine. There was no time to do what Alice had instructed about the leaves, so I left one or two whole Brussels sprouts behind. I hoped that would be good enough. At least good enough not to get an Incomplete today.

"Pretend you're chewing!" Alice said in a low voice.

Mr. Kreplach walked back into the classroom just as Akshay fell hard into his seat and moaned in pain. He shifted his weight to his non-bunchy butt cheek.

"That sounded like a satisfied moan, Ashkay. All done then?" Mr. Kreplach looked around at everyone's closed and chewing mouths. "Excellent! Excellent!" Then he caught sight of my bowl and Akshay's bowl. "Minerva, you and Ashkay need to work a bit harder next time. Maybe do a few more of Madame Bouche's nummies to really let the Brussels sprout love in."

I nodded and took my bowl to the sink. It was impossible not to notice how Mr. Kreplach kept mispronouncing Akshay's name. I just couldn't understand why he didn't realize it. Didn't he ever pay attention to what Akshay wrote on the top of his papers? I'd be pretty mad if a teacher kept calling me MANerva or something. Mr. Kreplach clapped his hands to get our attention.

"From now until lunch, you may have quiet free time. Please use that time to read, do homework, or watch videos, as long as they are food or cooking show videos. But no socializing, this is work time," Mr. Kreplach said. "And if any of you are interested in history, just this morning, Miss C. in IT uploaded all the old St. Julia Child videos to the server. You can learn even more about our school's patron saint from her original cooking shows!"

That sounded pretty interesting. Even when I didn't like the food they were making, I still loved watching cooking shows.

Back at my desk, I scrolled through the videos until I found one where St. Julia roasted chicken. My dad makes the best roast chicken in the entire world, with the crispiest, most delicious skin. He read an article by Helen Rösti, a super famous food writer who writes for *The New Porker*, that explained how to use a hair dryer to dry out the chicken skin before sticking it into the oven. It always comes out perfect. St. Julia didn't use a hair dryer in the video, but she did have a funny disagreement with a thick-accented little man about whether you should wash your chicken before roasting it. The man with the accent said he never washed his chicken. If any germs survived in a 425-degree oven, he thought they deserved to live. I giggled.

When the chicken video finished, the next video in the queue started to play automatically. I read the title: "1995 Clip: Julia Child on Fast-Food French Fries." I rolled my eyes. I didn't even need to watch it to know it would be a lecture on how awful fast-food french fries were and how you need to slather all fries with spices and fungus and precious metals just to make them acceptable as a food.

But before I could click to a video that wouldn't lecture me, the autoplay stopped, and a black dialog box popped up with a crossed knife and fork: "This video has been removed for violating the standards of St. Julia Child Elementary and Middle School."

That was weird.

I hit refresh several times, but I kept getting the same message.

I was about to raise my hand to ask Mr. Kreplach about

it when I felt something damp on my chest. I looked down. A huge wet spot was spreading out from my Hawaiian shirt pocket. The Brussels sprouts were leaking! Thinking fast, I grabbed a notebook and smashed it over my chest.

"I need to use the bathroom!" I blurted, and bolted for the door.

CHAPTER 11

It took some time, but I managed to flush all the Brussels sprouts down the toilet. My shorts were made out of that special moisture-wicking material, so their pockets dried almost instantly, but my shirt was still a little damp. I blotted at the pocket with a wad of paper towels until I heard the teakettle whistle for lunch. Dashing over to the coat hooks to grab a water bottle from my backpack, I realized that this was the first time I was going to the lunch tables in a really long time. While I dug around for the sandwich I secretly packed that morning, I tried to squelch a shimmer of nerves at the thought of seeing Patricia and Cindy.

We're not supposed to bring food from home, but the lunch monitors don't pay much attention to what we're eating. They're mostly there to prevent food fights and make us clean up our trash. Still, it can be risky, so it's not something I can do every day.

Just inside my backpack, resting on top of my secret

sandwich, was another unsigned note. This one said "Pro tip: line pockets with plastic sandwich baggies next time. P.S. Nice work today!" At the bottom of the note was the same shield as on the other note.

I jammed the note into my shorts and bolted for the lunch tables. Halfway across the quad, I noticed kids whispering and staring at me. A few even pointed. I couldn't help myself, I looked over at Patricia's table. She caught my eye and immediately turned back around again and huddled with the rest of her table. Two boys at the table stood up to look at me and snicker. I slapped a hand over my damp pocket and shook my head. I swear, people at this school make the biggest deal out of every little thing.

At our table, Willa, Alice, Ralph, and Akshay stopped talking as I sat down.

"Um, hi," I said. "I know I, uh, haven't been here in a while, but I can still sit here, right?" I fiddled with my paper lunch bag under the table. I felt very twitchy and out of place.

Maybe they were fine with having me in class but didn't want me sitting with them because I had ignored them for so long. I couldn't even think of a way to bring up the subject of the notes now.

They exchanged looks.

Then Akshay leaned across the table. "Did Patricia really make you eat raw fish heads at her birthday party?"

"Wait—what?" I almost dropped my secret sandwich on the ground.

"I heard it was snails *still in their shells,*" Alice said.

"Ugh." Willa shuddered. "Escargot."

Ralph plastered his hands across his mouth, but a muffled "HOARFFFFFFF!" still made it through.

I stared at all of them. "So," I said slowly as all the staring and whispers sank in. "Patricia told everyone about her birthday party." I knew Patricia and I weren't friends anymore—just thinking that out loud in my head gave me a stomach wrench—but I didn't think she'd go and tell people everything.

They nodded. Silent.

"Well, it wasn't fish heads or snails," I said finally. I told them about the crème caramel with raisins, the salt-baked fish, the squashed macaroni and cheese, and finally the green-pepper-infected grilled cheese sandwiches.

"She tricked you with macaroni and cheese *and grilled cheese?*" Akshay exploded. "That's so mean!"

Willa and Ralph nodded, too shocked to say anything at all.

"Wait." Alice held up a hand. "You're saying that you could taste the green peppers even after she took them off?"

Miserable, I poked holes in my sandwich with my fingernails. "It's like I have a defective tongue."

"Um, no—it's like you're a *supertaster!*" Alice corrected me.

"A what?"

"A supertaster—someone who tastes things more strongly than other people because of something to do with their genetics. Get it?" she said, her eyes dancing. "It's like how I'm a supersmeller!" she added, poking me in the shoulder, as if every syllable had an exclamation point.

I rubbed my shoulder. "A supersmeller? Wait, is that why—"

"I wear a gaiter and nose clips?" Alice finished for me.

I nodded.

"Yeah," Alice said. "I need to wear them because I can smell *everything*. Well, maybe not everything, but definitely every food thing. And it's so loud up my nose that I have to find ways to shut it all out. If I can't, it's really hard for me to get through a day of school without feeling like I'm about to die from all the gross food smells. Like, really, totally die."

"Die?" I tried to raise an eyebrow, but then I remembered that I've never been able to do that.

"I'm actually serious," Alice went on. "Your olfactory sense, which is basically everything up your nose except boogers, smells things around you to warn you of lurking dangers!"

"Okay," Akshay said. "You've talked about your supersmeller nose for years, but I don't remember you mentioning lurking dangers."

"I mean like poisonous gas or something on fire," Alice explained. "Your nose is supposed to smell that kind of stuff way stronger than anything else. Like an alarm for your body. But once your brain sorts out what you're smelling and decides that you're not in danger, it tells your nose to stop noticing the smell so much."

"Your olfactory system adapts," Willa said, pushing her black braids over her shoulder. "Just like the Borg in *Star Trek*."

"It's *supposed* to adapt, but my nose doesn't," Alice said. "So I'm a supersmeller all the time. And if you can taste things like green pepper when it's no longer there, maybe you're a supertaster, Minerva."

"Wow" was all I could say. Then my stomach squeezed itself back into a knot. "And everyone's still talking about it? Like, the whole entire school? Still?"

The table went silent again.

“Patricia kind of keeps telling more and more stories about you,” Alice said quietly. “You know how bullies never stop until they get a reaction out of you. And sometimes not even then.”

I closed my eyes, unable to deal with the thought of how many years of stories she could have to tell about me. “And everyone’s laughing at me.”

No one met my eyes.

“Not everyone,” Akshay said. Then he looked right at me. “We aren’t.”

All the RETCH kids shook their heads.

“We don’t think it’s funny at all,” Ralph said.

I twisted around until I spotted Patricia again. She was sitting with Cindy and the girls from her birthday party. As if she could feel me staring at her, Patricia glanced over. She nudged Cindy, who also looked at me. Janelle whispered something in Patricia’s ear. Their whole table exploded in laughter.

My eyes got too blurry to see anything else. I turned around just as two kids from one of the Becoming a Real Foodie classes walked up.

“Hey, is it true you cried over grilled cheese sandwiches until your mom came and got you?” one of them asked, a nasty smile smeared across his face.

“Man, if you cry over grilled cheese, there’s no way you’ll ever pass out of RETCH,” said the other one.

I clenched my sandwich into a squooshy bread ball, but before I could respond, Ralph swung his legs around the bench and stood up.

"Come here," he said, crooking a finger at the BARF kids. "I got a secret."

Mystified, the BARF kids leaned in.

"HOARRRRRFFFFFFFFFF!" Ralph roared in their faces.

The BARF kids jumped back.

"What's your problem?" one asked angrily.

"That's the sound I make right before I throw up," Ralph explained, "so you might want to leave Minerva alone and get out of here. Just in case."

The BARF kids looked at each other and turned to walk away.

"HOAAAARRRRRFFFFFFFF!"

Both BARF kids broke into a run. So did Ralph.

"HOARFF! HOARFF! HOOOOOOOOOAAAAA-RRRRRFFFFF!" he yelled, pelting after them.

"I think they'll leave you alone now," Alice said. "Ralph's really good at sounding super realistic."

I shook my head, not knowing if I wanted to laugh or cry.

"So, do you really think I could be a supertaster?" I asked, unballing my sandwich to see if there was anything edible left. "It kinda makes it sound like I have superpowers."

Alice smiled. "Who knows? Maybe you do."

"HOOOOOOOARRRRRFFFFFFF!"

Ralph and the BARF kids streaked past again.

"Anyway, here—" Alice said. "I think you're ready." She dropped another folded piece of paper on the table in front of me and then darted off to catch up with Ralph.

"Ready for what?" evaporated on my lips as the teakettle whistled the end of the recess-lunch period. I jammed part of my squished sandwich into my mouth, chewing hard and fast, and started walking to the classroom. I was about to unfold the note when I was slammed from behind. The note flew out of my hands and onto the ground.

"Ooops—sorry!" a third-grader called as he ran past.

I grabbed the note and stuffed it into my pocket to keep it safe. I'd have to read it later.

After we got through Persuasive Writing and Social Studies, Mr. Kreplach told us to use Science to work on our Food Science Fair projects. I opened my science notebook and looked at what I had written over the summer: "What Makes Grilled Cheese So Good, the Bread or the Cheese?: An Analysis of 14 Grilled Cheese Sandwiches." The chart I had neatly drawn with a ruler and pencil was mostly empty. Over the summer I had selected and chewed my way through six of the fourteen test sandwiches, but after Patricia's party, the idea of doing any more research on grilled cheese made my stomach sour like chunky yogurt.

I raised my pencil, then hesitated. I needed a different

topic. Setting my pencil down, I rummaged in my desk and uncapped a thick black Sharpie. I took an experimental sniff of the tip and then squeaked out an *X* across the entire sandwich chart. Then I turned to a clean page and wrote, "What Is a Supertaster?"

I checked out a computer tablet from Mr. Kreplach and started doing internet searches. While an article on supertasters was loading, I idly clicked over to the school server to see if the St. Julia Child french fry video was available yet.

But I couldn't find it.

Puzzled, I re-scrolled through all the videos about St. Julia Child to double-check. But the french fry video wasn't even listed, like it had been removed instead of just blocked. Weird.

I shrugged it off. Maybe there were four-letter words in it. That's usually why cooking videos got blocked by the school. Apparently, chefs swear a lot. I guess St. Julia wasn't any different.

Tapping my pencil on the edge of my desk, I tipped my head to the side and looked around the RETCH classroom.

Alice was toying with her nose clips in one hand, weaving her fingers in and out of the strap as she scribbled in a notebook.

Willa was hunched over her desk, reading her huge book. Her curtain of braids hid most of her face, but I could tell she was mouthing the words.

Akshay was testing whether he could sit on his sore butt comfortably. From the grimace on his face, he couldn't.

Ralph was quietly practicing his vomit noise behind his hand and writing stuff down. I couldn't wait to see his Food Science Fair project.

I felt a slight smile push its way across my face. And then, with a jolt, I remembered Alice's note. I looked over at Mr. Kreplach. He was deep into grading our papers with wide, sure strokes of his red pen. I slid the note out of my pocket and yawned louder than necessary to cover the rustle as I unfolded it in the cave of my desk.

It was a map.

And on the other side of the map was the same mysterious and strangely familiar LOPE symbol.

CHAPTER 12

As soon as the teakettle whistled at the end of the day, Alice bolted out of her desk and ran to the coat hooks while I was still fumbling and gathering my homework. By the time I got out of the classroom and swung my backpack on, Alice was halfway across the courtyard.

"Hey, Alice! Alice!" I called.

Alice waved at me over her shoulder. "Later!"

"Wait—I need to ask you something!" I yelled.

But she kept running.

I made a quick stop in the bathroom and was just drying my hands when I heard voices right outside.

"Oh my gosh, did you see that whole thing?"

I froze. Cindy's voice.

"Yeah, she's too weird even for Alice Who Only Eats White Food to be friends with," someone said. That was Britta, from the birthday party.

I glared at the bathroom door and put my hand on my

back pocket. I felt the folded note crinkle reassuringly. Alice was my friend, wasn't she? I mean, the notes proved it, right?

"Did *you* see how quickly Alice ran away from Minerva, Patricia?" Cindy again.

"Excuse me, please, but of *course* I did," Patricia said. My stomach clenched like a fist at her imitation of me. How long had she been doing that? It rolled out of her mouth too easily for it to be the first time.

"Excuse me, please," Britta and Cindy chimed in together, their voices singsongy and nasal. Like snotty geese. They laughed.

"How were you guys ever friends with her?" Janelle asked.

I held my breath and gripped at the wet sink as I waited for the answer.

"Honestly, I basically just felt sorry for her. If I hadn't been her friend all these years, no one else would have been. I was doing her a favor," Patricia said. "But she was becoming so annoying. I mean—the way she acted at my birthday party?"

I could hear the eye roll in Patricia's voice.

"She always needs so much attention," Cindy said. "Remember when you said you wanted to run for sixth-grade president instead of her, Patricia? How upset she got?"

"Minerva has a jealousy problem with me. She always has," Patricia said. "She can't stand the fact that I'm better at Eating, so she tries to make herself important in other ways.

Like saying she can taste things that aren't there. She thinks it makes her so special."

"I totally don't believe that tongue thing," Britta said. "She's lying."

"I think so, too," Patricia said.

"But she did know about the grilled cheese sandwiches, right?" Cindy said.

"Oh please, Cindy. I'm almost totally positive she saw me take the peppers out of the sandwiches. Didn't you see how she couldn't leave me alone through the whole party? She probably spied on me when I was in the kitchen. She's kind of a sneak."

I gripped the sink even tighter to keep from running out there and telling them how wrong they were. I *could* taste the green peppers and I *wasn't* a sneak!

"I don't know," Cindy sounded doubtful. "I thought she was in the dining room with us the whole time . . ."

"So, are you saying you believe Minerva?" Patricia demanded. "Or do you believe me? Because if you believe Minerva, maybe you should go be her friend."

As the girls walked away, I could hear Cindy promising that she was really Patricia's friend, not mine.

I thought about the map in my pocket. What if the map wasn't really a map? What if it was just a trick and it didn't actually lead anywhere? Maybe Alice *wasn't* my friend at all. Maybe she was getting me back because I never stood up to

Patricia for bullying her. And when she found out I fell for it, Alice would laugh at me in front of everyone. Just like Patricia.

Never in a million years did I imagine that Patricia would do what she did, but I ended up being all wrong about her. What if I was wrong about Alice, too?

At home, I closed my door and spread the map across my desk with shaky hands. The map looked like it was leading from school through the big park next to the playground and ending at the small park next to the train tracks, which was a few blocks from my cul-de-sac. An *X* marked the spot at a tree that was carved with a heart, and there were initials inside the heart—wait, no, those weren't initials. I grabbed the magnifying glass Hugo used for pill bugs and took a closer look.

Inside the heart was a time: 4:30. I looked at the clock. It was already 4:15. I could get there in time if I ran. But what if it really was a trick? I sat down on the edge of my bed. But what if it wasn't? I took a deep breath, stood up, and grabbed my sunglasses.

"Going on a walk!" I said, sprinting out of the house and cutting through our vegetable garden without waiting for a response.

At the end of the cul-de-sac I slowed a bit so I could recheck the map. To get to the park near the train tracks,

I had to cross the bike bridge that arched over the creek running below. I tucked the map back into my pocket and jogged off.

The creek that cuts its meandering path through my neighborhood starts in the dark, piney mountain range northwest of Muffuletta and tumbles into the marshy bay a few miles south. When we had a good, wet winter, full of sure and steady rain, the creek flowed fast and loud, and the water was so clear you could see all the way down to the creek's rocky bottom.

I stopped in the middle of the bike bridge and looked down. We hadn't had rain in a long time, and the water below was the murky color of gravy. Instead of rushing toward the bay, the creek moped around the banks, as if waiting for the next big storm to finally get it moving in the right direction.

In the tiny park on the other side of the creek, slants of sunlight cut through the branches of the evergreen trees and cast spiked shadows on the ground. Although Hugo had dragged me here many times to stand on the bike bridge and watch the trains clatter by, most people didn't linger on the bridge or in the park. It wasn't much of a park, really. It had a tiny grove of thick, gnarled oak trees, a scattering of towering redwoods and sequoias, and a single bench. The bike path cut through it, leading cyclists and walkers over the train crossing and onto Stanfork's campus. Off to one side of the path was an enormous boulder, with a plaque commemorating the founding of Muffuletta. I looked around at the familiar setting. There didn't seem to be anything here that would make it an obvious destination for a mysterious map.

I brushed off leaves and needles and ran my fingers across the raised lettering on the plaque: MUFFULETTA: A FOOD-TOPIA FOR ALL.

I stuck my tongue out at it. "All except picky eaters."

I climbed on top of the boulder to get a better view of everything around me.

Then I heard it: *"HOARFF!"*

I knew that *hoarf.* But it seemed to be coming from above me. I looked up, searching the dense branches of the oak tree next to the boulder. I couldn't see anyone. Or anything.

"Ralph?" I called in a loud whisper.

"Password!" hissed a voice from above.

I looked at the map again. "I don't know the password!"

"Oh, shoot, sorry: What food do you hate the most?"

"Succotash!" I didn't even need to think about it.

"And what sound do you make when you are made to eat it?"

I thought about a steaming bowl full of short green beans, carrots, corn, red pepper, and lima beans.

"BLEAURRRRGAHHHHP!"

A rope ladder fell from above, nearly smacking me in the head. I paused for half a second, thinking about the ladder swinging and swaying. I didn't even know how far up it went, and if I fell, it would definitely be concussion city for me. But I had to know what all this was about, so I took a deep breath, set my teeth, and climbed.

When I reached the top, I hoisted myself through a planked floor and found myself in an airy, weathered treehouse completely hidden by the redwoods surrounding it.

"Hi," Alice said. All four members of my RETCH class were standing there and grinning at me.

"Whoa," I breathed. In a corner of the treehouse was a stack of board games and a battered basket of books. A table was attached to the tree trunk, and strewn about were wooden stumps of various sizes for sitting. Ralph motioned me aside as he pulled the rope ladder up and latched the trapdoor.

"You're right on time for the pledge of allegiance," Akshay said, putting one hand on his stomach and clapping the other over his mouth.

All the other RETCH kids did the same thing.

"I pledge allegiance to the bowl

"and the united plates of pasta

"and to the resistance

"of every veg, except for Akshay-who-actually-loves-quite-a-lot-of-vegetables—"

"BUT I HATE BRUSSELS SPROUTS TO DEATH AND I THINK MOST MEAT IS SUPER GROOOOOOOSS!" Akshay yelled behind the hand muffling his mouth.

"—one clubhouse

"in the trees

"with grilled cheese and french fries for all."

"Welcome to the League of Picky Eaters," Alice said. She pointed to a small banner draped over a branch. It had the now-familiar symbol scrawled on it: a coat of arms containing the letters LOPE.

Realization dawned on me. "League of . . . Picky . . . Eaters? L-O-P-E?"

Alice nodded. "Because of your services to your fellow RETCHmates, we've decided to make you our newest member."

"Services? What are services? What have I done? I basically ignored everyone for an entire week! Or more!" After going so long not talking to anyone at school, now so many questions were trying to fight their way out of my mouth all at the same time.

"You helped me get rid of my oatmeal," Alice said.

"You gave me a piece of your pizza," Ralph said.

"You rescued me from the horrid Brussels sprouts," Akshay said.

"And you've never told on any of us," Alice said.

I looked at Willa, who never said a word. She met my gaze and gave me a smile and a nod.

I sat down hard on a stump. It was just right for a stool. "So, this is like a club?"

"A league," Akshay corrected me.

"But how? Why? When?"

Alice nudged Ralph and nodded. Ralph reached behind the books in the basket and pulled out a large green binder. The League of Picky Eaters coat of arms was on the front. Once again the symbol bounced around in my brain as something familiar, but how was that possible? I had never heard about any of this before! I gave my head a slight shake as Alice handed me the binder. "Read the first page."

I flipped it open to a note scribbled on a torn and grease-spattered sheet of paper.

Dear Fellow Picky Eater,

Over the years, I have made it my job to reach out to the picky children of Muffuletta. The League of Picky Eaters was created to help get kids like you through tough times.

Look for the treehouse in the redwood grove near the bike bridge.

Find the binder. Bring others. Make plans. Together you will survive school.

Stand picky, stand proud.

Guardian of the League of Picky Eaters

"But where did it come from?" I asked, paging through it.

Everyone exchanged looks.

"We don't know," Alice said.

"What do you mean?" I asked.

Alice, Akshay, and Willa looked at Ralph, who was staring dreamily off into space. Akshay cleared his throat. But Ralph's focus on whatever he was seeing didn't waver. Alice nudged him with her foot. Still nothing.

"HEY RALPH!" Willa yelled, shocking me and, judging by the blush on her face, shocking herself a bit as well.

"What? Oh. What?!" Ralph said, startled. He looked around at all of us. "What was the question again? Sorry, I was thinking about the fluffiest mashed potatoes and how you have to get butter just the right temperature to melt in them before the potatoes go all cold and lose all chance of being delicious."

Akshay sighed. "Minerva asked where the note came from." He pointed at the binder.

"Oh, yeah," Ralph said. "It's the weirdest thing. Last year, I found it in my backpack one day. Way down at the bottom under a bunch of stuff. No idea how long it had been there."

"Did you ask your parents?"

"No way," Ralph said. "They hate how bad I am at Eating. When they learned I was put in RETCH this year, my dad cried. He was so disappointed in me." He looked down. "It made me feel real lousy."

I bit my lip. I wasn't exactly happy with my parents at the moment, but at least they didn't get that upset about me testing into RETCH.

"Anyway," Ralph said. "I told Akshay about the note right away—we've been friends since practically forever—and then we spent hours looking for the treehouse."

"I almost got run over by two bikers and a screaming maniac of a kindergartner on a scooter before we finally found it," Akshay added.

"So you guys didn't start the League of Picky Eaters?" I asked, still trying to wrap my head around everything.

Alice shook her head. "No, and the binder doesn't actually say who started it, but it's full of tips and tricks to use at school and at home. That's where we got the idea to use pockets for the Brussels sprouts."

"And how to grab full bowls or plates of food and pretend they were empty while a teacher was distracted," Akshay added. "I mean, a lot of this stuff is what we've been doing at home for years, but some of it is really helpful."

"Also, just *how* to distract a teacher with lots of questions or weird noises, like my fake barfs, or even Akshay faking all sorts of accidents," Ralph said. "A lot of the notes have dates—some even going back fifteen years—and there's one in there from four years ago saying that Mr. Kreplach is particularly worried about accidents in the classroom, so he's easy to distract that way."

Akshay grinned. "Being known as a klutz has its advantages!"

"And see? There's a lot of different handwritings, so there have been lots of members over the years," Willa said, suddenly appearing over my shoulder and pointing out a few pages as examples. "Check this out. It says that Principal Butcher is their super-mean RETCH teacher, so the League must go waaaay back. I didn't even know she was once a teacher at St. Julia."

"Wow." I flipped to the front of the binder and touched the plastic sleeve protecting the note.

"Willa and I only found out about the treehouse because she followed Ralph and Akshay here after school one day," Alice said.

"Not on purpose," Willa added quickly.

Akshay snorted.

Willa gave him a look. "Fine. Not completely on purpose anyway. I was really into this detective series, and I wanted to practice tailing people without them knowing it. And"—she shot a smug grin at Akshay—"they didn't know it."

Now it was Akshay's turn to roll his eyes.

"Obviously we were going to tell you guys at some point. Jeez," Ralph added.

"How long have you all been friends?" I asked, realizing just how little I noticed outside my friendships with Cindy and Patricia. *Former* friendships, I corrected myself.

"Well, Willa lives across the street from me, so we started playing together soon after I moved here," Alice said.

I pondered over quiet Willa becoming friends with Alice, the Spuddy Bench yodeler. It made a weird sort of sense.

"And me and Willa were reading partners in second grade," Ralph said. "I guess the four of us all started becoming friends around that time, right?" The others nodded. "We all knew we were the worst eaters in our classes—it was sort of a bond."

"In fact, we predicted we'd all be put in RETCH," Akshay added. "So after we found the binder and decided that we should become the new League, we started practicing a lot of the tips and tricks at home."

"Basically we spent all last summer meeting up and preparing how to get through this year," Ralph said.

"Yeah, but we didn't know they'd mess with the cheese pizza at lunch," Willa said. "The one thing we could look forward to eating at school."

Everyone went quiet for a moment. High up in the oak tree, I could hear redwood needles from the surrounding trees dropping on the treehouse floor.

"Hey, look," Alice said, breaking the silence. "Even if we spend the whole lunch period de-egging our pizzas, we're going to figure it out. We're all in this together."

"Oh, that reminds me," Akshay said. "I've been thinking about that! I made some diagrams showing different ways to cut them up based on egg distribution. We just need to swipe some pizza cutters." He pulled a piece of paper out of his back pocket. I noticed that almost all his fingers had Band-Aids wrapped around them.

"I ran into some trouble with the pizza cutter," he explained when he saw me looking, unfolding the paper and spreading it out.

But I only half listened to what Akshay was saying about his diagrams. I kept turning Alice's words over and over in my head. Like flipping pancakes on a Saturday morning: warm, golden, and delicious. *We're all in this together.*

The map hadn't been a trick.

It had been an invitation. I clasped my hands together and gave them a quick, happy squeeze before turning my attention back to Akshay and his bandaged fingers.

CHAPTER 13

Several days filled with homework and chores and baby-sitting Hugo went by before I could get back to the League treehouse.

I crunched through piles of twigs and dry needles and climbed up the boulder. Tipping my head back, I took a really deep breath and bellowed, *"BLEAURRRRGAH-HHHP!"* Then I waited for the rope ladder to drop down. Nothing happened. I cleared my throat and tried again. *"BLEAURRRRGAHHHHP!"* Still nothing.

"BLEAURRRRGAHHHHP!"

"BLEAURRRRGAHHHHP!"

"BLEAURRRRGAHHHHP!"

A mass of birds flapped away, squalling at me for disturbing them. I heard a snort. Whirling around, I saw Willa standing on the bike path, watching me. Her hand was over her mouth, and her eyes were wide, like she hadn't meant to let the snort out.

"Oh, hi," I said.

Willa pointed at the branches above and said in a low voice that I had to lean closer to hear, "No one's up there yet."

My cheeks burned. How dumb could I be? I started to stammer out an apology, but Willa went on, still speaking softly. "That's the best Ralph impression I've ever heard in my life." Her amber eyes took me in fully as she seemed to consider whether she wanted to go on. "You might almost reach the back row of a largish theater with voice projection like that." And then, before I could react to that, she disappeared around the knotty oak trunk. I jumped down and followed her.

"If there's no one else in the treehouse, this is how you get up," she said, pointing at a bunch of knots going up the trunk, as well as stumps of wood that must have once been branches. "Start with these as your handholds and footholds until you reach actual branches. I'll show you." She clicked her backpack straps together around her chest and started climbing up the trunk, her hands and feet easily finding the appropriate leverage. I stayed on the ground, my stomach twisting slightly.

When she reached the first level of branches, Willa looked around for me. "Are you coming?"

"Um . . ." I said. "I am not sure if . . . that is, I'd—"

"Afraid of heights?" Willa asked, pulling herself up onto another branch.

"I'm afraid of concussions," I said. "It's, uh, sort of been a recent thing."

"The rope ladder?" Willa said, pausing her climb to look down at me.

"I was nervous about that at first," I said, "but then I did it and it was fine and ladders are easier than trees and I've never been a great tree climber maybe because we don't have a lot of trees on our street to practice on or—" I stopped myself mid-babble.

"No, I meant, I'll drop you the rope ladder when I get up there," Willa said.

"Oh, okay. Yeah, thank you," I said, relieved that I didn't have to climb the tree but at the same time wondering why I didn't keep my babbling mouth entirely shut. Willa was so much quieter than Alice, Ralph, and Akshay. And sometimes when I get around people who don't say much, my mouth gets very fast and ends up stumbling over itself.

I made my way back around the trunk to the boulder just in time to hear Willa call, "Heads up," which was followed by the rope ladder dropping down. I went cautiously up the ladder, feeling less shaky in my climb compared with the first time. I knew Willa was watching me. As much as she didn't say, I got the feeling that she saw everything.

When I got to the trapdoor opening, she stepped back to give me room to pull myself onto the floor of the treehouse. "'Wisely and slow. They stumble that run fast,'" she said.

I couldn't tell if that was good or bad, so I just said, "Um, thanks?"

Willa nodded, but didn't say anything else. She looked steadily at me. And then my mouth took off without me again. "Okay, I don't know what that means, can you tell me what it means? What you just said? Like is it good? Or is it bad? Or is it just like somewhere in between?"

Willa sat down on a stump seat and let out a soft chuckle, like tumbling water. "It's from *Romeo and Juliet*—it means being patient is safer than being impatient and rushing things."

"Oh. Yes. I guess it is. I'm impatient a lot, though."

Willa shrugged. "I don't know anyone who isn't, but repeating that to myself helps me sometimes." She paused, using a fingernail to pry at the acorn she had in her hand before continuing. "Like when I want to rush through a test or something? It makes me remember that being fast or first isn't always good, especially because I'm more likely to make mistakes when I go too fast."

"Slow and steady wins the race," I said, giving what I felt was a wise nod.

Willa gave another chuckle. "Exactly."

"So how do you remember all those quotes so well that you can just pull them out whenever you want to?"

Willa blinked, surprised by my question. "I don't know, actually—they just tend to stick to my brain when I read them. Or hear them. But the ones I remember best are usually the ones I don't understand at first. I spend a lot of time taking those lines apart and putting them back together until I can figure them out."

"Like math problems," I said. "Or science." I thought about what I loved the most about mysteries.

"Sort of, yeah—I never thought of it like that." She started to say something else and then stopped herself.

"What?" I asked, so much wanting to keep her talking and saying interesting things.

"I was just going to ask—what did you mean when you said being afraid of concussions was a recent thing?"

"Oh, that," I said. "Well, my family has this tradition on weekends. We set up our card table in the living room and we eat dinner while watching a science or nature program together. My mom calls it having a picnic in the living room, but with TV. And also not sitting on the floor. Anyway, there was a program about concussions and football players and CTE and it was really interesting but it was also kind of sad and scary, so I ended up reading a lot about concussions because—"

"Because you thought that knowing more about it would make it less scary?" Willa asked, nodding.

"Exactly! But it also kind of backfired, and now I'm just more aware that concussions exist, so I'm more nervous about them, too. It doesn't exactly make sense, I know."

"It makes sense to me," Willa said. "It's kind of what happened with me and Camp Shakespeare."

Now it was my turn to be quiet and let her talk on.

"I really didn't want to go. I don't like getting up and talking in front of people. Like, when we have to give speeches in school, I have a stomachache for weeks before it's my turn. I hate it almost as much as I hated those roasted beets."

I nodded. It had been another "stuff your pockets" day in RETCH. By now I knew to be prepared with pockets *and* plastic baggies.

"And," Willa went on, "that's exactly why my parents sent me to Camp Shakespeare. To do a lot more public speaking. They wanted me to 'get over' my fear. Just like they want me to 'get over' all the things I hate to eat."

"Did it work?" I asked after Willa said nothing for kind of a long time.

Willa made a face. "Not really. I still don't like public speaking. I really hate being the center of attention. But there was something . . . I don't know." She shook her head. "There was something about learning the lines inside and out and then performing them that made me feel powerful. When I was at camp, I didn't feel as freaked out as I do when I have to read a report in school. That made me want to do it a lot more. Maybe even be an actor someday."

"Is that why you have a line for every occasion?" I asked.

Willa half smiled. "I don't know if I have a line for *every* occasion. Mostly they just sort of come to me at certain times when I . . . like, when I can't find my own words, I guess."

I nodded, then had a sudden thought. "What was the food like at Camp Shakespeare?"

Willa tipped her head at me. "You ask a lot of questions."

"I do?" My face got hot again. This was the longest conversation I had ever had with Willa, and I didn't want to be nosy.

"It's okay, though. I kind of like that about you. The food wasn't bad, actually. Also, no one paid any attention to what I ate. I could eat french fries every night for dinner if I wanted. No parents to make me eat a balanced meal with the 'right' amount of vegetables and protein and stuff. My parents are really into balanced meals."

I didn't ask anything else. Instead, I sat there enjoying the happy, glowy feeling of Willa saying she "kind of" liked something about me. I couldn't remember the last time Patricia said or acted as if she liked anything about me.

Willa gathered her homework and settled herself at the trunk-nailed table. I went over to the basket and pulled out the green binder. I really wanted to ask Willa if she had any idea how the note got into Ralph's backpack, but I decided I had asked enough. Instead, I read the binder and started adding some tips of my own, and the two of us settled into a silence that was way less awkward than I would have thought it could be, almost as if the silence itself was another friend in the treehouse.

The green binder had a section giving tips about the

various parents in town. Like, who makes you clean your plate, who doesn't force you to eat your sandwich crusts, and who tries to trick kids. I recognized several names, but not others. Some of these parents had kids who had grown up years ago.

Cindy's mom is totally one of those tricking parents. A few years ago she gave me a bowl of yogurt for dessert and told me it was ice cream. I think she adds steamed, chopped broccoli to her brownies, too. I added her name to the binder and wrote the date down as reference for future members.

After about an hour, Willa stood up, stretched, and packed up her backpack. "I should probably get going. I want to start dinner before my mom gets home so she'll have more time to help me with my math."

"Okay," I said, and then I thought of something. "You know, math is my favorite subject, so if you ever need help, you could ask me."

Willa looked at me for a long time. And it wasn't uncomfortable at all this time. I just waited until she was ready to talk.

"Okay," she said. "Maybe I will."

She stopped at the trapdoor. "You have to leave now, too."

"Why?" Had I not been a member long enough to be trusted in the LOPE headquarters alone? No one ever mentioned rules like that. How long before they'd trust me?

"Because the last person out has to bring the ladder up

and then climb down the tree trunk way," Willa explained. "Sorry. It's so we can keep other people from stumbling upon the treehouse."

"Oh," I said. Of course that made sense.

"So unless you want to climb down by your—"

"No. It's fine, I'll leave with you," I said quickly. I was definitely not ready to climb down the scarier tree trunk yet. I put the green binder back in the basket and grabbed my backpack.

After Willa pulled up the rope ladder and joined me on the ground, she said in her soft voice, "If you want me to teach you how to climb up and down the trunk someday, I can."

"Okay," I said. "Someday."

CHAPTER 14

One day at school the following week, Willa took me up on my offer to help her with math, so that afternoon we walked home together. Alice was supposed to join us, but she had to stay after to talk to Mr. Kreplach (again) about not wearing her nose clips in class.

"He just doesn't appreciate the kind of advanced nasal technology I've got going up in there," Alice had told us with a sigh, then did a quick jig next to Mr. Kreplach's desk. She called them tiny jigs of joy and did them whenever she was overly frustrated. Her elbows jutted out from her sides, and she shuffled her feet back and forth with such a super-quick intensity that her shoes squeaked on the floor. "Mark my words," she said. "One day my nose will do something great."

Mr. Kreplach walked into the classroom with the biggest coffee mug I had ever seen. He looked exhausted.

"Alice," he said, "please sit down." He turned to look at me and Willa. "You two can go home now. I need to talk to Alice alone."

We each gave Alice small waves. Right before the door closed behind us, we heard her say, "Mr. Kreplach, you just don't appreciate the kind of advanced nas . . ."

"Mr. Kreplach's going to need a bigger cup if Alice ends up doing one of her tiny jigs of joy," I whispered. Willa just smiled.

On the way home, I chattered on about how weird the squirrels in the park act at night, the way only some crosswalk buttons give you a feeling of satisfaction when you push them, and others don't, and all my theories on what the seemingly empty building across the street from the police station was used for, since it must be used for something to have all those satellite dishes and barbed wire fences. Willa was quiet, but she listened in a way that I could tell she was really listening and not just tuning me out and nodding without hearing me. I ran out of things to say, and after a few blocks in complete silence, I asked Willa how she got so good at climbing trees. She told me all about the rock-climbing wall in town.

"It's called the Rock Salt," Willa said. "And it's supposed to look like this giant salt crystal, but it's just a big wall painted white." She explained about the shoes you wear and the colorful handholds and footholds drilled into the wall and how there's a rope around you at all times so you can't fall and get a concussion.

I was so interested in what Willa was telling me and how

much she was telling me that I didn't even say another word the whole rest of the way to her house.

"Come on in," she said, pulling out her keys and grabbing the mail from the mailbox. "My parents are still at the clinic."

Inside, Willa dropped her backpack on the kitchen table and took off her shoes. I also took off my shoes, lining them up to the side of the front door, and set my backpack next to Willa's.

"Is it okay if I use your phone to call my mom and let her know I'm here?" I asked. My mom wasn't overly anxious about me being out and about on my own, just as long as she had a general idea of where I was most of the time.

Willa nodded and pointed at the kitchen phone. "Go ahead. I'll be right back," she said, and disappeared upstairs.

I called my mom, telling her where I was with as few words as possible. I was still a bit upset with her and my dad and that entire conversation I wish I'd never heard.

"Yes, I'm fine. I'm doing homework. I'm at Willa's house. Willa Lewis. Okay. Yes. I know. Yes, I *know*. I'll be home by five, okay?"

Willa's house was quiet. And it wasn't just a lack of noise. Absolutely everything about it oozed quietness. The colors in the living room, from the furniture to the walls to the area rugs on the hardwood floors, were grays and browns and muted greens. Walking in the door felt like walking into calm, if you can even do that, whereas my house, by comparison, seemed like it screamed its head off the moment you stepped foot in it. Here, there was no mess. Nothing was out of place. Everything was neat and tidy. It was kind of like Patricia's house in that way. And yet I didn't feel on edge or like I'd break something super valuable if I so much as sneezed. At Willa's house, I felt welcome.

"Hey, do you mind if I start a load of laundry before we get to math?" Willa called down.

"No problem. And I can help, if you want," I called back. Family laundry was one of my chores, too.

"That'd be great, thanks." Willa came back downstairs carrying a bulging laundry basket and wearing . . . pajamas?

"I always change into my pajama bottoms as soon as I get home," Willa said, noting my look. "It's just so much more comfortable."

I have a word for an idea that is both mind-boggling and great, so my brain simply *groggled* at this idea. Of course Willa was right about pajamas being much more comfortable than real clothes, but I never thought about changing into my pajamas until, well, closer to bedtime, really. I wasn't even sure if my parents would let me eat dinner in my pajamas. Maybe on the weekend. Mother earth—this was something to try for sure!

I helped Willa load her family's laundry into the machine

in the mudroom at the back of the house. Outside the window, a lemon tree leaned against the side of the house. The yellow fruit was heavy, pulling some branches low.

"That's so cool that you have your own lemon tree!" I said. "Do you make fresh lemonade all the time?"

Willa glanced up and frowned. "We make lemonade when the landlord hasn't come by and already stripped the tree for herself."

"Ugh, landlords," I said.

"Yeah, I mean," Willa said, grabbing another piece of laundry. "I know it's technically her tree because she owns everything and all that, but still. And my parents would never complain about it, of course."

"I get it. I mean, my parents go out of their way not to tell our landlord when something breaks, because they don't want to give him a reason to raise the rent on us. They kind of want him to forget we exist."

She shrugged. "My parents keep saying we'll buy our own house when the prices come down but—"

"But it's actually cheaper to rent than to buy around here," I filled in for her, having heard this same argument from my own parents a lot.

"Yeah," Willa said.

Back in the kitchen, we sat down at the table, and after ten minutes of reviewing greatest common factors and lowest common multiples, Willa exclaimed, "Oh, of course!" She scribbled in her answers and grinned at me. "Thanks."

I smiled back.

"Now for the rest of my homework," Willa said, and started hauling stacks of books out of her backpack.

"Is that all homework?" I goggled.

Willa shook her head, "Oh, no, these are just for fun. I want to be a writer when I grow up, so I read everything."

"I thought you wanted to be an actor," I said, puzzled.

"I want to be a lot of things," Willa said. "An actor, a writer, a detective—"

I remembered what Willa had said about following Akshay and Ralph to the treehouse because she was reading a detective series.

". . . and a veterinarian, like my mom and dad," Willa said, ticking off a list on her fingers. "I'm going to try everything and see what I like best."

"Wow," I said. I hadn't thought too much about what I want to be when I grow up. Except maybe not picky.

I glanced at the clock. "Oh, shoot, I better get home."

Willa nodded and walked me to the door. "Thanks, Minerva," she said. She looked like she wanted to say more, but she had gone quiet again.

"Sure," I said, shouldering my backpack. "See you at school."

I had gone about a block when I heard footsteps slapping the sidewalk behind me. It was Willa.

"'Friendship is constant in all other things,'" she gasped out. "That's my last Shakespeare quote of the day, okay?"

"Okay," I said, smiling. Willa smiled back, then turned and ran home.

That was a quote I definitely understood.

CHAPTER 15

Focusing on my Food Science Fair project was hard when I really wanted to hang out at the League treehouse all the time. But the Science Fair was getting closer and closer, and I was starting to run out of time to finish my project. As much fun as I was having every time I got together with the other League members, I still needed to prove to my parents and everyone at St. Julia Child that the reason I was so bad at Eating could all be blamed on being a supertaster. It wasn't me, it was science!

After spending hours reading through so many tons of articles about supertasters, I dug up two tests that were supposed to tell you if you were a supertaster or not. One of the tests had to be ordered online with a credit card, which, being a sixth-grader, I did not have. I was no longer giving my parents the silent treatment, but I still didn't want to be around them that much because when I was, all I could think of was what I overheard the night of Patricia's party. The night they said it would be "easier" if I wasn't a picky eater. So when I wasn't at school or at the League treehouse, I stayed in my room and tried to avoid long conversations. I hadn't even told them about my new Food Science Fair topic, and I didn't want to get into it. All I needed for the other test was stuff I could scavenge around the house, so that seemed to be the best choice.

One afternoon I gathered up blue food coloring, index cards, and a hole punch and went across the hall to the bathroom. I needed to be able to examine my tongue, and the light over the mirror was the brightest in the house.

Hugo was sitting in a tub full of bubbles, pretending to eat fish tacos from his floating food truck.

"Do you want a fish taco, 'Nerva?" he asked as I unscrewed the top from the little food-coloring bottle and set it on the pink tile countertop.

"Not right now. I have to do some experimenting," I told him.

I took the index card and punched a hole in it. Then I stuck out my tongue and squeezed a few drops of the food coloring on it until I got it good and blue.

According to the directions, I was supposed to put the index card over my dyed tongue and count the number of bumps I saw in the punched hole. Most people call those bumps taste buds, but I learned that it's more correct to call them papillae because your actual taste buds are a mess of microscopic cells *inside* the bumps. It's pretty cool knowing stuff most other people don't.

I leaned in closer to the mirror.

The directions said that the bumps would be easy to count because they'd stand out pink and shiny from your blue tongue. I held the index card against my tongue and looked at the bit of blue I could see through the hole.

I squinted. I was having a hard time seeing the bumps, so I put my nose right up against the mirror. But that made everything blurry. And it fogged up the mirror.

"What are you DOING, 'Nerva?" Hugo demanded. He was standing in the tub, his small hands planted on his hips. A snow-white mousse of suds coated his body from the neck down.

"I'm trying to count bumps on my tongue, but I can't see them that well," I said.

"I can count! I can count almost all the numbers!" Hugo raised his arms. White bubbles drifted down around him.

"Do you want to help me?"

He thought for a minute, then said, "After I undrain."

He released the tub drain and crouched low to watch the bathwater glugging lower and lower. I tapped my fingers on the tile countertop. "Come on, Hugo."

"Just let me watch the squirrel," he said, crouching naked in the nearly empty tub and staring at the drain. When the rest of the water finally swirled away, I wrapped Hugo in a hoodie towel and put the index card on my blue tongue again.

Of course, Hugo was going to have questions.

"Why is your tongue blue?"

"It makes it easier to see the bumps."

"Can I have a blue tongue?"

"No."

"Why?"

"Because."

"Why?"

"Because."

"Why?"

I said the only thing I knew that would get him to stop.

"Because, it's a Halloween costume."

"I DON'T LIKE HALLOWEEN COSTUMES!"

By that time, my talking and saliva had washed away all the food coloring, so I had to dye my tongue all over again.

I stuck my tongue out and put the index card over it. "Now," I said, hoping he understood. He got so close to my face I could smell that he had eaten sardines on toast for lunch again. I took extra care to breathe through my mouth only.

"Twenty-five!" Hugo announced with an air of triumph. And then he gave me a full-on baby fish-mouth kiss on my nose.

I recorded Hugo's count in my notebook and rechecked my research. One article said supertasters usually have at least thirty papillae per punched hole area, but another article said twenty to twenty-five. So which was it? Was I a supertaster or not?

"Blargh!" I smacked my head with both hands.

I couldn't avoid it any longer. I was going to have to ask my mom for help buying that other supertaster test. It was the only way to find out the truth of my lie detector tongue and complete my project.

My mom was in the kitchen putting groceries away. "Why is your tongue blue?" she asked as soon as I opened my mouth.

"Because it's Halloween, Mommy!" Hugo said, his arms outstretched. "Don't you even KNOW that?!"

"I'm doing experiments," I said. "For my Food Science Fair project."

"Yes, Halloween spearmints," Hugo said, patting my arm. "Like gum."

"Hugo, will you go watch *Chef Muffintop's Mini Kitchen* so I can talk to your sister, please?"

Hugo was in the living room turning on the TV before my mom had even finished her sentence.

Mom pointed at a chair at the kitchen table. I dumped myself in it. She pulled out another chair, rested her folded hands on the table, and took a deep breath before she spoke. "Because you clearly don't want to talk about it, your dad and I have given you space to work through whatever it is you're going through. But now I'd really like to know what's been going on with you."

I shrugged and examined the table. There were fresh scratches on one of the legs nearest me.

Our cat, Needles, uses the table legs to sharpen and shed his claws. Last Christmas we got the cats the tallest scratching post we could find. It was covered in carpet and rope and had three ramps and soft places to sleep. Bean immediately jumped on the highest level and squirmed ecstatically around in the catnip we had sprinkled all over the post. Needles took one tiny sniff at it and went right back to scratching the table.

Patricia was over once when Needles trotted into the kitchen and went through his usual scratching routine.

"Wow, that's bad," she said, looking at the deep grooves he left behind. "You guys should get a new table."

"We can't," I said.

"Why?"

"Because tables are . . ." I stopped myself from saying what my parents told me. A new table is too expensive. I don't think Patricia or anyone in her family understands "too expensive."

"Because they say Needles will probably just do the same thing to a new table," I said.

"My family doesn't like cats," Patricia said, looking at the table with distaste.

"Minerva?" my mom said. I knew she wanted me to look

at her. But I also know that as soon as you look a grownup in the eye, you get to feeling so uncomfortable that you'll spill all your guts. Even when your guts aren't anyone else's business.

I kept my eyes lowered as I ran my fingers over the splintered wood. It did look pretty awful, but Needles couldn't help being who he was. And I loved him, no matter what he did.

"Minerva, please look at me when I'm speaking to you."

I looked up before I could stop myself.

My mom didn't have on her mad face. Instead, she looked confused and a little sad, which made me feel even worse about everything.

"I get the feeling you haven't been hanging out with Patricia and Cindy since Patricia's birthday party," she said.

I opened my mouth, but before I could say a word, she held up a hand and said, "You don't have to tell me about it unless you want to, but it might make you feel better if you do."

I pushed my finger harder into the rough parts on the table leg.

Needles was being Needles.

I was being me.

"It's just . . ." I started, and then the whole story of Patricia's birthday party came stumbling out of my mouth.

"That wasn't nice of Patricia or, frankly, her mother.

At all," my mom said, referring to the birthday party. She glanced toward the phone.

I knew what she was thinking. "Please don't call them —it makes things so much worse when you do that!"

"But honey, it's not okay. That sort of teasing from Patricia—it's bullying. She's being a bully."

"I know. And that's why I'm not friends with her anymore, which should make *you* happy—you've been hinting around for years that I shouldn't be friends with her. So? Now I'm not!" My anger was coming back again.

"Okay, okay," my mom said. "I understand why you're upset and angry, but you're taking that anger out on me and your dad all the time now, and all we want to do is help you anyway we can."

"Help? *Help?!*" I said. "You don't want to help me—you want me to get better grades in Eating to make your lives easier. Well, I'm a picky eater. I'm in RETCH, and I'm sorry if that ruins your lives!"

"Minerva, what on earth are you talking about?" my mom said. "Ruins our lives?"

"That night after Patricia's party—I heard you!"

My mom looked puzzled. So I went on. "I heard you and Dad talking in the kitchen about how much easier your lives would be if I was good at Eating."

"Easier for *me?*" My mom frowned and then sighed. "Oh,

honey, no." She rubbed at her eyes. "I was saying that it would be easier for *you*, just overall and in school, if you liked more foods."

"But don't you understand? I didn't *choose* to be picky! I don't know why I'm like this! But I am, and I can't control it! And that's why I want to find out if I'm a supertaster—maybe that will explain everything, and everyone will just shut up and leave me alone about it and stop expecting me to be something I'm not!"

And with that, I finally started to cry. But it wasn't a sad cry as much as a get-everything-off-my-chest-which-includes-all-these-stored-up-tears cry.

My mom came around the table. She pulled me into her arms and held me tight against her chest until my sobs quieted down and turned to shudders. It felt so good to let go and cry hard and loud. Not like the way I cried in Patricia's bathroom, where I tried so hard to shove all my sobs back down my throat, scared that everyone would hear me.

Hugo padded over, his eyes wide. He was still wearing his hoodie towel and nothing else.

"'Nerva, I think your tongue turned you blue all over, which means sad, and I don't want you to be so sad again anymore."

"Okay." I gave him a watery smile to show him I was

already not blue, and I wiped my nose with the back of my sleeve.

Mom wrinkled her nose at my sleeve but just said, "Oh, Minerva, I'm so sorry about all this—I'm especially sorry that Eating is so difficult for you these days. You love Math and Science, and it really shows in your grades for those classes. I just wish your struggles in Eating didn't overshadow everything."

She sat there a moment, thinking. "Maybe there's a way we can make things easier for you at home. Just so you don't feel so attacked all the time."

"You could let me decide what we have for dinner," I ventured.

"Minerva, we're not going to eat grilled cheese sandwiches every night."

"No, I mean, like, you and Dad always get to choose what you're going to make, right?"

My mom nodded, still not catching on.

"Okay, so that's great for you guys. If you decide that you're hungry for grilled steak and mushrooms one night instead of roasted scallion chicken, then that's what you make. But I never get to choose. I'm just supposed to be hungry for and eat what *you* choose for me."

"So . . ."

"So, let me choose some nights. Not all, but some."

Mom considered this, then nodded. "That seems reasonable. But then you should help with the cooking, too."

"No problem!" I actually loved cooking. I could make everything exactly the way I liked it. No surprises. "And also—"

"There's more?" Mom smiled.

I took a deep breath. "I don't want to have to eat three bites of anything I don't like. It's not going to make me like it. In fact, it's probably just going to make me hate whatever it is even more."

My mom didn't say anything, so I went on.

"If I want to try it, I will. But if I don't want to, I won't. Okay?"

Mom gazed at the bougainvillea outside the kitchen window. It was in full bloom, and the afternoon sun seeping through the fuchsia flowers made the entire kitchen glow pink and bright.

"Okay," Mom said at last.

"YAY!" I picked Hugo up and danced around the kitchen with him.

"But Minerva, I'm still going to serve you stuff that you don't like. Maybe someday you will try it and like it," Mom said.

"HEY I'M VERY FIVE!" Hugo roared in my arms.

I put him down again.

"Why did you do that? Dance with me!" Hugo demanded.

So I did.

Because it was for school and in the name of science, my mom said she would get the supertaster testing kit for me. The best part was, I didn't even have to pay her back. "If this helps you feel better about things, it's worth the money," she said. I showed her the online store I found where you can order all sorts of really cool science lab supplies, like test tubes, graduated cylinders, and—

"Ooh, look! Dentist tools!" I pointed at the screen. "Can we get those, too?"

"I think we're going to stick to the testing kit today," Mom murmured, entering her credit card information.

Excuse me, please, but I definitely have to come up with a reason why I desperately need dentist tools of my own. Like, next year I could totally do a Food Science Fair project on tooth decay or something. I could even use my own teeth for it! My mom keeps all my baby teeth in her jewelry box. Most of my baby teeth didn't fall out on their own, so Dr. Garfin had to pull them out in his office. And ever since he showed me that first tooth he pulled, its superlong root still attached, and explained that my baby teeth roots weren't dissolving the way other kids' roots did, I had thought about how awesome it would be to be a dentist.

"Okay, you're all set, Min," my mom said. "The kit should be here in a week or so."

"A week or so?" I repeated. "But that's forever from now! Can't we do overnight shipping or something?"

"Do you have an extra twenty dollars I don't know about?" my mom asked.

"No," I grumbled.

"Well, then I guess you'll just have to be patient." My mom smiled at me as she got up from the computer. "Find some way to distract yourself."

"You know I'm not patient, and I'm also really sick of not knowing if I'm a supertaster or not!" I called out as she left my room. "Mom? Did you hear me? I said I'm really sick of not knowing if I'm a supertaster or not."

"A week, Minerva," she called back.

"Well, I *am* really sick of it," I said to myself as I wrote the delivery date on my calendar and circled it in blue and gold marker. That's the day I would finally know why my tongue was the way it was. Maybe I could even get it put into my school records, like a doctor's note: "Please excuse Minerva from liver, green peppers, and all other gross foods. She is a supertaster."

What would it feel like to know I was a supertaster for sure? I hopped over a plastic apple and parts of a hamburger from Hugo's cooking set to stand in front of the mirror.

"Minerva," I said, pointing a stern finger at my reflection, "You are *NOT* a supertaster." I hunched my shoulders up, stuck out a panting tongue, and tried to look weak, pathetic, and tired.

Then I straightened up and looked at my reflection again.

"Minerva!" I announced, *"YOU ARE A SUPER-TASTER!"* I pumped both fists in the air and flexed my arms. I grabbed Hugo's favorite pink blanket from the foot of his bed and draped it over my shoulders like a cape.

"By night, she reads books under the covers and does almost all her homework, but by day, she fights for the rights of picky eaters everywhere—she's the *SUPERTASTER!*" I leaped up on my bed.

MRRRRAAAAAAAAWWWWWL!

"Oops, sorry, Beanbag," I panted, using my favorite nick-name for our little black cat. "Didn't see you there!"

Bean gave me a reproachful look from big yellow eyes. I stroked her head until she curled her compact body into my unmade bed again and started to purr. Then I hopped back to the mirror and did a few more, quieter rounds of:

"Supertaster!"

"Not a supertaster."

"Supertaster!"

"Not a supertaster."

The thing is, it's pretty impossible to pretend to know something when you actually know that you really don't know it yet but will know it soon. Thinking all that out made my head spin. But all of a sudden I had the best idea about how to decorate my Food Science Fair project board.

I dug some construction paper out of a desk drawer and settled down cross-legged on the floor with a pair of scissors. I snipped out red, blue, and yellow stars.

"POW! BIFF! WHAM!"

CHAPTER 16

"Minerva, it's not here yet—just go. Go outside, go for a walk, go for a bike ride, just do something instead of asking me every five minutes if your test arrived!"

I had only asked her four times that morning if the mail had come, but I guess it was four times too many, as my mom was now starting to leave the room every time I walked into it. Instead of pointing out (again) that it had been about ten days since she ordered the test kit, I decided that the best thing would be to make myself scarce for a while. I headed out to the treehouse and found Ralph doing homework at the table and Alice curled up on a corner reading a thick graphic novel about zombies living on a farm. She looked up and smiled as I came up the ladder.

"Hey, Minerva—what's up?" she said.

"Not much. My mom kind of kicked me out of the house because I wouldn't stop bugging her about the supertaster kit."

"Still not here?"

"Nope," I said, grabbing the binder and pulling up a stump closer to her. I didn't want to bother Ralph, who was pursing his lips and frowning at his papers.

Alice pointed to the binder. "Have you added any tips of your own yet? You can, you know. You're one of us."

"Oh, I did, already," I said. "Here—" I flipped to the page where I had written in my first tip and started reading.

"Baked potatoes are a good place to hide anything you don't want to eat. The most important thing to remember is that after you close the potato skin around the green beans, or whatever you have, give it a slight smoosh with the heel of your hand to make it look empty."

"That's a great tip—baked potatoes. I never would have thought of that," Alice said.

"Works best if your parents don't eat your potato skins," Ralph said, looking up from his work.

"Oh, no!" I said, my stomach sinking. "Did that happen to you?"

"Yeah. Before loading our dishwasher, my dad stands at the sink to scrape anything left on our plates into his mouth," Ralph said. "He's a human garbage disposal, and he was not thrilled to get a mouthful of broccoli with my potato skin."

"Did you get in a lot of trouble?" I asked.

"Nah," Ralph said. "They're used to me trying to get rid of food. They gave me a talking-to and took away my screen time."

“I’m so sorry, Ralph,” I said. I felt stupid for not realizing that there might be parents who would eat the potato skins. My parents just composted ours.

“It’s okay, but if you’re really sorry, you could help me with my math,” Ralph said, pointing at his homework. “Willa says you explain everything so clearly.”

“Sure,” I said. I was happy to do anything to help.

“Sweet!” Ralph crowed.

We worked until Ralph jumped up and yelled, “I finally get it! Oh my gosh, I *get it!* You are the *best,* Minerva! Thank you!”

I grinned. It felt so good to help the League members; they had already helped me so much. I picked up the binder again and added another tip about sneaking food under the table to family pets. But I made sure to note that you might have to make covering noise. For instance, our Bean is the sweetest tiny love of a cat you could ever want, but she growls like a wild thing when she’s chewing away at a piece of meat.

“Is anyone hungry?” Alice asked. “I was thinking about going to Amy’s for a snack.”

“Oooh, yeah!” I said. “Ralph?”

But Ralph didn’t respond. He was scribbling away, his face puckered in concentration.

“We’ll bring him something back,” Alice said, waving away Ralph’s silence.

Amy’s was only a few blocks from the treehouse, so it

wasn't long before we were sitting in a booth, unwrapping twin grilled cheese sandwiches. I was happy to see that I wasn't the only one who thought grilled cheese sandwiches weren't just the perfect meal, but also the perfect snack.

Alice sighed. "Amy's has the best grilled cheese in the entire world."

"Maybe even in the entire solar system," I agreed.

"Or galaxy."

"Or cluster," I said, looking at Alice.

"Or supercluster!" Alice said, looking right back at me.

"OR WALL! OR UNIVERSE!" we said in unison, and then started laughing.

"I have never met anyone else who knew the hierarchy of space," Alice said. She took a sip of soda.

"My dad calls it a *tower*—that's a math term where everything fits inside each other, like nesting dolls. He taught it to me when we were learning about neighborhood, city, and state in Geography," I said. "I thought we just stopped at our galaxy. I didn't know there were names for places beyond that."

Alice nodded. "I used to think universe came before galaxy, but my older brother, Ty—he wants to be an astronaut—explained about cluster, supercluster, wall, and *then* universe."

"It's weird to think of that distance being so everywhere out there. Sometimes at night I look at the stars and feel . . ." I trailed off.

"Small?" Alice finished.

"No, not small, exactly. More like lost, I guess. And sort of scared. I mean, just the idea that space keeps going on and on forever—there's something so lonely about it. I can't explain it."

"I get it. It's sort of creepy to think of something having no end," Alice said. "Not creepy, like a horror movie—but something that makes you feel a bit on edge when you really think about it."

"Yes, exactly!"

I ate a few more bites of my sandwich, thinking about dark skies and stars at night.

"We should have a sleepover in the treehouse!" I said suddenly. "With Willa, too."

"In the treehouse?" Alice repeated doubtfully.

"Yeah," I said. "Under the stars, with sleeping bags and snacks and everything." It would be so much better than any sleepover at Patricia's house.

"I don't think my parents would let me spend the night in a park," Alice said slowly. "Also, no bathroom."

"Oh, yeah," I said, coming back to earth with a thud. "That would be a problem." My parents probably wouldn't let me either, come to think of it.

"We could still have a sleepover," Willa said, suddenly turning around in a booth behind Alice.

Alice and I jumped.

"Oh my gosh!" I said, laughing in shock. "How long have you been there?"

"Just a few minutes," Willa said. "But you didn't notice me at all, did you?"

"Nope," Alice said.

"Epic eavesdropping detective skills." Willa grinned. "So what do you think? We could still have a sleepover, couldn't we? Maybe even outside?"

"In my backyard!" Alice said as Willa slid into the booth with us.

"Under the stars, with sleeping bags and snacks and everything," Willa said, repeating my words.

I nodded my head hard. "Yes, absolutely."

Akshay was in the treehouse when we got back. We offered him some of the fries we brought back for Ralph, who was still working away on his homework.

"Thanks," he said, stuffing a few into his mouth. "Man, I wish we had these at school."

"Yeah," I agreed. "I actually wanted to run for class president so I could convince Principal Butcher to put them on the menu."

"Yesss!" Akshay said, and pumped his fist in the air.

"But then," I said, "I decided not to run."

"Why not?"

"Because Patricia said she was going to, and I was going

to help her and I don't think—" I stopped. It had been such a nice day. I didn't want to talk about what happened way back then.

"Hey, Akshay," Alice said, purposely changing the subject. "You're still wearing bandages on your fingers?"

But Akshay kept serious brown eyes on my face. "You should still think about it, Minerva."

"Or," said Willa, tapping her teeth with a pen, "maybe there's another way to get french fries on the menu."

"Maybe." I couldn't bear to remember all the plans I'd made before the school year started. The plans I had given to Patricia as a birthday present.

"Akshay, your fingers?" Alice said, trying again.

A few days ago had been foie gras day in RETCH, and in the immersion part of the lesson Madame Bouche showed us how to make liver lobes. First we cut the liver shape out of brown felt; then we sewed the pieces together and stuffed them with cotton balls. They looked like little brown pillows.

"If you sleep with these on your beds every night, you will have lovely liver dreams!" she insisted as she walked around to check our work.

Madame Bouche was not at all pleased to discover Ralph coloring on his liver lobe with a Sharpie. Ralph explained, "They're liver spots, like my grandpa has on his hands."

"You know that in order to make foie gras, geese and

ducks have their food forced down their throats. It's abuse," Alice said when Madame Bouche examined her assignment.

"Oh, my dear, their tiny animal brains have no idea what's going on," Madame Bouche said, dropping Alice's liver pillow and moving on. I gasped, and Alice stuck out her tongue at Madame Bouche's spangled purple back. Wow, Madame Bouche was a true monster. I looked over at Willa, who looked more enraged than I had ever seen her.

Mr. Kreplach had just finished handing out the Eating half of the assignment—foie gras sandwiches—when Akshay howled "My fingers!" and dropped his liver pillow. "I pricked my fingers! WITH THE NEEDLE!" Mr. Kreplach and Madame Bouche immediately clustered around Akshay, trying to help him. Or trying to quiet him down. It wasn't clear which.

During the distraction Willa and Alice slipped around the room to gather up all the foie gras sandwiches and hand them over to me. I stuffed fistfuls of the sandwiches behind a set of culinary encyclopedias on the bookshelf. Akshay dramatically raised his howls of pain a notch to cover any noise we might make.

Now Akshay responded to Alice's question by waving his bandaged fingers in the air. "This is all for show. They're fine."

"I still can't believe you intentionally poked your fingers

with that needle," I said. "I can't even handle shots at the doctor's office!"

"You know, the thing about being so accident-prone is that after a while most of the stuff just doesn't hurt as much. You sort of build up a high pain tolerance," Akshay said. "And really, eating that foie gras would have been far more painful."

"What did your parents say?"

Before Akshay could answer me, we heard Ralph mumble, "Dang, these are as good as my aunt's." He shoved some fries into his mouth and kept working without acknowledging any of us.

"My parents are used to it," Akshay said. "I've been like this since I was a baby. See this?" He pointed at a scar just above his lip. "I fell through a chair when the seat cushion collapsed, and I banged my mouth on the metal frame. I was three. That was just the start. I've broken both my arms and sprained my left ankle at least four times."

"Have you ever had a concussion?" I asked.

"Once. When I fell out of the top bunk at our cabin," Akshay said.

"Was it scary?" I asked.

He shook his head. "It was more annoying than scary, really. My parents had to keep waking me up every hour all night long so I wouldn't go into a coma. I was super tired and grumpy the next day, but I was fine."

I was impressed. The last time I got a splinter, I screamed so loud when my mom tried to dig it out that our next-door neighbors came over to check on us. It was so embarrassing.

"Hey, look," Akshay said, unzipping his backpack. "I brought something for the treehouse." He pulled out a plastic food container and set it down. I eyed it.

"That's my mom's bhindi masala," Akshay said, catching my look. "It's okra with onion and tomatoes—it's amazing. But don't worry, that's not what I brought for the treehouse. This is what I brought for the treehouse!" He lifted a tall box out of his backpack.

Willa clapped. "Yes, Jenga! I am so good at this, guys!"

"Ralph," Willa called, "wanna play?"

Ralph didn't answer.

"He really gets into his own world sometimes," Akshay said, shaking his head. He opened his container of bhindi masala and started eating it with a plastic fork.

"Do you want to try it?" Akshay said. "It's totally okay if you don't. We all have different things we like that the rest of us don't. And we don't pressure each other in the League."

"Yeah," Alice said. "Last summer Ralph invited us all over to his house to grill stuff, but first he asked what we liked."

"And I'm not a full vegetarian," Akshay said. "Like my family doesn't eat beef, but they do eat fish, chicken, and lamb. I just don't like any kind of meat. It all commits texture violations in my mouth, so I couldn't eat any of the grilled meat. Even the idea grosses me out."

"Texture violations?" I repeated.

"Yeah, you know—it's like when you put a certain food in your mouth and it feels all wrong in there. Like, your mouth shudders," Akshay explained.

"Oooh, that's exactly the reaction I have with something like oatmeal or tapioca, and even bananas. It's . . . squicky." I said. *Squicky* was another of my invented words—it smashed together *squirm* and *icky*. I used it a lot.

"Exactly," Alice said, "and Ralph didn't pressure Akshay to eat any meat. Instead he made sure to have food that Akshay would like—to make him feel comfortable and welcome."

"His dad grilled zucchini spears and eggplant for me," Akshay said. "And even a few king trumpet mushrooms, which don't shrink or get all wet and mushy like other cooked mushrooms."

"That's really nice," I said, remembering how Patricia pretended to have food that would make me comfortable at her party, but it turned out to be the exact opposite.

Akshay's bhindi masala actually smelled kind of delicious—rich and spicy. "What else is in it?" I asked. To keep from being surprised in that bad raisin-in-an-oatmeal-cookie way, I always like to know all the ingredients of something before I eat it.

"Okra, onions, tomatoes, ginger, and spices," Akshay said.

"It doesn't look slimy—I thought okra was supposed to be slimy."

"It can be," Akshay said. "But my mom slices the okra and lets it sit before cooking. I think it might dry it out a bit, so there's really no slime at all."

"Maybe I'll try it next time," I said.

"Whenever you want. Just let me know. My mom makes it a lot," Akshay said.

The four of us played several very loud rounds of Jenga while I asked questions about the binder.

"But isn't it strange that we don't know how the note got into Ralph's backpack?"

"It is weird, but we have no idea," Alice said.

"We have theories," Willa added, sliding a Jenga brick out.

"Right: like someone broke into Ralph's house, stole nothing, and left a note behind just because," Alice said.

"Or it was aliens from a picky planet," Akshay said.

"Or Ralph discovered how to time travel and left it for his past self to find," Willa said.

"Or it was picky-eating zombies living under his floorboards who feel bad for us because it turns out that they are the only zombies who don't like brains, and they know how it feels," Akshay said.

"That's my theory," Alice said, waving her graphic novel about the zombie farmers.

"I mean, it could be . . ." I said.

Alice, Willa, and Akshay waited.

"Like, what if it was . . ." I tried again, thinking hard. "Oh, I don't have any idea!"

"That's exactly where we all are with it," Akshay said. "Welcome to the club. Again."

"It's just so *weird!*" I said.

"Sometimes it's best not to question the weird when you can just embrace the weird," Willa said.

Alice jumped up, her arms outstretched. "Yodel-ay-yodel-ay-del-yo-lady-HEY-oo-oo-AH-HEEEE!" she yodeled, then turned to us with a wink. "Like that?"

"Yes, exactly," Willa said calmly, as if Alice yodeled every day. I looked over at Ralph, who didn't give any sign that he had heard a thing. Maybe Alice *did* yodel every day.

"Hey, Akshay?" I asked.

"Hey, what?" Akshay smiled, concentrating on another Jenga piece.

"How come you don't tell teachers when they get your name wrong?"

Akshay's smile dropped a bit at the edges.

"I mean," I said in a rush, "it must bother you."

"Oh, it does. Like *a lot,*" Akshay said. "But . . . I don't know. I guess I'm just sick of telling them they're wrong and no one actually ever paying attention. Or caring."

"It's so wrong, though," I said.

"Yeah, it is wrong," Alice added. "I mean, they never have problems with food names like sauerkraut, avgolemono, and bagna cauda, but they can't get your name right?"

"They also never have problems with my name or yours," I pointed out to Alice. She nodded.

"Yeah, like, if I were a food, they'd care more about getting it right," Akshay said. "Sometimes," he went on, fiddling with a Jenga piece, "they make me feel like it's my fault for having a 'different' or 'difficult' name." Akshay put air quotes around *different* and *difficult*. "And so they do stuff like give me a nickname without my permission, like The Mouth did, to make it easier for them."

Willa had told us that *bouche* was *mouth* in French, so we all started calling Madame Bouche The Mouth when she wasn't around.

"But," Akshay went on, "they don't ever think about how 'easier' for them always makes me feel out of place, or like I don't belong there."

"It's not right to make *anyone* feel that way," Willa said quietly. "About anything."

"Nope," Akshay said. "And the whole name thing upsets my parents so much, I've stopped telling them about it."

"We should start calling Mr. Kreplach, Mr. KRAPlach and see how he likes it," Alice muttered.

Akshay gave her a slight smile.

"People sure have all kinds of ways of making other people feel strange and out of place and unwelcome!" I said, yanking out a Jenga piece and making the whole puzzle crash down. We all jumped at the noise.

"Sorry," I said, blushing.

"What about? It's how the game is played," Alice said. "I'm totally okay with you losing that one!"

I smiled.

"Play again?" Willa said. Akshay, Alice, and I nodded, and we all started rebuilding the tower.

After a few more games I figured I should head home.

"Bye, Ralph!" I called, stepping onto the ladder.

Ralph finally glanced up. Then he looked around in surprise. "You're leaving already? Akshay! Willa!" he said, waving. "When did you guys get here?"

Willa snorted, and Akshay rolled his eyes. I just laughed and waved goodbye.

CHAPTER 17

The Friday of the backyard sleepover, Madame Bouche fluttered into the RETCH classroom wearing a silky dress that had multiple layers, each a different shade of blue. She was carrying a box of rolled-up yoga mats, which she dropped on the floor with a *thunk* before turning to us, her arms spread wide.

"Today, my precious pickies," she trilled, "we will do an immersion lesson in scallops!"

Waves of barely muffled groans spread across the classroom, punctuated by a few "HOAR-OH-OARFFs" from Ralph. Madame Bouche eyed him.

"I ha-AH-ve the hicc-UH-ups," Ralph said.

Madam Bouche flicked her hands at him, as if dismissing him as unimportant, and said, "Now, everyone—quick quick—I need you to move all the desks and chairs against the wall so we can create an ocean floor."

Wondering, as usual, what we were in for on this immersion day, we all dutifully shoved desks and chairs out of the way. Madame Bouche unrolled blue and green yoga mats on the cleared space and flipped on a music player. Sounds of crashing waves filled the room.

"Now, everyone find a bit of ocean floor and lie down on your backs," Madame Bouche ordered. "Today you will imagine yourselves as hungry little sea otters floating through the ocean!"

Akshay called out, "Wait, you said we were on the ocean floor, but sea otters float on top of the waves."

"Shhh-shhh-*shhhh*!" Madame Bouche commanded, flapping her hands at him and handing out bowls of sautéed scallops that Mr. Kreplach had prepared before leaving for his staff meeting.

"Lie down and hold those bowls on your chest, just like you are furry, adorable, *hungry* widdle sea otters swimming on your backs and holding a scallop shell you scooped up for your din-din."

It's safe to say that the fishy smell steaming up from the assignment wasn't the only thing that made many of us gag in response.

Next, Madame Bouche withdrew a large spray bottle from her bag. "Now, prepare yourselves to breathe in that wonderful salty ocean air," she said as she tiptoed around the class, spritzing water into the air over our heads.

"Ptooey-ptooey," Alice spluttered. "Exactly how much salt

is in that water? Because everyone should be watching their sodium levels and—"

"Otters love scallops, and so will you!" Madame Bouche said, raising her voice until she drowned Alice out.

Akshay popped up on one elbow and said, "You know, scallops are bottom feeders who eat all the nasty garbage in the ocean, even stuff from other fish. So when we eat scallops, we're actually eating poo—" But before he could finish, Madame Bouche charged over and gave him a vigorous squirt in the face.

Akshay "accidentally" inhaled the water spray and then proceeded to roll around the floor in a dramatic coughing fit. While Madame Bouche clapped him desperately on the back and tried to get him off the floor, Willa and I quietly darted around the class, grabbing everyone's bowls. I tossed handfuls of scallops out the garden window, and Willa handed the empty bowls back around. Just as I flung the last handful, Mr. Kreplach came back into the room. I stepped quickly away from the window, wiping my greasy hands on the back of my jeans, but out of the corner of my eye I saw two feral cats squeeze through a crack in the wooden fence and streak toward the discarded remnants of our bottom-feeding assignment.

"Well, well, well!" Mr. Kreplach said, beaming at our empty bowls. "Isn't this nice to see! Madame Bouche, you have truly worked miracles on this picky lot lately." Madame Bouche preened and fluttered her blue draperies in delight. Then Mr. Kreplach looked at the rest of us. "It's nice to see you finally growing up and trying to be better eaters. After all, sixth grade really is long past the time of eating like spoiled preschoolers."

Preschoolers. That made me mad, and I wanted to say something back. Something about how we couldn't help what we liked and didn't like. And how my Food Science Fair project would explain everything. Once I proved I was a supertaster, there would at least be a scientific reason for my freakish tongue. In fact, maybe everyone in RETCH was a supertaster. And maybe, just maybe, people would finally accept that we were never going to be good at Eating and they should all stop judging us for it.

I opened my mouth, but was interrupted.

ROWWWWOWWWL!

Everyone turned to Ralph, who spread his hands wide. "That wasn't me, honest!"

HSSSSSST! HSSSST! ROWWWWOWWWL!

The noises were coming from the garden. And as the volume of the squalls, hisses, and yowls increased, they got even more vicious and threatening.

"What in the world?" Mr. Kreplach strode over to the windows.

My heart clutched in my chest, and I looked wildly around

at the class. The cats outside! Eating all those scallops! We were about to be discovered!

"Are those . . . cats out there?" Mr. Kreplach said, opening the wooden door and peering into the garden through the latched screen door. Madame Bouche peered out as well.

"Ugh," she said. "I detest cats—nasty, sneaky little beasts they are! You just know they're always hiding something."

"I knew I didn't trust her," Willa said in an undertone at my side. "What kind of person doesn't like cats?"

"Seriously," I muttered.

"Shoo!" Mr. Kreplach said, cracking the screen door open a smidge. "Shoo!"

Madame Bouche raised her water bottle and fired off several shots through the screen.

"How odd—were they fighting over food in a . . . vegetable garden?" Mr. Kreplach said, frowning.

I wanted to collapse to the floor in a puddle of relief. Mother earth, that was a close one.

When school got out, Willa, Alice, and I made plans to meet up at Alice's house just as soon as we collected all the stuff we'd need for the backyard sleepover.

"Sleeping bag, pillow, and pajamas," Alice listed on her fingers. "Anything else?"

"Flashlights?" I suggested.

"Absolutely!" Willa said. "Good idea. Oh, hey—what about dinner?"

"So, um, last night my dad said he'd make a bunch of grilled cheese sandwiches—enough for all of us," I said uncertainly. "Would that be all right with you guys?"

The sleepover had been my idea, but it was also the first one I was going to since Patricia's birthday party. I didn't want to seem bossy or controlling. I wanted everything to go okay. I needed everything to go okay.

"Sounds great," Willa said.

Alice nodded. "It's too bad Ralph and Akshay can't make it. They're gonna seriously miss out!"

I could smell hot melted butter as soon as I walked in my door at home. My favorite smell. On Fridays my dad didn't have to teach, so he usually beat me home from school. Most Fridays, he would go straight to his "study" and keep working. But today I walked into the kitchen and found him standing over the stove, easily flipping sandwiches with a spatula.

"Wow, Dad, those look as good as Amy's," I said, grinning. "Almost."

"*Almost* as good as Amy's, huh?" he said, keeping his eyes on the skillet. "Well, that's something to work up to."

I put an arm around his waist, careful to stand back from the hot stove. "Thanks, Dad."

He set the spatula down and turned off the burner. Then he put both arms around me and pulled me in for a hug. "Happy to do it," he whispered into the top of my head. "And also, you know you can call us if you need to come home."

My stomach gave a slight hitch. "Okay," I said quietly and then, before he could say anything else, I added, "I better go get ready."

I took a quick shower, gathered up my stuff, and set everything on the kitchen table. Hugo came running out of the living room and threw himself at me. "I will miss you for the rest of my life! You will come home if they are mean again!"

I decided to ignore the second part and hugged him back. "I will miss you, too."

"My room is lonely without you," Hugo told me.

"I know. Hey, maybe you can get Bean and Needles to sleep on your bed. They will if you're really, really quiet, and if you remember not to squeeze them."

Hugo considered this. "Okay," he said, and rampaged down the hall. "I'LL START BEING QUIET RIGHT NOW!" He slammed into our bedroom.

I kneeled down and looked under the kitchen table. Bean was curled up on one of the chairs, almost completely hidden in the shadows if you didn't know where to look. I put out my hand to pet her soft, black fur. She made a little *whirrup* noise deep in her throat and rolled over on her back, front paws bent like a rabbit. "You might want to hide really well tonight," I whispered. "I won't be here to protect you from his love." Bean sniffed at my head and started licking my hair, like she always does when my hair is wet from the shower or swimming. "I'm not coming back home tonight, Bean. I'm not. But it's going to be okay." I stood up and gave Bean a few final strokes under her chin. "It's going to be okay," I repeated to myself.

Just a few minutes later, my mom parked on Willa's and Alice's street. Across the street from Willa's, Alice's house was small, neat, and cozy looking. Not at all like Patricia's, which was so enormous that every space inside felt empty and cold, even when the air conditioning wasn't turned on. And in the winter, when the heater gasped on and blew forced hot air everywhere, it felt like the warmth never quite filled the rooms. My eyes focused on Alice's front door. It was painted red with black polka dots—just like a ladybug! It seemed exactly like the kind of front door Alice would have: crazy, unexpected, and ultimately amazing.

My mom unbuckled her seat belt and started to turn toward me. I knew she wanted to say something, just like my dad did. Something about being able to call and come home if I needed to. I couldn't bear to think about that possibility, so before she could say anything, I flung open the car door. "Thanks, Mom! See you tomorrow! Good night! Sleep tight! I love you!" I grabbed my stuff and ran across the street. As I made my way around to Alice's backyard, I held my pillow against my chest and slowed my feet and my breathing.

The backyard was empty except for a huge tent set up smack in the middle of it. "Whoa!" I whispered.

The front of the tent unzipped, and Alice stuck her head out. "Hey, Minerva! You're here! Dude, you gotta get in here and check this out! Willa's parents brought it over for us!" Alice said.

Willa popped her head out next to Alice's and swept her hand to me in a grand gesture. "'How now, spirit! Whither wander you?'"

I felt a warmth wash over me. Alice's and Willa's exuberance snuffed out the last worry in my stomach. It *was* going to be okay.

"Come on in!" Alice said. Then she cupped her hands over her mouth and did an abbreviated yodel of happiness through them. "Yodel-ay-yodel-ay-del-yo-lady-HEY!"

I slipped off my shoes and stepped inside. The tent was big enough for all of us to stand up in and had a lot of floor space. Plenty of room to spread out our sleeping bags. The sun, getting lower in the sky, filtered through the green nylon and actually made it feel like we were high up in the trees.

"We usually only get it out for camping in the summer, but my dad said it's good to air it out every once in a while, so it doesn't grow mildew," Willa explained.

"It feels like the treehouse," I said. My voice was hushed. Like I didn't want to disturb . . . anything.

"And look—" Willa unzipped a panel at the top of the tent, exposing a netted opening. "We even have a skylight! We'll be sleeping under the stars and everything!"

I shook my head in happy disbelief. I couldn't wait until it got dark.

Before setting up our sleeping bags, we decided to eat our dinner. Alice's mom had brought out paper plates, napkins, a bucket full of ice, and cans of grapefruit-flavored sparkling water. Alice spread out a picnic blanket to protect the tent's floor from food and grease stains. I plopped down on the red and white checkers and handed around my plastic container of grilled cheese sandwiches.

"Knock, knock!" a voice called from outside. Willa's mom stuck her head into the tent. Dr. Lewis wore her curly black hair in a soft puff instead of in braids like her daughter, but Willa had her mother's deep-set amber eyes. "I thought you girls might want these as well." She handed in three rolls of foam. "The bedrolls will make the ground less hard."

"Thanks, Mama!" Willa said, stacking the bedrolls in a corner.

"Yeah, thank you!" Alice and I echoed.

"Also," Dr. Lewis went on, "I have this for you." She pulled a bowl from around her back. "Fruit salad! I know you're having grilled cheese sandwiches, but try getting a little fruit into you as well. The doctor orders it." She winked with a grin at us.

I smiled back shyly. When I had gone with my mom to the vet for the cats' checkups, I had only met Willa's dad. I hadn't met the other Dr. Lewis before.

"How are Bean and Needles doing these days, Minerva?" Dr. Lewis asked me.

"Oh," I said, impressed that she remembered their names. I mean, she must see so many animals at the clinic. How could she keep them all straight? "They're good. Really good. But um, Dr. Lewis, I was just thinking about something recently, and since you're a vet and everything, you might be able to answer this. Can you explain why Bean likes to lick my hair?"

"Well," Dr. Lewis said, pursing her pretty red lips, which were shiny with gloss. "In my considered and medical opinion, I would have to say that the reason Bean does that is because"—she paused here and looked very serious before cocking her head—"sometimes cats are just weird." Her face broke into another smile.

I grinned back as Willa snorted. Dr. Lewis gave us another wink and walked out to the backyard and across the street.

After we were stuffed full of sandwiches and fruit—I only ate the strawberries and blackberries, but Alice and Willa ate the cubes of cantaloupe I didn't like—Alice folded the picnic blanket and set it in a corner of the tent. We unrolled the foam bedrolls and spread our sleeping bags on top, arranging ourselves so that we'd be lying in a circle, with our three heads in the center of the tent. When we were on our backs, with our heads sunk into our pillows, we could all look up at the skylight and see the purpling sky above us.

Alice popped into a sitting position and pulled out her flashlight. She clicked it on and held the beam under her chin, filling her face with shadows and hollows. "Okay, guys, it's time to tell *gross stories!*"

"What are gross stories?" I asked.

"Instead of scaring each other with ghost stories, we try to gross each other out with gross stories!" Alice explained. "Like, what's the grossest thing you ever had to eat?"

"Ooh, I'll go first," Willa said, grabbing the flashlight and sticking it under her chin. "So there was this time when my grandmother was visiting, and she made this dish that my mom loves from her childhood in New Orleans. It's called étouffée." Willa pronounced *étouffée* with a lilting accent, just the way our teachers were always trying to get us to do with various dishes at school. I was impressed.

"Étouffée is made with crawfish and a roux sauce and served with rice—" Willa went on.

I shuddered. I don't like lobsters. They look like giant water bugs to me, and crawfish are basically tiny freshwater lobsters. Another name for crawfish is actually mudbugs, because they live at the bottom of rivers, ponds, and streams. Mother earth, I can't handle that.

"Was the roux made with butter and flour or oil and flour?" Alice interrupted.

"Butter and flour," Willa said. "Because it's a Creole recipe, rather than a Cajun one. Anyway, my parents told me I used to really like it when I was younger, but this time . . ." Willa paused dramatically and looked at us, her eyes wide and staring. "This time I asked what *étouffée* meant."

Alice found her voice first, and it was raspy and dry with fear. "Wha—what does it mean?"

"It means—" Willa paused again and looked us each in the eye before screaming, "SMOTHERED!" Alice and I both jumped and screamed with her.

"And," Willa said, lowering her voice again, "I just couldn't get it out of my head that the crawfish had died—that it had smothered to *death* in the étouffée—like this." Willa flopped onto her back and thrashed her arms and legs around before slowing them to a few twitches and then finally dropping them to the ground and lying still. She rolled over and continued her story. "And I couldn't eat it, and my grandmother was pretty upset with me for a long time."

"Wow," Alice and I both said. A chill ran down my spine just thinking about it.

"Your turn," Willa said, handing me the flashlight.

"Okay. My story is not going to be nearly as good as Willa's, but it also involves fish," I said. I pulled my hair off my shoulders and tied it up in a ponytail.

Willa and Alice stretched out on their stomachs and waited for me to continue.

"You know that restaurant downtown—La Snobbiste Y'Eat?" I waited for them to nod before I went on. "Well, we went there for my dad's birthday last year, and they had one of those fancy menus where you don't have a choice. It's just one appetizer, one entrée, and one dessert—chef's choice."

"Prix fixe," Willa nodded, pronouncing it *pree feeks,* and again I marveled at her French accent.

"Right," I said. "So I thought the appetizer was going to be okay because it was tapenade—you know, olive purée—on toast. And I don't really mind that. But when I tasted it, this stupid freak tongue of mine—"

"Supertaster tongue, not stupid freak tongue," Alice reminded me. "We're going to find out soon that you have a *supertaster* tongue, which means it's smarter than the average tongue. Just like my advanced nasal technology, here." She patted the side of her nose affectionately.

"Okay, fine," I said, smiling and rolling my eyes. "My stupid *supertaster* tongue—"

Alice sighed.

"Could tell there was something fishy going on in the tapenade. Literally." I looked at them. "The chef made the tapenade the traditional Provençale way. That meant *with anchovies!*"

"Ewwwwww!" Alice and Willa shrieked.

"But wait, that wasn't the worst part. I scraped the tapenade off as best I could and tried to eat just the toast, but I could still taste the anchovies. And then the main course came: poached salmon."

"What was it—fish lovers' night?" Alice said in horror.

"So I started picking at the salmon. My parents were already mad at me for scraping off the tapenade—they even said Hugo was better behaved, and he was in a highchair—so I was going to try to eat the salmon. I figured I could put a small bite in my mouth, swallow it down with water, and then eat something from the bread basket. I didn't want to ruin my dad's birthday."

"Wait—shh—" Alice held up her hand. "Did you hear that?"

"What?" Willa asked, looking around.

"Maybe it's nothing. I just thought I heard something outside," Alice said. She grabbed a can of sparkling water and popped it open. "Okay, Minerva—go on."

"Right, okay—where was I?" I asked.

"You were taking a bite of salmon," Willa prompted.

"Oh, yes!" I remembered. "So I cut a bite of salmon with my fork and—did I mention that the skin was still on the bottom?"

They shook their heads. And Willa clapped her hand over her mouth. "Oh, no," she moaned. "I know exactly what's going to happen."

I nodded for emphasis. "When I brought the bite to my mouth, I saw that part of the salmon where the pink part meets the skin, and it was—" I paused, just like Willa had. "GRAY!" I screamed.

Willa and Alice yelled with me, and Alice rolled around on her sleeping bag for emphasis. "Gross! Gross! Gross! I hate that gray part!" Even though it was one of the grossest memories I ever had, I couldn't help laughing.

"Okay, Alice," I said. "Your turn."

Alice took the flashlight and was deep into her story about discovering that shrimp have a digestive tract that isn't always removed before cooking when she stopped suddenly.

"I just thought of something," she said. "All our stories have to do with some kind of fish. I mean, isn't that so creepy?"

I hadn't thought of it, but she was right—it was totally creepy. Another chill skittered down my spine.

"Hang on—what's that?" Alice said.

"What? Did you hear something?" I asked, hugging my pillow against my stomach.

"No, I . . . smelled something," Alice said, sniffing the air.

"I don't smell anything," Willa said, also sniffing.

"Yeah, it's something," Alice said. She stood up and went closer to the flap. She sniffed some more, then lifted the flap. "It's—oh my gosh!"

"What? *What?!*" Willa and I said.

"It's SARDINES!" Alice yelled, and pointed outside the tent. "SARDINES ARE OUT THERE!"

Willa and I scrambled to our feet just as Alice took a flying leap out of the tent.

"Ty! I know you're out there! TY!" Alice yelled. She was holding her nose now and looking around the backyard. "YOU GET BACK HERE AND CLEAN THIS UP!"

Right outside the tent, placed in such a way that any one of us could have stepped right in it if we got up to go to the bathroom in the middle of the night, was a plate of sardines. They had been dumped from their can and were sitting there in their horrible fishy oil.

"Oh, hi." An older boy's face popped out from behind some hydrangea bushes. "Were you looking for me? What's going on? Something wrong? Man, you guys can scream loud." It was Alice's older brother, Ty. I remembered him from when he went to our school a few years earlier, but now he was in high school and just as popular there as he had been at St. Julia Child.

"Ty, I'm serious," Alice said, stomping over to him. "Clean that up, and don't spill it on the tent or our shoes, or I'm telling Mom."

"Okay, okay. Chill," Ty said, grinning at all of us and clambering out of the bushes. He was tall and lanky, with white-blond hair like Alice's. But instead of blue eyes like Alice's, his were brown. "Don't get your nose all out of joint. Get it? *Nose*?"

"TY-Y!" Alice yelled again.

"Shh-shh. Okay, look, I'm cleaning it up, okay?" Ty

carefully lifted the plate. The thick oil shifted sluggishly. I held back a gag. "And to make it up to you guys, I'll make popcorn, okay?"

"Okay!" I said immediately.

But Alice glared at him. "You can help *Mom* make the popcorn. I don't want any fish oil making it in there on accident."

"So you'd be okay with it if it wasn't an accident?" Ty asked over his shoulder as he walked back to the house, walking faster but still being very careful with the plate.

"TY!" Alice chased her brother into the house, the screen door slamming behind them.

When Alice came back out again, she was carrying a bowl of popcorn and wearing her nose clips.

"These are just a precaution," she said. "In case Ty tries to do anything else tonight."

She reassured us that the popcorn was fish oil–free. She had watched her mom make it. As we munched our way through the butter and salt, Alice told us about other pranks Ty had pulled on her in the past. Most of them seemed to involve hiding fish somewhere around her room and waiting for her to discover it.

"He even kept track of my times," Alice said. "On a chart."

"On a chart?" Willa exclaimed.

"Yeah. I think it kind of backfired on him, though," Alice said. "Because he started to get really excited about how quickly I would discover the fish. He'd stand outside my door with a stopwatch, and he'd actually cheer when I beat my own time. You'd think he was training me for one of his track meets or something."

"Wow, that sounds . . . wow," I said. Being a picky eater was bad enough, but I couldn't even imagine having an older brother who made a competition out of my pickiness.

"He's not so bad. In fact, he was the one who came up with that centerpieces tip in the League binder," Alice said.

Willa seemed to know what Alice was talking about, but I hadn't read that far in the binder. Alice explained that Ty had felt really bad for her one night when their mom made Swiss chard as a side dish.

"I was really struggling, both with that smell," Alice said, putting a hand up to her mouth, "and the taste. So when my parents were in the kitchen, Ty suggested that I dump my chard in the centerpiece on the table."

"Ugh," I said, slapping my hand on my forehead. "That would have been so helpful to me last Christmas! My mom always makes this humongous centerpiece out of pine branches and holly."

"Did she make some sort of greens for dinner, too?" Alice asked.

"Creamed spinach with onions and water chestnuts." I shuddered. "Man, I wish I had known about the League back then."

Alice and Willa exchanged glances.

"What?" I asked.

"It's just . . . I mean, I don't know if you would have wanted to know about the League back then," Alice finally said.

I wrinkled my forehead. "What do you mean?"

Willa fiddled with her butter-stained napkin and didn't meet my eyes. "Like, would they have let you be friends with us?"

"They? Who?" I had no idea what she was talking about. And then, with a jolt to my brain, I did.

"Oh, Patricia and Cindy."

Their names tasted awful in my mouth—green pepper, squash, and the gray bits of salmon all smushed together in a horrible casserole.

"I mean, Patricia sort of orders you guys around, right? And she thinks I'm a total freak, so . . ." Alice trailed off, giving me room to fill in the blanks in my own words.

"She would have made me choose between them and you. And—" My voice snagged in my throat. I swallowed.

"And they were your friends. You didn't really know us," Willa offered.

"I guess." I stared up at the tent skylight. The night was pricked with stars, like someone had taken a thumbtack to the sky.

Until this year, I had been convinced that being in the

same class with my best friends year after year was the best part of school. And that being in a different class from them would destroy my entire life. But being with Patricia and Cindy all the time also meant that I didn't pay attention to anyone else, much less try to make other friends. Akshay and Alice had been in my class in other years. And I had seen Willa at her parents' vet clinic a few times. But I never talked to them or tried to get to know them.

It had been easier to stick to what I was used to, instead of trying something new. Because what if I didn't like it? Or what if they didn't like me?

"Maybe I shouldn't have said anything," Alice said in a low voice.

I looked back at Alice. She was frowning at her fingernails.

"No, it's fine. I'm fine." I pushed a smile up my cheeks to prove it. "It sounds weird to say it, but it's almost hard to believe I was ever friends with them. Or maybe I just don't want to remember it."

Looking back on the past few weeks was like sitting down to your favorite dinner on a Friday and trying to remember what you had for breakfast the Monday before. You know you ate breakfast and you remember not liking it, but when you've got a big bowl full of bacon and Parmigiano-Reggiano cheese pasta steaming up at you, it wipes away all memories of that Monday breakfast.

"You know, we'd never make you choose," Willa said.

"Yeah," Alice added. "You can still be friends with them and with us, if that's what you want. Just, um . . . don't tell them about the League?"

I tried to imagine walking up to Patricia—who lately had started looking right through me whenever she saw me—and saying anything to her. My stomach whammied me the way it did in kindergarten when I fell from the monkey bars and got the breath knocked out of me. It felt like everything inside me, including all my air, was trying to leave my body through my spine.

"Still be friends with them?" I said, pulling in a breath at last. "No. They're not my friends."

We heard a horn as a freight train rattled through town a few blocks away.

In summer here, the night air gets so still you can hear the blasting horns even over the fan in my window. As soon as Hugo and I hear that first blast, we sit up in our hot, tangled sheets and whisper *"TRAIN!"* across the room at each other. Then Hugo tries to count the cars by sound alone. If it's late at night, it's usually one of the longer freight trains, and Hugo ends up falling asleep around car count fifty-three.

Once, Patricia was sleeping over at my house when the freight train came through. I saw Hugo pop up like always, but before he could say anything, Patricia crabbed from the floor, "Ugh, that's so loud! When you have air conditioning, you don't have to hear all that noise." Then she slammed her pillow over her head. Hugo scrunched back down into his covers. He didn't count the cars that night.

"They're *not* my friends," I repeated to Alice and Willa, remembering Hugo's face that night. "I just got too used to thinking they were. And it kept me from facing up to how they treated me. And how they treated other people."

"They're not nice," I added after a moment.

"No, they're not," Willa and Alice said together. They looked at each other and laughed.

"*You* guys are nice," I said, smiling.

Willa and Alice looked at each other again and said, "Yes, we are!"

All in all, I thought as I sank down into my pillow hours later, my eyes barely staying open, this was probably the best sleepover ever.

CHAPTER 18

"I don't WANT to be TASTED!" Hugo informed me, lowering his brows over his dark eyes.

It had taken nearly two weeks, but my supertasting kit finally arrived. Because my research told me that genetics were involved in whether or not I was a supertaster, I planned to test every member of my family to see if I could make a prediction about my own results. Then I would take the test myself.

Hugo sat on his bed with his arms crossed.

I slapped my hands over my eyes and dragged my fingers down my face and moaned. "For the gazillionth time, Hugo, no one is *tasting* you. I want *you* to taste this test!"

"I'm in KINDERGARTEN. We don't have tests in KINDERGARTEN. Mr. Lard says it!"

"Mr. Lard? You mean, Mr. Collard?"

Hugo rolled his eyes, something he had learned to do in kindergarten. "That's what I said! Mr. LARD!"

"Look, Hugo, this is all it is." Once again I pulled out the supertaster testing kit and showed him the four plastic vials of paper strips.

Three of the four groups of paper strips were flavored with different chemicals. Being a supertaster depended on how strongly you tasted the chemicals on each one. The fourth group were the control strips, and they had no chemicals or flavoring at all.

According to the instructions that came with the kit, if you were a supertaster, one strip in particular was supposed to totally gross you out. The second strip would taste salty or bitter or maybe even sweet to some people. And the third chemical strip would have a taste only if you could taste the first one.

I unscrewed the caps on the vials, which had color-coded tops and sides, so I was the only one who knew which test strip was which. That's called a blind taste test because you don't know what you are getting. It's the only scientific way to take the test.

"Look, Mom and Dad already took the test, okay? It's just these little pieces of paper. I stick them in your mouth and you tell me what you taste. That's all. Easy-peasy!"

Hugo's eyes widened to the size of dinner plates. "I like peas."

"Then will you please take the test for me? I have to test everyone in the family before I test myself."

"Why?"

“Because,” I said, squeezing my hands into a single fist and trying to remain as calm as mother earthly possible, “I need to know what kind of taster everyone in the family is to make a prediction for me. It’s called my hypothesis.”

“Then what?” Hugo asked.

“Then I test myself to see if my hypothesis is right or wrong.”

Hugo considered this. He nodded. “But after, you have to read me all the books.”

I exhaled. “How many is all?”

Hugo held up five fingers. “All.”

“Fine. All.”

For all four taste test strips, Hugo gave the same answer.

“Tastes like paper.”

“Tastes like paper.”

“Tastes like paper.”

He even chewed up and swallowed the last one, the control strip. “Tastes like paper.”

Hugo scuttled to the living room to choose five books. I wrote down his results and rechecked my research notes, highlighting the note about the gene that determines whether you are a supertaster. This gene comes in two versions: nontaster and taster. Everyone gets two of these genes, one from each parent, and their combination determines how strongly you taste things.

If I inherited two taster genes—one from my mom and

one from my dad—I would be a supertaster, which would explain why my tongue was so strange and why I wasn't good at Eating. However, on the opposite end, two non-taster genes would make me an undertaster, meaning my powers of taste weren't very strong at all.

Given that Hugo didn't taste anything on any of the strips, he was probably an undertaster. I snorted as I wrote that down. It's pretty easy to like everything you eat when you can't taste how gross it is.

Only twenty-five percent of the population are supertasters, twenty-five percent are undertasters, and the other fifty percent are known as "average tasters." To be an average taster, I'd have to get one taster gene and one non-taster gene from each of my parents.

I flipped through my logbook and reread my parents' results. They both seemed to fall in the average taster category—they tasted things on the test strips, but nothing was too strong for them. This meant they each had one taster gene and one non-taster gene.

I sat back in my chair and chewed on my pencil.

I could end up being any of the outcomes. I could get two non-taster genes and be an undertaster like Hugo (which was unlikely, based on the performance of my lie detector tongue my entire life).

I could get a taster gene from one parent and a non-taster gene from another and be an average taster like them.

Or I could get a taster gene from each parent and be a supertaster. This was the only result that made sense to me. It would explain what was wrong with my tongue, and I'd have superscience to back it all up!

It was time to find out if I was a supertaster or not.

It was time to find out the truth.

But first, my hypothesis. I took the pencil out of my mouth and wrote my prediction in my clearest, calmest, most unhurried handwriting.

Then I reread it.

Three times.

I reorganized and counted the vials again. They were all there, stuffed with the paper test strips that would finally tell me yes or no.

I chewed my pencil some more as I frowned the situation out. Everything was ready and in place for me to test myself, but it still felt like something was missing.

With a rustle, the LOPE map to the treehouse peeled off the wall and drifted down to my desk. It had been doing that a lot lately. I had gone through almost an entire roll of my purple sparkly tape trying to keep it in place, but it just didn't want to stay put.

I hunkered down on the floor and pulled a shoebox out from under my bed. This is my box of precious things. It's also where I keep extra rolls of purple sparkly tape so Hugo can't find them. The last time he got at my tape, he used up three whole rolls turning his stuffed cow into a sparkly purple mummy.

As I dug around the box for my last roll of tape, I pulled out a menu from Amy's Delish Diner, a postcard from the president of the United States thanking me for writing to her, and a rock named Fat Tum Tum that Hugo had "rescued" from the beach and given to me. I finally found the tape under the LOPE notes from Alice and a brochure from the Rock Salt, the rock-climbing place, which Willa had given me just last week. The map forgotten for the moment, I sat down on my bed and thought about how, over the past few weeks, each day in RETCH had started to feel like an adventure. At the same time, the RETCH class also felt like something dependable and familiar. And safe.

I reread the notes. These notes weren't from Alice Who Only Eats White Food, as I had once thought of her so many ages ago. They were from Alice Who Sent Me Helpful, Encouraging Notes.

Alice Who Told Me About Supertasters.

Thinking hard, I pulled out the Rock Salt brochure and flipped through it, remembering how Willa didn't laugh at my concussion fear. How she offered to teach me how to climb the tree. I remembered her quote: "Friendship is constant in all other things."

And I knew what was missing from my experiment.

CHAPTER 19

A few days later I creaked open the screen door, which, I couldn't help but suddenly notice, had quite a lot of holes in it. "Hi," I said.

Alice stepped in. "Hey. Um, I ran into Willa on the way over and she told me to tell you she's running a bit late."

"Oh. Okay," I said.

And then we stood there in a silence that went on for an entire week.

I started to panic. I don't know what on mother earth made me think it was a good idea to invite Alice over. But why was this so weird? I had been to her house. We had a sleepover together. And everything was fine and comfortable when we were at school or in the League treehouse. Yet now I felt seriously *un*comfortable. Inside my house, she would be able to see absolutely everything there was to see about me, and I didn't know what she would think of it.

"So, um . . ." I started to say, then stopped.

Alice looked around. "You have a very nice house,

Minerva." Her voice came out strange. Formal and stiff. Was she acting weird because I was acting weird? Or was she acting weird because she really didn't want to be here?

"Thanks," I blurted out. "It's kind of a mess right now."

My insides cringed. What a dumb thing to say. I mean, our house *was* kind of a mess. But between Hugo's blocks and train layouts and my dad's papers and exams and all the books of mine and my mom's lying half open on every available surface, it was always like that.

But I didn't have to point all that out to Alice. Like I was apologizing, or like I didn't want her to think we were always like this, even though that's exactly who we were. Maybe I should have cleaned it up before she came over. I sighed.

"It looks like my house." Alice grinned, sounding more like herself.

My shoulders relaxed, and my chest bloomed with warmth. "Do you want to see my room?"

Alice's face lit up. "Yeah!"

"Wait—let's get something to eat first. I, um, made a snack for us." I led the way to the kitchen and pulled open the fridge door. "Do you like cream cheese on celery?"

"You mean, like ants on a log but without the nasty raisins?" Alice asked. "That sounds perfect."

I pulled out the plate I had prepared and set it on the table with some napkins.

"Wow!" Alice said. She was staring at the scratched-up table leg. "Did an animal do that? Or your little brother?"

"Oh, um," I said, remembering Patricia's reaction when she first saw the scratches. And that was many scratches ago.

The warmth in my chest chilled a bit.

"Our cat Needles did that."

Alice took a closer look at the table leg and giggled. "It looks like he's trying to whittle it into a new shape."

"He's kind of an odd cat," I said. "My mom found him as a stray in her acupuncturist's parking lot. He was really tiny and sick and scared of everything, but then we helped him get healthy and used to people. Though he still kind of gets agitated by a lot of things."

"Cat-gitated." Alice snorted. I gaped. She liked to make up words, too! I'd have to add that one to my list of invented vocabulary. "Oh, so is that why he's called Needles?" she asked, munching on celery and cream cheese. "Because of where he was found?"

I nodded.

"That's a great name. I thought it was because of his claws! My dad won't let us get cats." She sighed. "But I have a hermit crab named Creature."

"Excuse me, please, but that's the best name ever! I've always wanted a hermit crab!" I said.

"Needles might eat it, though," Alice pointed out.

"Yeah . . . ew." I shuddered.

We wrinkled our noses at each other.

"Can I see your room now?" Alice asked.

As we walked down the hall, I called out, "Dad, Alice is here and we've had our snack and we're going to be in my room."

My dad stuck his head out of the laundry room and smiled. "Hey, Alice—nice to see you."

Alice gave him a wave. "Hi, Mr. Van Zoren—did you know you make amazing grilled cheese sandwiches?"

Dad grinned. "Do I now?"

Alice nodded vigorously. "It's, um, like . . . well, yodel-ay-yodel-ay-del-yo-lady-HEY-oo-oo-AH-HEEEE!"

Startled, my dad jumped back and dropped the towels he was holding. Calm as ever, Alice bent over, picked up the towels, and handed them back to my dad, who was staring at her with the widest eyes. I held my breath, wondering what he would say when he regained the power of speech. I don't think I ever told my parents about Alice's yodeling habit.

"That's—that was," my dad started, and then burst out laughing. "That's an amazing yodel you've got there!" he finally gasped, wiping his eyes.

"Thanks," Alice said with a wide smile. "I have found that there are times in life where the only way to express myself is with a yodel."

My dad grinned, shaking his head as I nudged Alice back down the hall.

I put my hand on the doorknob to my room, feeling nervous again. "Um, just to prepare you," I said, "I share a room with my little brother, so . . ."

"It's kind of a mess?" Alice finished for me.

I nodded.

"That's okay. I don't share a room with Ty," Alice said, "but my room is always a mess anyway."

We stepped into my room.

It wasn't "kind of" a mess.

It was a disaster.

Clothes were hanging out of half-open dresser drawers, Hugo's bed was a rat's nest of twisted sheets, stuffed animals, and random toys, and there were more books spread out on the floor than in the bookcase.

At least my bed was made. Sort of.

"Ah, home sweet home," Alice said, looking at me sideways.

I flopped down on my bed, giggling. "Oh, man," I said. "If you could have seen the time Hugo—"

"Hey," Alice interrupted in a hushed voice. "Who's that?"

I sat up and saw that Needles had pushed my door open. He was staring at Alice, his yellow eyes round and questioning.

"That's Needles," I said. "Wow, he usually hides from strangers."

Alice slid off my bed and crouched down on the floor.

She stretched her hand out to Needles, her fingers curled

under, just like my mom taught me to do whenever I meet a new dog or cat. They can sniff you without feeling threatened by you.

Needles hesitated. Then he pushed the rest of the way through the door to trot over and sniff Alice's hand.

"Hi, Needles," Alice whispered. "I like what you've done with the kitchen table."

Needles rubbed his orange-striped face against Alice's hand, then flopped to the floor at her feet, belly-up, and gazed at her from his upside-down angle. Alice scratched his head.

"Wow. He's showing you his belly," I said. "That means he likes *and* trusts you!"

I watched Alice pet Needles with long, gentle strokes. His purrs rumbled through his throat.

"Hey." I snapped my fingers. "I never asked you about your Food Science project—what are you doing?"

Alice looked up from petting Needles. "I'm figuring out the best way to slice up a potato so that it fries perfectly. Golden crispness on the outside and light and mealy on the inside. It's all about the surface area," Alice said. "Lots of math."

"Wow," I said. "I bet that wins Most Delicious at the fair! Oh, wait—french fries!"

"What?"

"That french fry video at school—the St. Julia Child one—did you watch it? As part of your research?" I asked.

Alice shook her head. "I don't think I know what you're talking about."

"There was this historical video on the school server," I explained. "It was supposed to be about St. Julia Child and french fries, but when I tried to access it, all I got was a dialog box that said it had been removed for violating school policy or something."

"That's strange," Alice said. "I wonder why. Maybe swearing?"

"Yes!" I said. "That's what I thought, too! Wait, maybe we could search for it right now. It could be on the internet, and if it is, maybe there's something in it that you could use." I jumped up, grabbed the laptop, opened a search tab, and typed in "Julia Child french fries." The video showed up instantly. I clicked play. By the time the video ended, Alice and I were both staring at each other, our jaws completely dropped. All thoughts of the supertaster test had evaporated from my mind.

"No way," I breathed.

"Play it again," Alice whispered.

We replayed the video four more times to make sure we were seeing and hearing what we thought we were seeing and hearing.

"Do you realize what this means?" Alice asked, grabbing my hand.

"No. Do you?"

"No, but it must mean something," Alice said. "Can you find a way to bring the video with us?"

I nodded. "I think so."

"Good, because we gotta activate the phone treehouse for an emergency meeting," Alice said.

The phone treehouse was a list of phone numbers for every member of the League. It was activated by calling the first name at the top of the list. Then that member called the next name on the list, and so on.

While Alice ran off to ask my dad if she could use our phone, I rummaged around in my pencil box until I found an old thumb drive. I started to stick the drive into the slot, but then I hesitated.

Kids were always talking about the things that could get you suspended at school. Some said you could get suspended for being fifteen minutes late. Or swearing. Or not washing your hands after using the bathroom. When I was in first grade, a third-grader told me I'd be *expelled* if I didn't return my library book on time. (I know now that he was trying to scare me, but just in case, I never had an overdue book.)

The french fry video had been removed for being against school rules, so maybe it was also against the rules to bring it back to school. Maybe it was against the rules to even know about it. Could you be suspended just for knowing something?

I sat back in my chair, the thumb drive still in my hand.

Maybe we should just forget about what we saw. Wasn't that safer?

But then I thought about how hard it was for everyone in RETCH to eat from the mandatory hot lunch menu. I thought about how Principal Butcher wouldn't put plain grilled cheese or french fries on the menu. I thought about the egg-covered pizza, Ralph's tears, and secret sandwiches under the table. This video could change all that forever.

"By day she fights for picky eaters everywhere," I whispered to the floor. And I shoved the thumb drive into the computer and downloaded the video. I still didn't know what we were going to do with it, but we would think of something. That's what superheroes do. I looked up at the League of Picky Eaters map taped back on the wall. Maybe we were all superheroes.

POW!

CHAPTER 20

With the phone treehouse activated, Alice and I got ready to head over to Amy's for my first emergency meeting of the League of Picky Eaters.

"Why Amy's?" I asked, slipping the laptop into my bag. My dad had given me permission to bring it. I told him that Alice and I needed it to work on my Food Science Fair project.

"Free Wi-Fi connection," Alice explained. "Plus, french fries!"

"But what about this?" I held up the thumb drive. "We don't need Wi-Fi if we have this, right?"

"That's backup," Alice said. "Keep it in a safe place."

"Backup for what?" I asked.

"I don't know yet, but big ideas always need backup," Alice said. "And we're going to have some big ideas about this. I can feel it."

I didn't know what the safest place was for the thumb drive. I briefly considered sticking it under my mattress, but remembering Hugo and my purple tape and how he was always getting into my stuff, I slipped the thumb drive into my pocket. It seemed like the safest plan was to make sure it was always near me.

At Amy's, all five of us crammed into one of the larger, semicircular booths.

"So what's up?" Akshay asked, drumming his fingers on the tabletop.

Alice nodded at me. "Show them."

I opened my laptop and joined the diner's Wi-Fi connection: CANTELOPE. I shuddered. My least favorite melon in the world. The browser window was still open to the tab with the Julia Child video, so all I had to do was hit play. The entire League leaned in to watch.

"'O, me,'" Willa said when it was over. She grabbed my hand and looked at everyone in turn. "'The gods!'"

I could tell from their shocked expressions that everyone felt exactly the same way.

"Yeah," I said, closing the computer.

"So what do we do with this?" Alice asked. "Because we can't just do nothing. We can't keep walking around Muffuletta knowing this and not saying anything about it."

"Take it to the police!" Ralph said, standing up like he was about to head to the station right that minute.

"And what would they do?" Akshay tugged him down. "There's been no crime."

"It is a crime. It's a crime against our taste buds," Ralph grumbled. "Making us eat—"

The table exploded in a confusion of crosstalk.

"Should we tell our parents?"

"Could we get suspended?"

"We should blast it over the school loudspeaker!"

"How would we get into the office to do that?"

"Willa knows how to pick locks!"

"Then we'll definitely get suspended."

"Wait!" Willa shouted over the noise. Everyone stopped talking and turned to look at her. Willa blushed but kept going. "Ralph is right."

"I am? I mean, I AM!" Ralph said. "About what, again?"

"We need to tell someone about this. But not the police. We should take it to Principal Butcher." Willa turned to me. "Minerva, you wanted to become class president so you could change the hot lunch menu, right?"

I nodded. "But how would this make me class president?"

"It wouldn't, because you wouldn't need to be class president to change the menu. Just show this to Principal Butcher," she said.

"But what if she suspends me?"

"Well, you're not the only one who knows about it. We all know about it now. She can't suspend all of us." Willa looked slightly worried for a moment. "Can she?"

Akshay shrugged. "It seems like principals can do anything they want," he said. "But that doesn't make it right."

"Wait—" Willa said. "Minerva said that the school pulled this from the server, right?"

I nodded.

"What if somehow this gets removed from the internet? It happens all the time when videos violate copyright."

"How do you know that?"

"I read about it," Willa said, then added, "You guys, I read *a lot*."

"Minerva downloaded it on a thumb drive," Alice said.

"Always good to have backup," Akshay said with approval.

By the time we all had to go home, we still didn't know what to do about the video. But we had eaten tons of tasty french fries trying to figure it out.

On the walk home with Willa and Alice, I suddenly remembered that I had forgotten the supertaster test. "Um, guys? Do you want to come to my house for just a minute so I can show you my Food Science project? You know, the whole supertaster thing? But only if you want to."

Alice beamed. "Show us!"

I turned to Willa, who smiled. "Lead on, Macduff!"

Alice and I said hi to my parents and Hugo, who were in the living room doing a jigsaw puzzle.

"Also," I said, "this is Willa!"

"Hi, Willa—we've heard a lot about you." My mom smiled. Willa gave them a wave and a smile.

After I explained about the taster strips and showed them my hypothesis, Willa said, "Okay, so after testing your whole family, you think you got two taster genes from your mom and dad, and that would make you a supertaster, right?"

I nodded.

"Well?" Alice said. "Are you?"

"I don't know," I admitted. "I haven't tested myself yet."

"Really? I would have done it as soon as I got the kit!"

Willa nodded in agreement. "I'm impatient, too."

"Well, actually, my dad teased me, saying it's scientifically unethical to test myself, so I thought maybe you guys could give me the test. Is that totally dorky?"

"Not dorky at all," Alice said.

"And even if it is totally dorky, so what?" Willa said. "We can all be dorky together. After all"—she leaped up on a chair and held out her arm—"there is more strength to be had in combined dorkiness than in any other kind!"

"Which Shakespeare play is that from?" I asked, giggling.

"*The Three RETCHES of Muffuletta*, an original play by Willa E. Lewis," Willa said, and swept us a bow with a mischievous grin. "Get it? Wretches with a *W* and RETCHES, like our class?"

"Wait, are *we* wretches?" Alice asked.

"Well, we're wretched in RETCH, so . . ." Willa held her hands out, palms up.

"I totally love it," I said. I really did. "So, you guys will test me? Help me prove I'm a supertaster?"

They both nodded.

"Awesome!" I said.

"Oh, but . . ." Willa said, hopping down from the chair and pointing at my clock. "It's getting late, and I have to get home. How about we give you the test right after we set up for the Food Science Fair tomorrow? It feels like the perfect time and place, you know?"

"Yes, definitely. Totally," I said. I was so happy that Alice and Willa agreed to be my testers that I didn't care when we did it, just that we did it together. I could be patient one more day before proving the superpowers of my tongue.

CHAPTER 21

Setup for the Food Science Fair took place in the afternoon, but the actual judging wouldn't happen until the next day. Alice and Willa joined me just as I finished arranging my panels. In addition to the superhero sound effects decorating my corkboard, I also made a yellow shield, with SUPERTASTER written across it in purple sparkly pen, which I stuck right in the middle of my center panel. I had been inspired by the LOPE symbol.

"Oh, wow—I didn't know you were doing a whole superhero theme!" Alice said, clapping her hands. "I love it!"

"I had a feeling you would." I grinned. Then I pulled out the vials from my backpack and set them on the table.

Willa pointed to them. "Ready?"

"Yes." I zipped up my backpack and pushed it aside. My fingers felt for the thumb drive. It was still where I had slipped it in that morning. I felt the need to carry it around with me.

"No peeking!" Alice said.

I closed my eyes and opened my mouth for the first test strip. "Hmm, it tastes a little salty?"

A second strip was placed on my tongue. "Okay, what about this one?" Willa asked.

"I . . . don't really taste anything on that one."

"How about this?" Alice asked. That was the third strip.

"I guess it's a little . . . bitterish. Sort of?"

With each strip, my stomach had slumped farther down to my ankles. I could taste the chemicals on the strips, but nothing was as strong or revolting as it was supposed to be if I had been an actual supertaster. But that was all wrong! I *HAD* to be a supertaster! I just had to be!

"Well, I guess that's it," I said after tasting the final strip.

Alice and Willa were quiet. Then Willa said, "So, not a supertaster?"

I shook my head, gritting my teeth against the rising disappointment.

"Are you okay?" Alice asked.

I stared hard at my corkboard instead of looking at them. If I saw the sympathy I could hear in their voices, I was worried that I'd start bawling. They'd never want to be friends with someone who acted like such a baby.

I whispered, "I just thought being a supertaster would explain everything. It would explain why I am like this." I waved my hand at my tongue. My *stupid* lie detector tongue that didn't have anything super about it at all. I mean, why else could I taste things so strongly? Why wasn't there a reason I could point to and say, "See! That's why!"? None of it made any sense.

"I guess," I said. "I'm just . . . Minerva. With no other explanation. Just Minerva."

"Yeah, but the thing is," Alice said. "I really like Just Minerva."

"So do I," Willa said.

I looked up. Willa was studying my corkboard as she chose her next words. "See, Just Minerva was nice enough to give Ralph her piece of pizza. Just Minerva was brave enough to flush Brussels sprouts down the toilet and hide foie gras sandwiches behind books and throw scallops out the window for feral cats to feast upon."

"Just Minerva became a member of the League of Picky Eaters even without being a supertaster. And it's not like we take randoms off the street." Alice grinned.

I forced a smile. "It's just, I don't know, some part of me really believed there was something amazing about my stupid tongue."

"Hey, I know what—you're all done here, so let's go see if anyone else has finished setting up," Willa suggested, plucking at my sleeve. "We still have time before the bell rings. There might even be something we can snack on."

Alice nodded, pulling up her yellow plaid gaiter. "Just in case," she said.

I picked up my pencil and wrote the final result in my logbook: "Minerva Van Zoren: average taster."

I sighed, then followed my friends. So much for being a superhero in disguise.

I knew I was acting kind of stupid. No one really has superpowers, of course. But still, thinking it made me feel like I could do anything. Like I could march into Principal Butcher's office, slam down the thumb drive, and demand that she change the school menu. *POW!*

Or, instead of feeling lurchy in my stomach every time I saw her, I could tell Patricia what I really thought of her. *BLAM!*

Willa and Alice stopped in front of a project. It was Mortimer's, a seventh-grader whose mom runs a fishing fleet up and down the coast. I wrinkled my nose. Ugh—fish. But as I read Mortimer's board, I saw that his project was not about fish, it was about thickening agents for tomato soups.

My interest perked up a bit. I find uncooked tomatoes revolting because their squishy rawness is, as Akshay would say, a texture violation for me. But as soon as you puree them into oblivion, strain out the seeds and skin, and make them into nothing even resembling tomatoes, I actually love them. I mean, tomato soup or sauce is basically just ketchup. I had a sudden memory of that tomato-based sauce in Akshay's mom's bhindi masala. It did smell amazing.

Mortimer offered us all taster cups of one of the soups.

"You test all of them to see if you can feel a difference in their textures. It's all about the mouthfeel."

Before I could take a sip, Patricia and her group of friends elbowed their way in front of us.

"Um, Alice, didn't you see that this is red soup?" Patricia said. "Or are you colorblind as well as being bad at Eating?"

pop

I felt a tiny bubble of anger at the base of my spine.

"She's not bad at Eating," I said.

I didn't say it very loud, but Patricia eyed me.

"You guys are in *Remedial Eating*, Minerva. That literally means bad at Eating."

I stared down at the soup in my cup.

"Why do you care?" Willa asked, way louder than was usual for her.

Patricia stared at her. And Willa matched her gaze without blinking.

"Whatever, weirdos," Patricia said, holding up three fingers on each hand and putting them on her forehead. "You're just three freaks in a pod."

She turned her back to us, picked up two taster cups of soup, and shoved another into Cindy's hands. "Here, carry this."

"But I—" Cindy started to protest.

"Obviously I can't carry all three soups, Cindy," Patricia said, rolling her eyes at the other girls, who rolled their eyes back and nudged each other sympathetically. "I only have two hands. Sheesh."

Without a word, Cindy put down one of the soups she was about to sample and took Patricia's instead.

They walked off.

"Man," Alice said, staring at their backs. Willa shook her head.

"I know," I said.

"And this one was thickened with a naturally occurring gelatin," Mortimer said, giving me another cup of tomato soup as if the whole scene hadn't just happened right in front of him.

I took a sip. What was that? I frowned. I took another sip. There was something—

"Can you tell the difference between the other two?" Mortimer asked. "One was thickened with bread, one with a roux of flour and cream, but this—"

"OH MY MOTHER EARTH!" I yelled.

"Exactly," Mortimer said, delighted. "I used—"

But I didn't wait for him to finish. I tore across the courtyard to where Patricia was lifting a cup to her mouth and about to die.

I dodged around some second-graders having a burp contest before I reached her.

"STOOOOOOOOOOP!" I hollered, and smacked the cup out of her hand.

KA-POW!

Tomato soup flew everywhere.

But she was holding another cup of soup, so I smacked that one, too.

BLAM!

And I smacked the one Cindy was holding.

SPLAT!

For good measure and thoroughness, I went around and smacked, slapped, and slammed all the cups of tomato soup from her group's hands.

Patricia stared at me, her mouth open. Rivulets of tomato soup streamed down her face and red hair.

Panting, I put a hand on her shoulder. "Are you okay? Did you drink any of it?"

Patricia sucked in a great whoosh of breath.

"HAVE YOU COMPLETELY LOST YOUR MIND MINERVA WHAT IN THE WORLD IS WRONG WITH YOU!?" Patricia screamed at the top of her lungs.

"Clams," I said. "There were clams. Your allergy. You could have died."

Patricia's mouth opened and closed like a beached walleye.

Everyone in the courtyard was watching us now.

"I saved your life," I explained again. "Because . . . clams."

There was a whistle blast. A yard duty monitor pushed through the crowd and grabbed our arms. "Okay, girls, let's go see Principal Butcher."

"No no no no no no no!"

I looked over to see Hugo hurtling over the kindergarten yard fence and barreling straight for us.

"You can't 'tack my 'Nerva!" he yelled, batting at the monitor's hand.

Surprised, the monitor dropped my arm and stepped back as Mr. Collard ran up and tried to hug-grab Hugo, the way kindergarten teachers are taught to do if kids need restraining.

Big mistake.

"DON'T TOUCH ME I'M DELICATE!"

I winced, and Patricia stared past the monitor at me.

"You and your brother are such freaks," she hissed.

I looked back at Willa and Alice, who were staring at me, their jaws dropped.

CHAPTER 22

"You." Principal Butcher pointed at Patricia. "Tell me what happened."

"I don't even know!" Patricia said. She put her hands over her face and sobbed dramatically. "I was just minding my own business, checking out the Food Science Fair, and Minerva totally *attacked* me!"

"I did NOT attack you! I saved your life!" I shouted, jumping to my feet.

"Minerva, if you raise your voice again, there will be serious consequences, do you understand me?"

"But I—"

"MINERVA."

Next to me, Hugo slipped one of his hands in mine and squeezed it until my fingers cracked. I sat back down. "Okay, fine."

"How exactly did Minerva attack you?" Principal Butcher asked Patricia.

"I was minding my own business, about to try some soup

from one of the projects, and Minerva lost it. She knocked all the soup out of my hands and my friends' hands, and, well, just *look!*" Patricia said, standing up.

I bit my lip. She looked like something out of the horror movies I wasn't permitted to watch.

Principal Butcher turned to me. "I've never known you to be violent, Minerva. What do you have to say for yourself?"

I took a deep breath.

"I was saving her life. There were clams in one of the soups, and she's *ALLERGIC* to them. Her throat would have swelled up and then suffocated her to *DEATH* in an anaphylactic shock."

"There weren't any clams," Patricia said, crossing her arms. "It was all just tomato soup."

"But I tasted clams! I did!"

"You *tasted* clams? But you didn't *see* clams?" Principal Butcher asked.

"Yes," I said.

Principal Butcher raised an eyebrow. I knew she did not believe me.

"I can taste things that aren't there now but were there before!"

Patricia snorted.

"You know I can, Patricia," I said, glaring at her. "Go ask Mortimer. He'll tell you what was in his soups."

"I WILL GET HIM!" Hugo jumped up and ran to the door.

"Hugo," Principal Butcher called, "I don't think—"

But he was already gone.

Principal Butcher turned to Patricia. "Patricia, where is your medication? Because Minerva is right—your clam allergy is quite serious. Your parents have assured the school that you would have it on you at all times."

"There weren't any clams in the soup," Patricia repeated, recrossing her arms over her tomato-covered shirt. "And besides, I didn't taste it, so even if there were clams in the soup, which there were *not*, I'd still be fine."

Hugo banged the office door open. He was dragging Mortimer behind him. The seventh-grader looked dazed. Interacting with Hugo can have that effect on people.

"Tell them about clams," Hugo ordered Mortimer, yanking on his arm.

"But it will ruin my results!" Mortimer objected.

"Mortimer, this is incredibly serious," Principal Butcher said. "It is school policy that anything containing an allergen has to be clearly marked. You should know that by now."

Mortimer went pale. "Well, um-m," he stuttered, "one of the tomato-based soups in my experiment is a bouillabaisse, which starts out with a shellfish stock that has fish bones, clamshells, and shrimp and lobster shells in it. The thickener for bouillabaisse comes from the gelatin that's released into the stock from the bones and things as they simmer. But then you strain out all the solids before you add the tomato broth and, um, everything else for bouillabaisse, like the fish and clams and shrimp and stuff."

"So the fish and clams and shrimp and *stuff* were in the soup at some point?" Principal Butcher asked.

"Yes, but just for flavor and ultimate thickening power —I took all the fish and, um, stuff out before I served it to anyone, so that's okay, right? Because no one actually ate a clam?"

Principal Butcher stood up and pointed to the door. "Mortimer, you will go immediately to put a sign on your project that clearly indicates there is shellfish in the soup. You will also write a paper about cross-contamination and turn it in to me tomorrow. Go. Right now!"

Hugo released Mortimer's arms, but he planted both hands on his hips and scowled at Mortimer like he was the reason for all the trouble.

"Patricia, are you one hundred percent sure that no soup went into your mouth?" Principal Butcher asked.

"Yes, I'm sure. Minerva had her freak-out before I could taste any of them," Patricia said, glaring at me.

I sprang out of my chair. "Which means I saved your life!"

"Minerva, this is your very last warning, and then I call your parents."

I sat back down and whispered, "I saved your life!"

Butcher cleared her throat and shifted in her seat. "It would appear that Minerva did indeed save you. If not your life, she definitely saved you from having an anaphylactic reaction. I'm still not clear on how she detected the clams, but you are very lucky she did."

I clapped my hand over my mouth so my "See!" wouldn't turn into a phone call.

Patricia sat there looking like she had taken an extra-large sip of sour milk. Excuse me, please, it's not like I was expecting a hug or anything, but it seems to me she could've acted a little more like she appreciated that I stopped her from dying a horrible clam death.

On our way to our classrooms, Patricia refused to look at me. Her face was stiff with anger. Everyone had already gone back to their classes, and our footsteps rang out on the pavement in the empty courtyard.

I couldn't stand it any longer. "You know, you could at least say thank you."

"Thank you?" Patricia scoffed. "For what?!"

"If it hadn't been for me, you could have died. I saved your life—even Principal Butcher said so!"

"You did not save my life. I didn't come close to dying or even getting sick at all," Patricia said, striding ahead of me.

"Still, if I hadn't been there—"

Patricia whirled around, her eyes narrowed. "You really

think you're so special and so smart, don't you?" she hissed. "Well, guess what? I'm not actually allergic to clams, which means you didn't even come close to saving my life, so HAH!"

I stopped walking. "What? Yes, you are too allergic!"

"No, I'm not. Okay? My mom just tells people that because I don't like clams and she doesn't want a tiny thing like that affecting my grades." She folded her arms and stared back at me.

Without thinking, I reached out to clutch at her arm. "Oh my god, you don't like clams! Now you understand! You're just like me! Man, I never thought about pretending to have an allergy. That's kind of a good idea. I don't know how my parents would feel about lying to teachers, though—"

Patricia twitched her arm away from me.

"I am NOTHING like you!"

"I just meant—" I faltered.

"News flash, Minerva—there's a HUGE difference between 'one thing' and 'everything,' or don't you understand anything?"

We were standing in front of the sixth-grade Food Science Fair projects.

Patricia flicked her eyes to mine. She sneered. "Oh my god, do you actually think you're some sort of superhero, Minerva? Because of your stupid tongue?"

I felt ice lurch down my spine.

"Well, you're not. And another thing, Minerva?" she

went on, tipping her head to the side and narrowing her eyes at me. "Carrying around a notebook doesn't make you class president, and you act like a loser at sleepovers. Why don't you grow up?"

The squashed look of hurt on Cindy's face as Patricia ordered her around flashed before my eyes. How long had it been since I was in Cindy's place? It felt like forever and also just this morning. Once you take a big step back, it's so much easier to see what something is like. But when you're surrounded by it, it's hard to know what's normal and what's awful.

And Patricia was awful. Plain and simple. The ice in my spine was replaced by simmering bubbles of anger.

I threw my shoulders back and looked Patricia square in the eye. "I gave that notebook to *you*."

"Yeah, great idea for a birthday present, Minerva. A used notebook full of dumb ideas. They're all in the trash where they belong."

The bubbles, now at full boil, coursed through my body and flushed across my face.

Patricia curled her lip until it almost touched her nose, saying, "I don't know why I was ever friends with you in the first place."

The burning tingled across my tongue.

"You know what, Patricia?" I snapped. "I don't know why we were friends either. Do you want to know something else?

You're absolutely right—you *aren't* anything like me. I don't order people around. I don't push people around. And I don't go out of my way to embarrass my friends and make fun of them. EXCUSE ME PLEASE, Patricia, but you? Are the meanest person on mother earth!"

BIFF! BLAM! SLAM! CRASH! WHAM!

Patricia looked surprised but recovered instantly. "And you are—you are in RETCH."

"That's right," I said stoutly. "And I'd take everyone in RETCH over you any day."

Without waiting for her reaction, I turned my back on her and skipped back to class, feeling bouncier, happier, and stronger than I had in a long time. I was ready for anything St. Julia Child might serve up.

Feral cats had been hanging around outside the classroom, trying to get in ever since scallop day. I had to nudge two away with my foot as I opened the door. "Is this a gagger which I see before me?" someone squealed as I walked in. I froze in place, still holding the door open. The two feral cats slipped past me before I could stop them. Shoot. That wasn't good.

"Dagger," I heard Willa hiss across the room, "It's a *dagger,* not a gagger."

Madame Bouche was standing in front of the class. She was wearing an elaborate brocade dress with fussy sleeves and puffed shoulders. And she was pointing at me.

"Wait . . . what?" I was totally confused, which was a

pretty typical feeling during a food immersion lesson, but this was far more bizarre than usual.

Madame Bouche gestured to me to take my seat.

"It's asparagus day, so she's performing lines from Shakespeare," Alice whispered, crossing her eyes. "Asparagus spears? Shake*speare*? Get it? She says we'll get so swept up in the language of Shake*speare* that it will make us want to eat everything in sight afterward."

"Seriously?" I asked.

"Mr. Kreplach says it's in the approved immersion curriculum," Alice said.

"Yeah," Willa muttered. "That's what she says she's doing, but she's totally messing up the quotes just to suit her purpose. It's horrible." She pressed her hands over her ears. "I'll bet she just did a web search for the lines she wanted. I'll bet she's never even read or seen a single play. The untrained *shouldn't mess with Shakespeare.*"

"This is kind of extreme, isn't it? Even for her?" I muttered back.

"Talkers are not good doers!" Madame Bouche announced, glaring at me.

I guess that meant I should shut up, so I did.

"A horseradish, a horseradish! My kingdom for a horseradish!" Madame Bouche said, smacking the back of her hand against her forehead repeatedly and sweeping around the classroom, peering under desks.

"Is she looking for a horseradish?" Akshay wondered in a loud voice.

"This is so stupid and wrong," Willa said. "It's my kingdom for a *horse*."

"To eat or not to eat: that is the question," Madame Bouche said. She perched on the edge of Mr. Kreplach's desk, threw one leg over the other, and made a thinking-very-hard face.

Willa groaned.

Right at that moment, one of the feral cats discovered the tassels on the hem of Madame Bouche's skirt and attacked it. Madame Bouche gave a little scream and aimed a kick at the cat. Her foot delivered only a glancing blow, but the cat gave a startled yowl and ran to a corner of the classroom. Willa gasped.

Madame Bouche pointed a long finger at her. "Oh, how sharper than an English cheddar it is to have a picky child!" She narrowed her eyes.

"'To thine own self be true!'" Willa quoted back in a louder voice than I'd ever heard her use in class.

Madame Bouche paused, gaping, then regathered herself. "Yes, um, well—where was I? Oh, yes." She raised a brocaded arm in the air. "Some are born gourmet, some achieve gourmetness . . ."

"Oh, yeah? Well, some have gourmetness thrust upon

them. And you know what? THAT'S NOT FAIR!" Willa was now standing.

"Friends, Romans, countrymen, lend me your ears of corn!" Madame Bouche said to the class, a hint of hysteria creeping into her voice. I wondered if she was going to start slothering soon. It seemed like she was close.

Willa climbed up on her desk, opened her arms wide, and shouted, " 'If you prick us, do we not bleed? If you tickle us, do we not laugh? If you poison us, do we not die? And if you wrong us, shall we not REVENGE?' "

"Yeah!" Akshay pumped his fist in the air and scrambled to stand on his desk as well. There was a look on his face that said he wasn't entirely sure what he was doing, but he was super doing it anyway.

"HOARRF!" Now Ralph was standing on his desk.

"I COME TO BURY CAESAR SALAD WITH ANCHOVIES, NOT PRAISE IT!" Alice yelled, climbing up on her desk. I had a feeling Shakespeare never said anything about anchovies on a salad, but it was hilarious anyway.

"How did you know—" I asked as I scrambled up on my own desk.

Alice shrugged, offering me a steadying hand as I stood. "Hang around Willa long enough and you're sure to pick up on a thing or two."

As a class, we stood on our desks, arms crossed. It was

defiant and huge and like nothing any of us had ever done before.

Right at that moment, Mr. Kreplach walked back into the classroom. "What is going on here?!"

Akshay jumped down, strode over to the chalkboard, and grabbed a piece of chalk from the rail. Without even pausing, he wrote "AKSHAY" in looming capital letters. He turned to face Madame Bouche and Mr. Kreplach. "My name is not Ashkay. And no, you cannot call me Shea. My name is Akshay, and that"—he jabbed a finger at the chalkboard—"is how you spell it."

Madame Bouche threw her hands up and screeched to Mr. Kreplach, "That's it! I quit!" and stormed out. Mr. Kreplach scrambled after her.

"'Lord, what fools these mortals be!'" Willa said, stepping down from her desk as the four of us clapped.

Willa took a bow.

CHAPTER 23

My second visit to the principal's office that day was more crowded than the first.

"Well," Principal Butcher said, glaring at us. "I hope you're proud of yourselves. There will be serious consequences for your totally unacceptable, insubordinate, and outrageous behavior today. In addition to having all your parents called, you have lost recess for two weeks. You will spend that time in the school gardens"—she smiled a smile that told us she was going to enjoy what was about to happen and we were not—"where you will spread manure."

Ralph opened his mouth.

"Not one SOUND," Principal Butcher said, pointing at him.

Ralph closed his mouth.

"Now I want all of you out of my office. Out!"

We trooped back across the courtyard to our classroom.

"You know what? That was the most fun I've ever had at

this school," Ralph said. "I almost don't even care about the manure. Not at all. Really, though, how bad do you think it will smell?"

"I can bring clothespins for everyone's nose," Alice promised. "They work almost as well as nose clips."

Akshay gave her a fist bump of thanks.

"At least we didn't get suspended," Willa said.

My spine tingled—not with anger this time, but with something else. Something bigger. I stopped walking. *Suspended.*

Willa stopped walking, too. So did Alice. We all stared at one another.

"Are you guys thinking what I'm thinking?" Alice asked slowly.

"You know we are," Willa said.

"What?" Ralph said. "What are we thinking?"

"So we're really going to do this?" I said.

"We are," Akshay said.

"'Once more unto the breach, dear friends, once more!'" Willa said.

"Will someone please tell me what we're thinking and doing?" Ralph demanded.

"French fries," Alice told him. "We're thinking about Julia Child and french fries. And we're doing something about it."

We ran to the coat hooks. I grabbed the thumb drive out

of my backpack, and the five of us went back to the principal's office.

Principal Butcher groaned when she saw us walk in together.

"What are you doing here?" she said. "I have seen enough of your entire class to last a lifetime!"

"We have something to show you," I said, pulling the thumb drive out of my pocket.

"What is that?" Principal Butcher asked, eyeing it like it was a particularly large bug she wanted to squish.

"Something I found out about St. Julia Child."

Principal Butcher sighed. "If I watch it, will you all leave?"

We nodded.

Moving aside a stack of PTO bumper stickers, she slid the thumb drive into her computer and clicked on the video file. St. Julia Child's plummy voice floated out of the speakers, telling an interviewer how much she enjoyed fast-food french fries. Not how bad they were. Not how un-gourmet they were. Not how *plain* they were. But how much she loved eating them just as they were.

Principal Butcher smashed her hand down on the space bar, stopping the video. Her brows snapped together. "Where did you find this?"

"That's Julia Child—the patron saint of this school—saying she likes fast-food french fries," I said. "Not sweet potato fries with gold leaf and smoked paprika, but plain old, regular french fries from a fast-food chain!"

"I know what it is. Where did you get it?" Principal Butcher said in a tight voice. She stood up and started pacing.

"It's from the internet," I said.

"It's not available on the internet. We removed it," she snapped. "It was barely on the server an hour before we took it down."

"You took if off the school's server, but I found it at home."

"At home," Principal Butcher said faintly.

I guess it hadn't occurred to the school that anyone would care enough about what Julia Child said about fast-food french fries to search it out. And I guess it hadn't occurred to anyone at the school just how much some of us hated the school lunch menu. Excuse me, please, but maybe the school should think more like picky eaters.

Principal Butcher cleared her throat and took a deep breath. "Yes, well, at some point St. Julia might have enjoyed fast-food french fries, but she also says in that video that she never eats them anymore."

"That's because she says they changed the recipe," I said. "They were better before, and she liked them before."

"But she didn't like them any longer," Principal Butcher said. "Because she quite obviously came to her senses, and that's all that needs to be said about it."

"But—" I was confused. I wanted to argue back. I knew that what was on that thumb drive was a big deal.

Willa stepped forward. "I don't think that's all we have to say about it, actually." She spoke loudly and clearly, without a hint of nervousness, and she held up a book she'd been carrying. I hadn't noticed it until just that moment. She flipped to a page and said, "This is from someone who worked with St. Julia Child on one of her television shows." She began to read: "'She had a hearty appetite and would try almost anything.'"

Principal Butcher looked smug.

Willa read on in the same loud, clear voice. "'She would taste a lot of stuff that she didn't like and would somehow make it disappear'—"

Principal Butcher looked even smugger.

"—'but not down her mouth.'"

Principal Butcher's smugness faltered a bit.

"And here is what she said when she was asked about what foods she hated," Willa continued, flipping to a different page. "'Cilantro and arugula, I don't like at all. They're both green herbs, they have kind of a dead taste to me.'"

Principal Butcher put a hand up to her mouth.

"And when the interviewer asked her what she would do if she was ever served cilantro or arugula, she said, 'I would pick it out if I saw it and throw it on the floor.'" Willa snapped the book closed. "According to the way this school defines picky eating, St. Julia Child herself was a picky eater. In fact, St. Julia Child might even have been placed in RETCH."

We all stared at Willa in amazement. She grinned at us. "I told you I read a lot. Plus," she said, indicating the book, "it's always good to have backup."

I took a step closer to the principal's desk. "Principal Butcher, is it really such a big deal to put plain french fries on the menu? After all"—I picked up one of the PTO bumper stickers and read the text aloud—"'What Would St. Julia Child Do?'"

Principal Butcher started mumbling to herself.

"This cannot get out. This goes against everything St. Julia Child stands for, and I will not let you *remedial eaters* besmirch this school's good name!" She shook a trembling finger at us.

"We're not trying to . . . besmirch the school's name," Akshay said.

"Yeah," Ralph added. "All we want to do is prove to you that regular french fries are okay to have on the menu."

But Principal Butcher wasn't listening. She muttered under her breath. "Can't let this get out . . . Reputation to uphold . . . ruinous! Ruinous!"

"You're the one who should be class president," I told Willa.

Willa looked surprised and then proud. "Okay." She smiled.

Principal Butcher stopped pacing and turned to stare at us. Her face looked disturbingly pale.

"A *RETCH* student as class president? At this school?"

"Um, we're not supposed to call it RETCH, remember?" Ralph pointed out.

Principal Butcher teetered to her desk, stretching out one hand to guide herself back to her seat. "Excuse me, I'm not feeling so—" But before she could finish her sentence, she sank to the floor in a faint, banging her head on the desk.

Everyone gasped, but instantly my brain flashed back to the science program on concussions. Instead of being terrified, I realized that I knew exactly what I needed to do.

I called 911.

By the time three fire trucks and an ambulance arrived, Principal Butcher was conscious, but not doing a lot of talking. When I asked them many times, the paramedics said they didn't think she had a concussion, but they wanted to take her to the hospital just in case. As they loaded her into the ambulance, one of the paramedics turned to me and shook my hand.

"That was fast thinking, young lady. You're quite a hero today."

Hugo shoved his way through the crowd just in time to hear that last part.

“My ’Nerva IS a hero! A supertasty hero! She’s Supernerva!” he announced, hugging me.

I grinned and looked over as the entire school watched the ambulance pull away from the carpool lane. My eyes fell on Patricia. She glared at me. All the attention I was getting was probably eating her up.

“Weirdo,” Patricia hissed at me.

I looked over at my RETCH class and thought about kissing Brussels sprouts, and Morty, the well-fed plant, and feral cats, and Madame Bouche’s scarves, and the treehouse. The biggest smile stretched across my face. It turns out that being weird is far more heroic than not being weird. And way, way more fun.

“Why don’t you go suck a clam, Patricia?” I said.

Patricia’s jaw dropped, and her eyes darted around to see if anyone had overheard. Then she leaned forward. “Don’t you dare think about ratting me out,” she said in a low voice. “Because it’ll be your word against mine, and who do you think they’ll believe?”

“I DON’T LIKE YOU!” Hugo announced, and stomped on Patricia’s foot.

Patricia gasped in pain and shock.

“Oops,” I said. “Hugo, you really should be careful where you’re walking.”

Then I dragged Hugo away before he could stomp on anything else.

CHAPTER 24

Principal Butcher spent the night at Muffuletta General Hospital for observation and was sent home in the morning. She wasn't at school the following day. Mr. Kreplach explained that her doctor told her to rest at home, but the Food Science Fair would go on as planned. So that evening I stood at my project and waited for the judges to come by.

"Now tell us, Minerva . . ." one of the judges said. He was so tall, he bent himself nearly in half to peer at my board. "Why did you choose this topic for your Food Science Fair project?"

I cleared my throat and gripped my hands together to remind myself not to bite my nails. Not in front of the judges. "I wanted to prove that the reason I'm a picky eater and not good at Eating is because I taste things more strongly than other people do. That I'm a supertaster."

"And yet," another judge said, flipping open my logbook, "your hypothesis was wrong. You're not a supertaster." She adjusted her glasses as she picked up my tester vials and peered at them.

"No," I said quietly. I kept my eyes on my hands. "I'm not."

I saw my parents standing with Hugo a little ways away, and I remembered something my dad told me once. I looked at the two judges and cleared my throat. "But in science, just like in math, we learn from our mistakes. We learn even when we get things wrong."

"Oh? And what did you learn?" another voice asked kindly. A third judge stepped out from behind my parents. She was wearing a white chef's coat and black-and-white-checked pants. It was Amy from Amy's Delish Diner! I had no idea she was a Food Science Fair judge! I wanted to tell her how much I loved her french fries, her ketchup, and especially her grilled cheese sandwiches. I wanted to tell her about our family's tradition of going to her diner the night before school started every year. I wanted to tell her that I could eat like myself only at her restaurant.

"Minerva," my mom prompted me in a whisper.

"What did I learn?" I repeated.

Amy nodded with an encouraging smile.

"I think I learned that supertaster or not, I'm a picky eater. I didn't choose to be one, but that's who I am." The judges were quiet, so I went on. "And maybe it means I will never be great at Eating, but that's okay. I'm great at other things.

Things I like. Things I think are important. Like math and science and—"

Willa and Alice were now making their way toward my project. "And standing up for myself and being a friend. I learned that I'm great at being a good friend. I'm really great at being me. And I think that's actually more important than being the best at any particular school subject." I took a deep breath. "Maybe I'll change. Maybe I'll be less picky one day. Or maybe I won't. But I'm not going to worry about that. I'm going to concentrate on who I am today."

My parents stepped up to give me a hug while Amy and the other judges consulted with one another. Finally, Amy opened a folder she was carrying and attached a blue first prize ribbon to my display.

"Congratulations, Minerva," she said, and she shook my hand.

"You chose a fascinating topic, and your research and method were certainly rigorous," the tall judge said.

"I'll be interested to see what you come up with next year," the third judge said. "You don't have to be good at Eating to be interested in food or food science."

"Also, being a supertaster isn't the only explanation for why a person might taste things as strongly as you do," Amy said. "Some people are just very observant and sensitive to all aspects of the world around them. Even the worlds inside them." She pointed at her mouth.

“Thank you!” I breathed, barely able to stop myself from screaming. I had never won first prize at the Food Science Fair. “I’m thinking of researching tooth decay next year!”

All three judges smiled at me and my parents and moved on to the next project.

“We are so proud of you, Minerva,” my dad said.

“Honey, you worked so hard. Even if you hadn’t gotten first prize, we’d still be proud of all the time and effort you put into this,” my mom added.

Hugo, who had somehow managed to stay quiet this entire time, popped up from under my table and demanded, “FAMILY HUG!”

The four of us moved in to hug each other, with Hugo squirming in the middle as he tried to find a way to squeeze each of us at the same time.

The next day, Principal Butcher was back at school, frowning whenever she saw me. So nothing had changed there, even though I did kind of save her life. However, a major, huge exciting mother earthly change came in the form of plain, regular french fries being added to the school lunch menu. No announcement or explanation. They were just there. And only the League of Picky Eaters knew why.

“I could live on these!” Akshay said, holding up a fistful and stuffing it all in his mouth.

As it turned out, it wasn’t just the RETCH students who

welcomed the new lunch item. In fact, so many BARF and GAG kids were eating them in such large quantities that a few parents, including Patricia's mom, demanded a meeting with Principal Butcher.

I was in the office waiting for Akshay when their meeting ended. He had accidentally rubbed his eyes after touching a chile pod in the garden, and the nurse was putting a milk-soaked washcloth on his face to stop the burning.

With a slam of the door, a group of parents stormed out of Principal Butcher's office. "I'll bring this up at the next board meeting for sure," one parent muttered.

"I will *not* have my child eating food that doesn't challenge him," announced another.

Patricia's mom glanced over and saw me standing there listening. She didn't say anything out loud, but her face said a lot of stuff. And none of it was nice.

"She's getting Patricia a clam tutor," someone said after the parents were gone.

It was Cindy.

"A clam tutor?" I asked.

Cindy nodded. "Four days a week. No one's supposed to know. Her parents are going to tell everyone they paid some special doctor to cure her clam 'allergies.' She swore me to secrecy."

I looked at her curiously. "Then why are you telling me?"

Cindy shrugged, "Because I'm kind of mad at Patricia right now. She's always ordering me around, and she never listens to me."

"You know, you could stop being friends with her," I said.

Cindy gasped. "Who would I sit with at lunch?" She took a step back and stared at me. "Patricia's right. You are weird."

"Oh yes, I'm very weird," I agreed.

CHAPTER 25

That afternoon, the League of Picky Eaters gath-ered at Amy's Delish Diner to celebrate the school lunch menu change.

"I still can't believe we did it," Alice said, sipping a thick milk shake that was swirled with ribbons of chocolate and caramel.

"I wonder what else we can change," Willa said, looking into the distance.

Rummaging through my backpack, I pulled out a black Sharpie and the brand-new purple notebook I had bought at the Flashlight Under Covers bookstore. I looked at it for a few seconds, then squeaked "President Willa's Ideas for the Improvement of the Students at St. Julia Child Elementary and Middle School" across the top. I handed it to Willa. "I was serious about what I said in Principal Butcher's office. I think you should be class president."

"That means giving speeches in front of people, doesn't it?" Willa said.

"But you proved you can do that, and you do it really well," I said. "Look what happened—both in RETCH and in Principal Butcher's office."

"Yeah. I heard that The Mouth is on rest cure for her nerves. She's not coming back until next semester," Alice said.

"I hope that cat kicker never, ever comes back," Willa said, frowning. "Maybe we can be co-presidents?"

I nodded, thrilled at the idea.

Alice grabbed my Sharpie and pulled a napkin from the metal dispenser. She wrote something on it and slapped it on the table for us to read.

"'Stand Picky, Stand Proud'?" I said.

"Yeah, let's see how that works for a presidential slogan," Alice said, throwing an arm around Willa's shoulders and mine.

Willa smiled. "Fine. Minerva, you can keep track of ideas." She opened her laptop. "Let's see what else we can find out about St. Julia Child. Just in case it comes in handy."

"Hey," Akshay said, looking over Willa's shoulder. "That's weird!"

I glanced up as Willa asked, "What's weird?"

"Is that really Amy's Wi-Fi network?" Akshay pointed at CANTELOPE.

"Yeah, why? We used it the other night," I said. Alice sniffed at her milk shake.

"Can't Elope?" Akshay said. "That's just a strange thing to name a Wi-Fi network."

"No, it's the melon," I said. "Isn't it?"

"That's not how you spell *cantaloupe,*" Akshay said.

"Oh," I said. "That is strange." I turned to Alice, but she wasn't listening. She was sniffing the fries on the table and frowning.

"Is Amy engaged to be married or something?" Willa asked. "So, like, can't elope means she can't run away to get married? But that's still a bizarre thing to name your Wi-Fi network."

"GUYS!" Alice interrupted loudly, sniffing rapidly. "Can't you [sniff] smell that? There's [sniff] something [sniff sniff] wrong!"

"Wrong?" Akshay repeated. "What do you mean? I don't smell anything."

Neither did I.

"Something . . . like rotten eggs." Alice looked around. "Like gas."

I flushed.

"Well, it's not me, and anyway whoever smelt it—" I said.

"Dude, not *that* kind of gas," Alice interrupted me. "*Dangerous* gas." And before anyone could say another word, Alice slid out of the booth and ran to the back of the diner.

We all scrambled to follow her just as she disappeared through the swinging doors to the kitchen.

"Um, are we allowed in there?" Willa said, looking nervous. "Isn't that for employees only?"

I put two fingertips on the swinging door and pushed it open a sliver. I could see Alice pointing at her nose and turning off all the burners. All the line cooks looked surprised, but Amy was listening intently to whatever Alice was saying.

"What's up guys?" Ralph said, appearing at our sides. His hair was wet.

Even though I had saved Principal Butcher's life and she'd put french fries on the menu, we all still had two weeks of manure duty in the garden instead of recess. Today Ralph and Akshay were playing Keep Away with their manure-filled shovels, and Ralph ended up slipping and falling right into the pile. Ralph had to run home and shower before meeting us at Amy's.

"So what's going on?" Ralph asked again.

"Alice said she smelled gas," Willa explained.

Ralph grinned. "Maybe it was something she ate? Because whoever sniffed it—"

"*Not* that kind of gas," I said, talking over him before he could finish. "She ran into the kitchen."

"Well, why don't we just go in?" Ralph said, pushing through the door. "Aunt Amy won't mind."

"Did he just say Aunt Amy?" Willa asked.

"Oh, mother earth," I gasped, as the realization hit me like a bucket of ice water. "It's not *can't elope*!" I bounded over to the counter and grabbed one of the laminated menus. I stared at it, pulling it away from my eyes and squinting. Finally I saw it. A huge watermark faintly in the background of the menu. It was in the shape of a shield. Or a coat of arms. I flapped the menu over my head as I ran back to Akshay and Willa. "It's Cante LOPE! Look!"

As Akshay and Willa gaped over the menu, Alice, Ralph, and Amy came back through the doors. Ralph was carrying a basket of steaming fries that were glistening with fat, and Amy had her arm around Alice. "If it hadn't been for you—if it hadn't been for that remarkable nose of yours, my girl, oh my goodness!"

Line cooks and wait staff rushed around the restaurant, opening windows and doors.

"What's going on?" Willa asked.

"This incredibly perceptive young woman sniffed out a natural gas leak coming from a tiny crack in one of my pipes! We've shut all the appliances off until we can get a crew out here to repair it, and we're ventilating to disperse any buildup. If there'd been a major buildup, we could have had an explosion!" Amy explained, hugging Alice.

"And I got the last batch of fries," Ralph said, grinning through a mouthful of hot potatoes.

Amy ruffled Ralph's hair affectionately. "Now, you share with your friends, Ralph. They're my best customers."

We all went to sit down as Amy headed back into the kitchen, calling instructions out to her staff. Ty, Alice's older brother, sauntered over to us. He had been watching the commotion with his friends from their table.

"What was all that about?" he asked Alice.

"My nose—this thing here," Alice said, jabbing at her nose, which was now getting quite pink from the number of times she had poked or smacked it, "just saved this restaurant! I smelled out some super dangerous gas!"

"Well." Ty grinned. "Whoever detected it ejected—"

"NATURAL GAS!" Alice said, raising her voice.

"Wow, nice job." Ty put up his fist for his sister to bump. "But you know, I think I'm really the one Amy should be thanking."

"Excuse me, please, what do you have to do with it?" Alice demanded. I couldn't help but notice that she had picked up one of my expressions. Maybe I would pick up yodeling from her.

"Well, if I hadn't put your nose through all that training with all that fish—" Ty shrugged and turned back to his friends, ending the discussion.

"Ty," Alice said, following him, "this is not about you. I have told you a hundred times, I have advanced nasal techno—"

"Wait. Ralph, we need to back way up," Willa said. "Amy, the chef of Amy's Delish Diner, is actually your aunt?"

"Yeah?" Ralph said, frowning. "Haven't I ever mentioned that?"

Willa and I goggled at each other. Akshay just dropped his head on the table with a sigh. Alice came back to the booth, sucking on a milk shake.

"I snatched my brother's," she explained with a grin. "He deserved it."

"Okay, Ralph," Akshay said, his voice slightly muffled. "Let me ask you this: Do you think your aunt Amy might have been the one to put the LOPE note in your backpack?"

Alice gasped. She had put down the milk shake and was staring at the menu. "Um, guys? Have you seen—"

"Wait, what?" Ralph interrupted Alice. "Why would she do that? She's a chef—why would she know anything about a secret League of Picky Eaters?"

"Maybe because *she* is the guardian of the League of Picky Eaters?" I said, trying hard not to shout.

"Was your aunt at your house around the time you found the note in your backpack?" Willa asked.

"Yeah. How did you know? She was there for dinner one night that week. She always brings me french fries from the restaurant. I *told* you guys she made good french fries!"

Akshay started thumping his head on the table and groaning.

I took the menu from Alice and pushed it in front of Ralph's face while Willa opened her laptop again.

"Ralph, look at the name of the Wi-Fi network. Look at the last four letters," I said. "And look closely at the menu. Or actually not closely. Pull it away from your eyes and look at the background. Look at what's behind the words."

Ralph frowned, looking from the menu to Willa's computer. His eyes widened. "Hey, is that . . . whoooaahhhh."

"It's the LOPE shield! I knew I had seen it somewhere before!" I smacked the table triumphantly. "Back when you guys gave me that first note, I thought it was familiar. But I had no idea why!"

Amy approached our table. She carried a bowl of fruit in one hand and a plate of raw carrots, celery, cucumbers, and zucchini in the other. "I know you all love the fries, but have some fruit and veggies, if you can stand them. Make your parents happy."

"Aunt AMY!" Ralph said, pointing an accusing finger at the watermark shield on the menu. Amy grabbed a piece of cantaloupe from the fruit plate and popped it into her mouth.

"I always have my eye out for my most special customers." Then Amy winked and walked away.

Ralph flopped back against the booth. He had a dazed look on his face. "Does that mean my aunt *climbs trees?* Isn't she kind of old for—WAIT—WAIT." He held up a hand as if we were about to interrupt him, even though there was no chance of that, since he was doing it quite well on his own. "Does that mean my aunt, my *chef* aunt, is a picky eater like me who also climbs trees? Or, at least, *was* a picky eater like me? Or something? Oh, I can't process this." He rubbed his temples until his pale skin reddened with the force of his fingers.

"Guys, I think that's why we've always felt welcome here," I said slowly. "There's so much on her menu that makes us feel it's safe to eat here! It's why she makes the *best* grilled cheese sandwiches! Because she *understands!*"

"Wait—but Ralph's aunt didn't found the League of Picky Eaters, did she?" Alice asked.

"It doesn't sound like it," Willa said. "Remember, the note is signed by the guardian of the League of Picky Eaters, not the founder."

"And she just told us that she looks after kids like us—kids in RETCH—the way she and her class were looked after, so someone had to have come before Amy and her class. Someone else must have been the founder—or a group of someone elses," Akshay said.

Everyone started talking at once. Everyone but me. I just sat quietly and listened.

When this school year started, I had only two friends, who turned out to be the opposite of friends.

I failed a placement test and got placed in the worst Eating class, which turned out to be the best Eating class.

I lost two non-friends and gained an entire treehouse league of real friends.

I thought this year was going to be awful. It turned out to be amazing.

And it was just getting started.

"Ralph, seriously," Akshay said. "How could you not tell us that Amy was your—"

"HOOARRRFFF!" Ralph interrupted, right in Akshay's face.

Alice was pushing up her nose so Willa could look in her nostrils. Like she expected to find some sort of strange equipment up there.

"You all are such weirdos," I said, shaking my head and grinning so hard my cheeks ached.

"Takes one to know one!" Alice and Willa sang back while Akshay and Ralph gave me the thumbs-up.

"Yeah, it does. It really does." I took a french fry, paired it with a zucchini spear, and took a bite. Not bad. I dipped the combo in ketchup and tried another bite. Even better.

POW!

ACKNOWLEDGMENTS

When you sit down to eat a delicious meal, it might be easy to forget the many hands that worked hard to bring that plate to you. There are planters and farmers, harvesters and drivers. Packagers, manufacturers, loaders, and shippers. There are the stockers and checkers in the grocery store, and there are the shoppers and delivery people, if you cannot go in person. At a restaurant or in your own house, there are the cooks and chefs, the servers, bussers, and dishwashers.

Many working hands is how a meal comes into being. It's also how a book gets made. And we consume both of them. Here are all the wonderful working hands that helped turn my manuscript into a hearty meal for you to enjoy.

First, I want to thank my agent, Jordan Hamessley. She was clearly exhausted with me filling up her inbox with picture book manuscripts, because one day she finally said, "Go. Write something longer. Maybe try a middle grade." Three months later, I was in her inbox again with the first draft of this book—my first ever novel. (I don't think I stayed out of her inbox as long as she hoped. But she told me to go write, and I do what she tells me!)

Next, my gratitude goes out to Dinah Stevenson, who offered on this this book via a simple, world-changing email, calling it "highly original and charmingly weird." Those words will forever be part of my bio.

Then there's Jennifer Greene, my Clarion editor, who pushed me to reach for more and try harder during the revision stage. Jennifer loved this book the way a parent loves a child—always trying to get them to be their personal best using direction, encouragement, understanding, and support. Everyone should have such an editor. Jennifer's gentle pushing is also the reason for one of my favorite scenes in this book. Can you guess which one it is?

Huge thanks also go out to the rest of the Clarion/HMH team who worked to get this book from manuscript on a computer to bound book on a shelf: Eleanor Hinkle, Maxine Bartow, Helen Seachrist, Emma Grant, Zoe Del Mar, Anna Ravenelle, and Susan Bishansky. Special thanks to Mary Claire Cruz, Kaitlin Yang, and Alyssa Nassner—all of whom made this book look delicious, inside and out. Deep gratitude goes out to Sahrish Nadim for her authenticity read, as well as to Grace Wynter for her authenticity read and for her enthusiasm for the book as a whole.

Childhood friends from whom I drew inspiration: Alice

and her knitting, Becca and the yodeling tape her parents played on a long car trip, Laura for her strength, Anna for her jigs of joy on the high school tennis courts, and finally, Suzanne and Nicole for their decades of support, love, and solid friendship.

Early readers and critique partners: Claire Bobrow, Joanna Ho, Molly McDonough, Natalie Mitchell, and Kellie DuBay Gillis. You all saw this book in the most basic of phases; when it was little more than prepped ingredients without a clearly defined recipe. Thank you for being my taste testers and cheerleaders. Your reads and comments are worth more than a Michelin star.

Author friends: Anne Ursu, Elana K. Arnold, Ishta Murcurio, Brandy Colbert, Karen Strong, Martha Brockenbrough, Dev Petty, Lindsay Lackey, Christina Soontornvat, Susie Ghahremani, Kristy Everington, Tara Hannon, A.J. Irving, Betsy Bird, Cassandra Federman. You all have given me so much support and wisdom over the years, and I am forever grateful that you exist in the writing world.

Amy Spaulding, for making me hungry for hamburgers as I was writing this and for whom I named the diner and secret heroine of this book.

Julia Child. I think she'd really get a kick out of this book—especially the idea of a school granting her sainthood and naming themselves after her.

Helen Rosner for bringing to my attention that the way

to get the best skin crackle on a roast chicken is to use a hairdryer.

My parents for supporting me and instilling in me a love of reading from the crib, my mother-in-law for always being on my side and staying endlessly fascinated by the intricacies of how book publishing works, and my big sister, Jennie, for cheering on my successes and for being loudly outraged on my behalf when I experience disappointments.

Bean and Needles who sat, slept, and purred by my side, on my pillows, or behind my laptop during the entire writing process and whose cattish quirks earned them starring roles in the book. I started my children's writing career trying to capture many beloved cats between the pages. I'm glad I finally succeeded.

My tripod of strength, support, and inspiration: Mark, Henry, and Arthur. You fill up my life with poetry and laughter, and the love you surround me with is the reason why I can and do write. First for you and then for the world.

Finally, I want to thank you, the reader of this book. Now that you hold it in your hands and have chomped all the way to the end, this book is no longer mine, it's all yours now.

At the end of their cooking show, Jacques Pépin and Julie Child used to say, "Bon appétit and happy cooking!" So to you—my hungry or picky—reader, I say, "Bon appétit and happy reading!"

FIND YOUR STORY

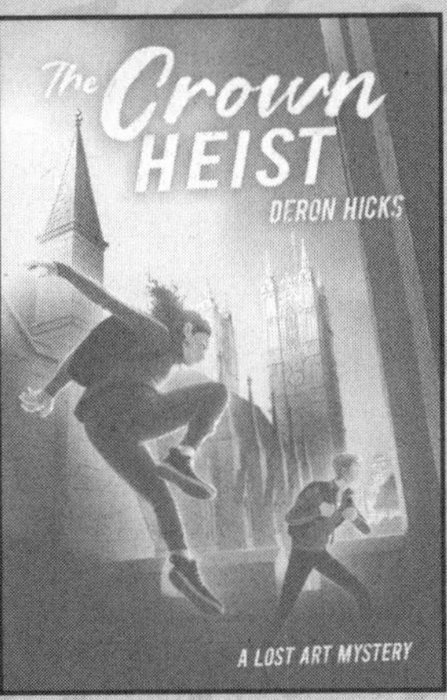

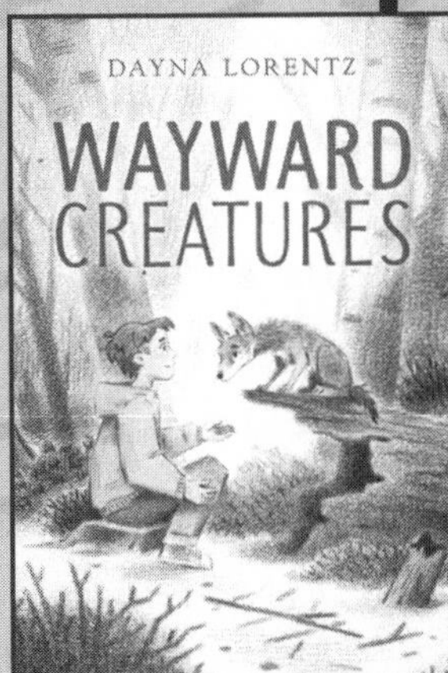

CATCH UP WITH HARLEM'S FAVORITE FAMILY!